LAND OF
THE BRAVE AND
THE FREE

Books by the Phillips/Pella Writing Team

The Journals of Corrie Belle Hollister

My Father's World
Daughter of Grace
On the Trail of the Truth
A Place in the Sun
Sea to Shining Sea
Into the Long Dark Night
Land of the Brave and the Free

The Stonewycke Trilogy

The Heather Hills of Stonewycke
Flight from Stonewycke
Lady of Stonewycke

The Stonewycke Legacy

Stranger at Stonewycke
Shadows over Stonewycke
Treasure of Stonewycke

The Highland Collection

Jamie MacLeod: Highland Lass
Robbie Taggart: Highland Sailor

The Russians

The Crown and the Crucible
A House Divided
Travail and Triumph

LAND OF
THE BRAVE AND
THE FREE

MICHAEL PHILLIPS

BETHANY HOUSE PUBLISHERS
MINNEAPOLIS, MINNESOTA 55438

Cover by Dan Thornberg,
Bethany House Publishers staff artist.

Published by Bethany House Publishers
A Ministry of Bethany Fellowship, Inc.
6820 Auto Club Road, Minneapolis, Minnesota 55438

Printed in the United States of America

Library of Congress Cataloging-in-Publication Data

Phillips, Michael R., 1946–
    Land of the brave and the free / Michael Phillips
      p.   cm. — (The Journals of Corrie Belle Hollister ; bk. 7)
      1. United States—History—Civil War, 1861–1865—Fiction. I. Title.
  II. Series: Phillips, Michael R., 1946–   Journals of Corrie Belle Hol-
lister ; 7.
PS3566.H492 L36   1993
813'.54—dc20   92–45107
ISBN 1–55661–308–3   CIP

To
Anke Peters,

one of the most special of God's women it has been my privilege and honor to know, with prayers for the deepening of His character and being within you all the years of your life. In you I have seen a heart that has always hungered for truth and the things of God. It makes me proud to know you, for you are truly a "daughter of grace." I love you.

The Author

Michael Phillips has authored, co-authored, and edited over 50 books. He is editor of the bestselling GEORGE MACDONALD CLASSICS series and has co-written several series of historical fiction with Judith Pella, all published by Bethany House Publishers.

Nominated for fourteen ECPA Gold Medallion awards, Phillips has received much recognition for his writing and editing. Sales for his books exceed three million, and seven of his titles have appeared on the *Bookstore Journal* bestseller list.

Phillips and co-author Judith Pella began the CORRIE BELLE HOLLISTER series as a team effort, but other writing projects have resulted in the mutual agreement that Phillips continue this one on his own. Phillips owns and operates two bookstores on the West Coast. He and his wife, Judy, live with their three sons in Eureka, California.

CONTENTS

Part One

CHAPTER 1

It's been sixteen days now.

Sometimes I feel that my prayers go unheard. There is no change. The peaceful face still sleeps, only sleeps. I continue to sit here, gazing upon those features, wondering who this is—who and why and how did it happen . . . what does it mean? And I continue to pray.

But I grow fainthearted. I wonder if God does truly mean to restore and heal and make alive again, or is this the time when he has stepped across, as he does in every life, into the tide of man's affairs to take another soul of his making unto himself?

If indeed this is such a moment, then my prayers are in opposition to his will and plan. Do I pray in opposition to his sovereignty?

Such difficult questions always seem to plague me—whether it be about an unknown face with sleeping countenance, or about mysteries in your word or uncertainties concerning your work among men and those who call themselves your people. No answers are quick to come.

And still the compelling in my heart grows stronger and stronger concerning this one whose being is presently in my hands, that pray I must. Surely this precious life about which I yet know nothing—surely it is not time for it to end.

My thoughts, as they so often do, beckoned me outside to the hills and fields and streams and trees I so dearly love. I grabbed up my New Testament, knowing that Mrs. Timms would watch over my charge well, and went out.

It was early afternoon. The sun was high and I wondered

where its warmth had gone from the summer of such a few short months ago.

I left the house and took the path eastward, then abandoned it altogether. I jumped the fence bordering it, struck out across the wide pasture where some cows were grazing at the far end, working my way up the slight incline to the thin wood about half a mile away. Notwithstanding the early November chill that hinted at snows and storms and fierce blasts of hail even now beginning their slow journeys down from the arctic, the day was a glorious one to be out. The thin breeze that kicked up every now and then foreshadowed almost more by odor than by feel the approaching winter, adding a tingling sensation in both nose and skin to the warmth of the sun's rays that was purely and deliciously pleasant. The great vault of blue overhead was unbroken save by a few slender wisps of white from the chimneys of some of the surrounding farms, but even these had diffused into nothingness before reaching a third of the way up against the horizon. Straight above me was nothing but the infinitude of distance, stretching into regions of space unknown by man, into the very heart of God himself.

I threw myself down in the springy, sun-warmed and sun-softened grass, breathed in deeply with pleasure, and let my eyes drift into the unknowable blue depth above me.

"Lord God," I whispered, "where *are* you up there? Where *is* your home in the heavens that people are so fond of talking about in the pious tones of their prayers, when I feel you so vitally alive in the tiny place within my own being I call my heart? Do they know you there too, Lord? Or do they look up and speak of you with such lofty grandeur because they have not yet learned to look for you in the still quiet places within their own beings?"

All about me was quiet except for an occasional distant baritone low of a contentedly feeding cow. God's voice is never easy to hear, never so readily discernible to the inner ears of my being as the sounds of his creatures are to the outer ears of my head. I often wonder why he made it so—that if he wants us to heed every whisper of his voice, why that voice is so soft to our human senses. But perhaps what he wants more even than our hearing him is our obeying him when we do *not* hear him. If his voice were *too* loud and his commands *too* unmistakable, perhaps the requirement upon our own wills would not be so great, and our obedience would thus be less.

Again, I found myself lost in obscure regions of God's unknowable purposes. And one thing I did know, that I mustn't lose sight of *my* purpose, which was clear enough, nor tarry too long before returning to it. I jumped up and continued my way toward the wood.

As I walked, my thoughts returned, as they often did, to reflecting on this terrible war and its claim on human life, on the untold suffering it has caused . . . and once again, as how many times before, to the question which haunts me: Did I make the right decision? Was my stand one that God desired me to take? Or was I then, and am I still wrong and out of step with the rest of God's people? If God did indeed speak with his still small voice into my mind and thoughts, into my heart and convictions, then why did no one understand? Why was their denunciation of me so unequivocal and vicious simply because I—one of their own, a comrade, a fellow member in the brotherhood of God's family— spoke out the truth I felt compelled to voice? If I was indeed wrong, as they say, why did they not take me tenderly to their bosom and, in gentlest love, seek to help me discover my error? If perchance I was right, why did they not humble themselves to hear my words, and themselves seek truth beyond their own selfish interests? But to cast me adrift with their heartless and cruel accusations, without so much as an inlet wherein to tether the leaking vessel of my faith, full of doubt and uncertain of the calling I was so sure of only a few short years before . . .

"God, O God—preserve me at all costs from bitterness and unforgiveness! Do not let me sink, my Father. Though I hear you not and see you not, do not leave me! Keep my soul safe and my mind clear and my heart uncluttered with hurts from the past. Lead me, O God, into your truth!"

Is *truth* too distant a commodity for God's people to care about? Why do one's *own* interests and one's *own* safety and one's *own* views and one's *own* future take preeminence over what is *true*? Surely among God's people it should not be so. Yet then why do I feel so alone and seemingly at odds with those millions of others who make up what we call the body of Christ? And what of those more millions on the *other* side of the fateful line between North and South who also consider themselves right? How two governments can feel it their duty to war against each other is not so difficult for me to understand. But how God's people on both sides can feel it their *sacred* calling to support this killing—that I will *never* understand. That it is right I *cannot* accept. That the truth of God is thus represented, I *will* not believe!

I sat down among the trees, took out my Testament, and opened it to the well-worn and familiar passage. I scarcely needed to read it, for the words were so deeply ingrained in my consciousness. Yet I never tired of letting the soothing words of the Master flow over me as a cool stream, my spirit uttering as I read the inarticulate longing of my deepest being that the Father of Jesus would answer, and answer mightily, the magnificent prayer of his son.

> They are not of the world, even as I am not of the world. Sanctify them through thy truth: thy word is truth. . . . Neither pray I for these alone, but for them also which shall believe on me through their word; that they all may be one; as thou, Father, art in me, and I in thee, that they also may be one in us: that the world may believe that thou hast sent me. And the glory which thou gavest me I have given them; that they may be one, even as we are one: I in them, and thou in me, that they may be made perfect in one; and that the world may know that thou hast sent me, and hast loved them, as thou hast loved me.

I could read no further. Every time I pondered with fresh wonder the depths of the Lord's words, I found myself lost in ever-deepening regions of sheer marvel and awe at the inescapable fact that Jesus was praying for *me* on the night before his death. Try as I might to think my way to the bottom of them, to peel off one more layer of their meaning, I found myself, as always, treading upon ground seemingly almost too holy to ponder, and knowing that in the prayer itself was the answer to my hunger: *It is enough . . . my Father knows how the fulfillment will come.*

Twenty minutes more I sat, my lips unmoving—this was no time for conscious prayer—though my heart heaved with the great prayer that was the very essence of my personhood. Then finally I rose, my spirit calm again, ready to continue my vigil at the bedside, and ready again to pray and not grow weary.

I made my way back to the house as I had come.

Mrs. Timms heard my foot upon the stair and met me at the door as I walked in.

"Mr. Braxton," she said excitedly as she came up to me. "I think she may be coming awake! I heard the faintest whimper, and thought I detected a flicker of her eyelash."

She turned, and I followed her with hurried stride into the sickroom.

CHAPTER 2

I walked quickly to the bedside.

At first glance there was no change. Still the sleeping form lay as I had left it. And yet, as the landlady had said, there were subtle hints of stirring.

I sat down on the edge of the bed and leaned down near the pale face whose every feature I had come to know so well. I knew those features well but their owner was still a stranger to me. I could see movement under her closed eyelids, followed by brief momentary wrinkling across her forehead. I knew she was dreaming. Though the distorted thoughts of sleep were clearly troubling, my heart leaped with the hope that they were the precursor to wakefulness.

I gently laid my hand upon the busily moving forehead.

"Father," I said softly, "I ask you one more time, in the name of your son Jesus—heal this precious child of yours and make her whole again. Breathe your life into her entire frame, into her entire being. Restore her to the fullness of the stature and health and vibrancy which are in your heart to give all your men and women."

For a moment I was silent. Then I turned to Mrs. Timms, where she stood observing but uncomprehending. "Leave me alone with her, will you please?" I said softly and with a smile to reassure her I meant her no ill.

"Of course, Mr. Braxton."

"Mrs. Timms . . . thank you for watching her so carefully while I was out. I think you are right and the time is at hand. Why don't you boil some water for tea."

"Right away, sir," she rejoined eagerly, then left the room.

I turned again to gaze upon the face below me.

For more than two weeks I had been studying this young woman's features, wondering who she was and whom she belonged to.

What caused such love within me for each human's individuality, I do not know. No doubt the Maker of myself and my curiosity and my love altogether put it into some corner of my being. I would like to think it is a little piece of himself that he put in me. He was teaching me to look upon others of his with the smallest shadowy foretaste of what *he* sees when he looks into each one of us with a love unlike anything we can fathom.

When and where and why God put it into me, these are things I need not know. But I do know that when I behold another face of man or woman, within my heart spring up depths indescribable of love for an individuality I can sense and feel is unique in all the creation of the world that I desperately want to know and experience and be part of that one. Ah, what depths of *life* lies unknown and undiscovered within each human soul! Undiscovered even by that soul itself. The souls of most men and women are asleep in a deeper slumber even than this young woman before my gaze at this moment. Asleep in the midst of their lives of seeming bustle and toil, even lives of seeming meaning and relationship and interaction with their fellows through the daily ebb and flow of life's events.

Yet most are asleep! They know neither themselves nor their Maker, nor those around them. They do not know *life* because they have never learned to *live*. They are locked away in dungeons of self and greed and guilt and uncertainty and fear. Their bodies and brains conduct the affairs necessary to the carrying on of what they "call" life, but because of their bondage to these inner demons with which they are afflicted, they do not truly know what that magnificent thing called *life* is.

My heart swells when I consider the Master's words: *I am come that they might have LIFE, and that they might have it more abundantly.* What words of joy and liberty and freedom he brought us! *Abundantly* . . . what can he have meant but the glorious sharing of *his* very life!

God, why do so few know this life, even so few of your own sons and daughters? Surely you do not mean it to be so!

Is this hunger within my own breast to know such life myself, and to see and discover it in others, and to bring it to those who do not know it—is this passion to know life and bring life and declare life—to *live!*—why my heart has so gone out to this young daughter of God who now lies in my very bed struggling literally against death itself?

From the moment my eyes fell upon her and I stooped down and picked up her frail and broken body in my arms, I knew I could stop at nothing to assist the Giver of life to bring life back to her.

Here was one who was not merely asleep of soul, but whose body itself lay at the very gates of death. And if perhaps I had been disappointed in the past, desiring to bring the words of life to those awake in body but asleep in their deepest beings, then here was one who could not turn me away because of the very desperation of her need.

I know you sent her to me, Lord—perhaps as a reminder that life is a good and precious thing to seek, even if I have often felt alone in the quest. Help me, Father, to never stop looking for the depths of life in the faces I pass by every day. Give me your words to speak, your smiles to smile, your hands of help and encouragement with which to bring your salt to the earth, and above all, your eyes to see deeply into all men and women—most of all into myself!—into those innermost regions where *you* see them and *you* see me. Give me eyes to see as *you* see, Father! I desire to see into hearts and to love with a love that is yours, whether or not those I see and those I love know and see with your eyes.

Again my eyes scanned the sleeping face. It was not, I suppose, a noteworthy or remarkable face in the way the world considers remarkable. But the world's eyes look only to the surface of things, and what is a face but the outward means by which a man or woman's inner being rises to the surface and escapes into the atmosphere of relationships? Men look to the outer, and, if they are satisfied to probe no deeper, then interact with that outer shell—dare I even call it a facade?—thinking it is all there is. Thus they rarely approach the region of true personhood in their approach with other individuals with whom they have to do.

But a face for me is far more, a gateway into the regions where personhood dwells. And when I gaze upon a face long enough, what but love can sprout and grow within my bosom! For each man or woman's personhood is a precious and wondrous thing—created by the hand of Love like no other in all the universe! The eyes are the windows. Try as they might to shut their houses tight against unwanted intrusions, every face has two wide, glorious, beautiful, radiant windows whose purpose, I believe with all my heart, is only partially to enable us to see *out*, but equally to allow others to see *in*.

The face before me was full, to my eyes, of personality and adventure! Though the windows were for a time closed, I could surmise that it had been many places and had seen and known and experienced much about which I could only guess. It was a tall face, and I liked that immediately. A tall forehead above the tan eyebrows, and a chin that extended a good way down below the mouth. It was a face with room, without limitations. I found myself hoping that perhaps the owner to whom the face belonged was like that, too—large of soul, expansive, able to reach high but at the same time able to feel deeply in the low valleys of life as well. I hoped it was a tall, growing, unbounded spirit.

The eyes, though closed, were wide-set above a perfectly straight nose. This also boded well, for they appeared to be eyes well out toward the surface rather than deep-set. They would not, I was sure, be prone to squinting and narrowness of vision. I had a feeling they would be hungering, probing, inquisitive, outlooking eyes, not inward, tight, self-focused. Oh, how I desired to see the eyes themselves!

The cheeks were full, though not plump. High cheekbones were visible, pale now from the loss of blood and the struggle for life. But I had the distinct feeling that those cheeks were well-acquainted with exertion and capable of high color. The lips I already had more than a passing acquaintance with in the struggle to get liquids into her mouth and down her throat. They were full lips. From the shape of her mouth, I got the impression that this young lady knew how to express herself and communicate, and probably found no trouble laughing as well. Unless I was gravely mistaken, here was one in whom *life* was indeed developing. Perhaps it was another of the reasons I so desperately besought the

Lord on behalf of her recovery. I knew there was something here too vital and alive and wonderful to allow this war to snuff out before God's time. Light brown hair falling below the shoulders filled out the top and surrounded the face. It had been dirty and full of bits of leaves and twigs, but I had done my best to wash it as she lay there, as I had, with Mrs. Timms' help, the rest of her clothes and person.

I sat a few moments longer.

I removed my hand from the forehead. The movement and twitching of its muscles had stopped. The eyes had similarly grown quiet. Again she seemed to be sleeping peacefully.

Then suddenly another change began to come. The eyes twitched again, but this time it was not in response to a dream. It was the twitch of a blink, then another, struggling to blink hard enough that the reflex motion would carry the lips upward.

Then—wonder of wonders!—the moment came! The lids slowly rose, cautious at first against the sudden infusion of light. They came up halfway, then shut again, seemingly resting for the final effort.

And then, all at once . . . the windows opened fully, and the light poured in!

CHAPTER 3

Such eyes they were!

My heart bounded with indescribable delight! The unknown face was suddenly alive with depths of being at which I had only till then been able to faintly guess. Such love flooded through me just at the wondrous sight! How could God put such love for others of humankind within my breast!

The light brown could not have been more perfectly suited to the hair that flowed from above it, and the dainty light brown eyebrows resting calmly above the two shining orbs.

For a moment I could tell the eyes were unfocused, as if the sleep yet lingered. They were blank and indicated no awareness in either direction—inward or outward. Then again came a crinkling of the forehead and the tiniest hint of confusion in the eyes. A blink followed. At last her gaze came to rest on my face, then found my own eyes returning their questioning gaze.

"Hello," I said softly. "My name is Christopher Braxton. I'm afraid you've had a rather serious accident."

"I . . . I don't understand," the voice faltered. "Where am I?"

To call the sound musical to my ears might seem trite or hollow. But what else could I call it but music? The music of a brook dancing and splashing and gurgling over stones, the music of wind through treetops racing moments ahead of the wind, the music of giant ocean waves crashing against a rocky shore—what are even these compared with the rich timbrelled variety of a human voice? And the sound of this one, which had, with her eyes, been asleep so long, instantly set the many-toned chords of my heart vibrating all at once. I could scarcely control the excitement in my *own* voice sufficiently to respond in a calm enough manner so as not to alarm her.

"You are safe and well," I answered.

"But where?" she asked, her eyes moving slowly about the room. "I . . . I recognize nothing." Her gaze drifted back, and again came to rest on me.

"Yes, I know." I smiled. "And you do not recognize me either." She nodded, and seemed for a moment trying to smile, but the bewilderment she felt was even stronger and kept the upper hand.

"You are in my own room, not far outside Midlothian. This is a farming community, but I merely board here. You need have no fear of me—the matron of the house is in the next room."

"But why . . . what happened to me . . . why am I here?"

"You do not remember?"

"No, I remember nothing."

"You were apparently shot—in the back, just under your right shoulder blade."

Her right hand came out from under the blanket, and immediately her face winced in pain. Her left followed, crossing over her chest where she lay on her back, trying to feel the wound. She could not reach it, however, but the hand discovered the bandages and splint with which I had attempted to make her shoulder immobile.

"You lost a great deal of blood," I said. "I thank God I discovered you when I did."

"Where did you find me?"

"Alongside the road to Richmond, about half a mile from here. There was no sign of horse or anyone else. My first thought was that you had been somehow wounded in a skirmish from the Union siege. But there has been no fighting anywhere near here. What happened . . . do you know?"

"I'm sorry, I . . ."

Her brow wrinkled once more and her eyes closed tightly in what I knew was an intense effort.

"No, I'm afraid I just can't recollect anything of what happened," she said after a moment, opening her eyes again.

"No matter, Miss Hollister," I said. "I'm certain it will all come back once we get some solid food inside you. It's been hard enough, unconscious as you were, to get broth and water into your mouth—"

"Excuse me," she interrupted.

I stopped.

"That name you just said?"

"Hollister?"

"Yes. Who did you mean?"

"Why . . . *you*, of course, Miss Hollister. There was a letter in your pocket. It's over there on the dressing table."

Her whole face mirrored back only bewilderment with my words. "I . . . I'm afraid I don't know that name," she said.

I returned her troubled and inquisitive gaze. "I suppose I simply assumed from the envelope that the letter had been sent to you."

I rose, went to the dressing table, and returned with the letter. I handed it to her.

She reached up from the bed, took it with her left hand, and stared for several moments at the writing on the envelope. At last she read the name aloud, though softly.

"Corrie . . . Corrie Belle Hollister."

A few seconds more she looked at it, then up to me, her eyes watery and pleading.

"Please, you've got to tell me," she said. "Who is this Corrie Hollister? Why . . . why was I carrying a letter addressed to her?"

"I don't know," I replied.

She looked down again at the envelope, then dug with her fingers for the letter inside.

"What does the letter say?" she asked.

"It was not mine to read," I answered.

She looked quickly over it, read half of the first page, then let it fall from her hand to the bed.

"What is it?" I asked.

"I don't know," she said, shaking her head. "None of it makes any sense to me."

"Who's it from?"

"I don't know."

"May I see it?" I asked.

She handed it to me.

I turned the single sheet over, looking for the signature at the bottom.

"It's signed *Almeda,*" I said. "Do you know someone by that name?"

Again she shook her head. "No. I don't reckon I ever even heard the name before."

"Not the kind of name you'd forget," I said.

"Not likely," she said.

"Well, then," I said cheerfully. "If we can't clear up the mysteries of the letter or your wound, at least you can tell me one thing so I'll know what to call you. What *is* your name?"

A long silence followed. When at last I saw her lips trying to speak, they quivered and her eyes filled. The tears were in earnest this time, and from their midst the large brown eyes flitted about in growing panic. I could see a great cloud of fear begin to engulf her as she spoke.

"I don't know, she said, then closed her eyes and began to weep softly."

CHAPTER 4

When I reentered the bedroom about five minutes later, I had a cup of tea and a bowl of warm chicken soup on a tray. I thought it best to let her shed her initial tears of grief, shock, and bewildered dismay alone. She did not know me nearly so well as I knew her. She had been conscious now for a mere ten or fifteen minutes, and it would take some time for her to become accustomed to these strange surroundings.

"Well," I said, "I'm sure we will untangle the mystery of your identity and the letter and everything else well before evening. But in the meantime, we must get you eating again! You have no idea what I've been through keeping you alive!"

She looked up, wiped away the tears with the handkerchief I had left with her, then attempted the first smile I had yet seen. And the sight was worth the wait!

"I am sorry to have been such a bother to you," she said.

"Did I say you were a bother?" I rejoined. "Not at all! I only said it was a difficult challenge to get water and broth into your stomach! And now that you are awake, I want to lose no time in getting something more substantial into you. There is a great deal of strength to be regained, besides just your memory."

"Will I remember?" she asked, in a tone of deep worry and doubt.

"Of course you will. You are probably just not altogether awake yet, besides no doubt being famished. Everything will come back to you very soon, I am sure. But it does perhaps explain the large lump I found on your head, in addition to the wound. From everything I was able to determine, I think you were riding a horse

27

at the time. You were probably thrown and struck your head. There was a large rock not far from where you lay."

"And you found me there, just along the roadside."

"Off to the side, in some brush, near the rock, as I said. It can't have been long after it happened when I came by because the blood was still wet underneath you where it was soaking into the grass."

I saw her give an involuntary shudder at the words.

"I'm sorry. This is hardly the kind of talk to give you an appetite, is it!"

I set the tray down and proceeded to prop her up to a sitting position with several pillows behind her. I took the cup of tea and handed it to her. Then I sat down beside her on the bed, the bowl of soup in my hand. "Now you may not like this," I said, "but I'm not sure I trust that left hand of yours yet, and I don't want to lose a drop of this good soup of Mrs. Timms'. So I'm going to feed you."

She smiled and took the first spoonful willingly, then followed it with a sip of tea.

"That is good," she said. "I reckon you're right . . . I *am* hungry."

I refilled the spoon and sent its contents after the first.

"But how do you know I'm not left-handed?" she said.

"Simple," I replied. "Because of the callouses and ink stains on the fingers of your right hand."

She glanced down, turned her right fingers over, and seemed to take in my observation with interest.

"I also know that you are a writer," I said. "Of letters, perhaps . . . I don't know. But the callouses and stains are too deep and permanent to have been made from mere occasional correspondence. And you are much too old to still be in school, although I have wondered if perhaps you are a teacher, for that *could* account for it."

"Why do you think this is from writing?" she asked, holding up the fingers as much as she was able without pain.

"The signs are unmistakable. I know them too well." I showed her the first three fingers of my own right hand, bearing all the same signs of black ink and thick pads of flesh. "I write too."

She sighed deeply, then took another spoonful of the soup.

"Perhaps you are right," she said. "But I recall nothing of how these marks got here any more than why my shoulder hurts."

She ate awhile longer in silence. I knew she was thinking, but I had not so much as a guess where her thoughts might be. How lonely her perplexity must have been in those first hours of wakefulness! At length the bowl was empty. I was delighted with her appetite. All signs pointed to the fact that this was a healthy young woman.

"Do you think I *am* this Corrie Hollister?" she said as I placed the empty bowl on the tray.

"I think that it may be likely," I answered. "Why else would you be carrying a letter addressed to her?"

"Maybe I'm the Almeda who wrote the letter to Corrie Hollister."

"That could hardly be. The letter was already postmarked, all the way from California. *Are* you from California?"

"I . . . I don't know." Again she was silent. "Was there nothing but the letter?" she asked after a minute.

"No, that was all you had," I answered. What other suspicions I harbored would keep. I had given her enough to ponder for one day, and it would be better for her memory to come back to itself of its own volition. If I needed to show her what else I possessed, the time for such a revelation would have to be just right.

"I'm sorry, but that lump on my head must be worse than either of us thought. I've already forgotten *your* name, and at least one of us should know who the other is."

I was delighted to see that she had a sense of humor too! "Christopher Braxton," I said, laughing.

"And what do you want me to call you?"

"Believe it or not, some people used to call me Rev. Braxton, but I never could get used to that."

"Reverend! Are you a minister?"

"I once thought I wanted to be, but I'm not so sure anymore. I used to be pastor of a church. But it seems a long time ago now. I suppose, if you want to know, I'm in the process of trying to figure out who I am too, and *what* I want to be now that the ministry to which I had given my heart is no longer open to me."

"I'm sorry," she said.

"I am too. But new doors in life are constantly opening before us. And so I anticipate the future eagerly, even though I may not know any more of where I am going than you know where you have been."

"You still haven't told me what to call you?"

"Well, now that we've dispensed with the *Reverend*, there's always Mr. Braxton, which Mrs. Timms very respectfully addresses me as. But there again, there is a discomfort in that too."

"How so?"

"I never felt anyone had a right to be *Mister* Braxton except my father. So I suppose we're left with the name he gave me—Christopher—which I suppose I like best of all."

"You don't consider it too informal for a stranger to call you by your given name?"

"You forget, you're hardly a stranger. I've known *you* for over two weeks."

"But I *am* a stranger. You don't know who I am!" The chicken soup was already doing its work of restoration. A sparkle of fun danced in her eyes where the tears had been only a short time before.

I laughed. "Well, it would seem you have me there!" I said. "But to answer you, no—I do not consider it too informal at all. I have never been one to stand on pretenses, and I have never been accused of being formal."

"In that case, I will call you Christopher," she said.

CHAPTER 5

Regrettably the words I had spoken about the speedy return of Miss Hollister's memory were not to be fulfilled. After another week, it became clear that the problem was more severe than I had anticipated.

By then she was up and about the place and regaining her health and color and vigor admirably. Notwithstanding, the wound in her shoulder and apparent concussion on her head continued to exercise their toll, and she remained in bed at least half of each day. But I made sure she walked about and got some fresh air and ate as much as she could, and gradually I could see strength returning to her frame.

It did not, however, seem to be bringing back her memory, and as the days progressed I became increasingly more deeply concerned. That she was indeed Corrie Hollister I was all but certain, though I still had not shown her why I believed the name of the envelope to be hers. Somehow I had not felt the time to be right, though I sensed it would be soon.

I did not know much about amnesia, other than that it could be total or partial, and that it could last but a matter of a few hours or days or could be indefinite. I knew sometimes memory came back slowly by degrees, and sometimes all at once, usually triggered by some thought or event having to do with how it originally was lost in the first place. The more time that passed, the more my concern grew, but also I hoped that in time the restored health of her body would lead to restoration of her mental faculties as well.

Her convalescence did offer the opportunity for us to talk a great deal, and it was curious to discover those places wherein her mind was still active, and those mental rooms which had temporarily been cut off from her use. Of herself and her family and her personal background and recent past, she could recall nothing. Even as I began calling her by name, she seemed to resign herself to the appellation as a fact, but it did not appear to strike a chord of familiarity or recognition within her.

And yet when it came to matters of the spirit, there seemed to be no lack in her individuality and expressiveness whatever. I was delighted, in fact, to find what kind of spiritual and moral fiber she was made of, though I had reason enough to expect it and was hardly surprised. Her sensitivity to the things of nature around her was perhaps heightened by the loss of something so close that we all take for granted. And along with this I knew from the very first that she was a young woman of God's design and making, a true daughter of her Father in heaven. Her awareness of God's life within her was neither stilted nor shy, and it expressed itself in the most refreshingly simple and childlike, loving and trusting ways. But there was nothing child*ish* about the childlikeness of her faith. She was a deep and profound thinker about the things of God, and I found her a wonderfully adept sharpening instrument for my own ideas and questions, even doubts. Here was someone who really *thought* about things, like I did myself! *Thought* without being afraid of asking questions and looking at hard things that seem fearsome to most people.

Even though she had no idea who she was, *I* knew who she was—this young woman was one of God's own! In all my years as a Christian and among Christians, never had I met one so in harmony with my own desire to search for and discover ever more depth in the *ideas* of both the spirit and the reality of the application and *practice* of those ideas.

From the first day with her, I recognized the combination immediately—this was a *hungry* soul—hungry to grow and learn, not in the least self-satisfied, desirous to press ever deeper into the character and heart and being of God . . . to *know* him!

Not a sophisticated soul, I could tell that too . . . no airs, no pretensions, no guile. Hungry . . . eyes wide open for all life could teach, for all life might mean.

How does one encounter such an appetite for *life* in a human breast and not be drawn to it, and not want to share in its pilgrimage to the high places of God? I had been around staleness and stagnation of the spirit so long, how could I not relish in the mere anticipation of *knowing* this lady's heart?

Six days after her awakening, I packed her up comfortably in the wagon, and with a lunch prepared by Mrs. Timms we headed into the countryside. It was her first excursion away from the house itself, and I judged that she was strong enough for an afternoon away from the bed.

"Where are we going?" she asked softly from where she lay padded in the back of the wagon amid as many blankets and pillows as I could get together from the house.

"Out . . . out away . . . to the country, to the hills, wherever our gallant steed should take us!" I replied, turning around and speaking to her with an enthusiasm that matched the joy in my heart.

"Sounds like an adventure," she replied. "Are you sure I am up to it?"

"You, Miss Hollister, I have deduced from my observations, are one I doubt would be daunted by anything!"

"I've never been wounded before."

"How do you know that?"

She was silent. "Hmm . . . you're right. I reckon I don't know that, do I?"

"Unless you are remembering more than you think," I suggested. "In any case, yes, I *do* think you are up to it."

"I still feel so weak, not nearly myself."

"Ah, there you are again, making comments that hint in the direction of your past. It seems as if, though your mind is not recalling its facts, your emotions are sensing things you used to feel."

"Is that a good sign?"

"I think a very good one."

"You still haven't told me where we are going."

"I don't know. I just wanted to get you out of the house, under the blue and white of God's sky, let you feel the wind in your face and feel the autumn chill and smell its smells. I know how you love God's creation, and it will refresh your spirit."

We rode on quietly for a while. I kept the reins tight so that our pace would be slow and the bouncing at a minimum. I took us probably not more than three-quarters of a mile from the house, then stopped and jumped down.

"You stay just where you are until I have a place ready for you," I said.

I tied the horse to a tree, then got several of the blankets and spread them out on the dried grass of the meadow. She started to rise.

"Wait," I said. "I don't want you reinjuring that shoulder trying to climb down."

"I'm fine. I can—"

I jumped up onto the wagon wheel beside her, and before she had a chance to finish, I slid my hands under her knees and back where she lay and scooped her into my arms. A moment or two later she was on the ground adjusting the blankets around her.

"I'm sorry," I said, noting the crimson in her face. "I didn't mean to embarrass you. But I have to admit I am very protective where that shoulder of yours is concerned."

"I must have lost a heap of weight," she said, giving a nervous little laugh. "You picked me up like I was a feather."

Now it was my turn to laugh. "Believe me, Miss Hollister, compared with the lifting I have done in my life, you *are* scarcely more than a feather! I worked my way through seminary hoisting hundred-pound bags of wheat all day long at a granary."

She said nothing, and the thought turned me introspective for a moment. "Although in retrospect," I added, "I suppose even that wasn't the hardest work I ever did."

"What was?" she asked.

I couldn't help smiling ironically. "Trying to feed people starving for the truth," I said. "People who had no idea how desperately hungry for it they ought to have been."

I paused. "Actually," I went on pensively, "perhaps the hardest work of all was trying to figure where truth was myself . . . *after* all that happened."

We opened the basket and laid out the simple fare provided for us by my landlady.

"Father," I prayed, closing my eyes, "I thank you for this glorious and wonderful day you have given us to enjoy. Thank you for the clouds above that move about as if delighting in the antics of the wind, the breath from your mouth. Thank you for those gentle breezes down here, chilling our cheeks and carrying into our nostrils those fragrant aromas from your thousand growing things, rousing us to life itself. Thank you, Father, that you do not allow us to rest, but always keep the winds of your spirit blowing through our inner houses to clean and purge and refresh. Thank you for your sun, the very picture of the fiery light of life which is the essence of your being. Thank you, God, for life itself! And I thank you for my sister, for protecting and preserving and restoring her life, for leading me to her. I ask you, Father, in the name of your son Jesus, to invigorate and fully energize her body, to utterly heal her wound, and to restore the fullness of her memory in your perfect time. Thank you, Father, for your goodness to us—in all ways. Amen."

"Amen," she repeated softly.

We began to eat awhile in silence. Neither of us, however, seemed particularly intent upon the food.

"Thank you for praying for me, Christopher," she said at length.

"Of course," I replied.

"Nobody's ever prayed like that for me." She caught herself, then glanced up and smiled. Such a beautiful and innocent smile of sheer delight in the moment. "At least, I don't *remember* ever being prayed for like that!"

"Sometimes I tend to get carried away when I pray," I said. "God's goodness is just so huge, it occasionally overwhelms me."

"I could feel that as you prayed," she said. "You really *know* God, and talk to him just like he truly *is* your father."

"What else is he?"

"But I don't remember hearing anyone talk so . . . I don't know—I reckon it sounded almost bold the way you were talking to him, like you knew he was not just listening, 'cause maybe we all do that, but like you knew without doubting it at all that he was gonna answer what you asked for."

"I suppose I do believe it," I said.

"Hearing you pray for me with such confidence, well, I reckon it makes me believe it too."

"I'm glad to hear it," I said.

"There is one thing I'm not glad about, though," she added.

I looked at her with concern. Then she smiled, and I saw that it was nothing I needed to worry about.

"Even though neither of the names are ones I altogether feel comfortable with, I reckon being called *Miss* Somebody still sounds a mite stranger than just having one name to get used to. So if you're still thinking I'm the person on that envelope I was carrying, especially if I'm calling you Christopher, don't you think it's high time you were calling me Corrie?"

"If you like," I laughed. "I will do so with pleasure."

"I do like."

"Then Corrie you shall be!"

CHAPTER 6

"Why are you doing all this for me?" Corrie asked after she had finished with as much lunch as she could eat.

"You mean helping you get back on your feet? What else could I do? Are we not commanded to do whatever we are able for our fellows?"

"But you have taken care of me night and day, for weeks. Surely you don't do this for everyone you meet."

"I do not often meet young ladies near death from gunshot wounds."

"You know what I mean," she said, not to be deterred from her interrogation. "There is something different about you. I know it. Even if I cannot remember who I am or where I have been, I can tell that you are unlike people I've known before, even if I can't remember them. You must know it too."

I felt myself squirm with embarrassment. She had turned the spotlight of conversation straight into that region where I was least comfortable that it should be—pointing at me!

"We can't talk much about me," Corrie added. "There's nothing we know of to talk about! So now I want to know about you. If we don't know why *I'm* here, I want to know why *you're* here taking such good care of me, someone you don't even know."

"But I *do* know you."

"There you go again trying to sidestep my question. I said it before, you know what I mean."

I laughed, thinking to myself that this was a determined and forceful young lady, a side to her I hadn't yet seen. "I suppose I do," I said.

I paused. "I have always had a great longing to help people," I went on at length.

"Why? Where did it come from."

"It's a long story."

"I'd like to hear it."

"If I tell you where it came from originally, I'll never get around to answering the question you just asked about why I'm here now with *you*."

"You'll tell me about the first part of it someday?"

"If you like."

"I insist you do. As much as you long to help people, I want to know *about* people."

"Why?"

She became very thoughtful. "Hmm . . . I don't know. It's something I just feel inside, like every person has a story to tell that I'm supposed to find out about."

"Another clue to your past?" I said.

"I reckon so. Which is all the more reason why I want you to promise that you *will* tell me *your* story someday, where the thing came from inside you that wants to help folks."

"All right . . . I promise."

Corrie smiled, satisfied. She'd won the exchange and knew it . . . and I knew it too! This young lady could match wits and hold her own with anybody!

"Now tell me why you're here now, and why I was lucky enough to have whatever happened to me happen where you'd find me."

I took in a deep breath and thought for a minute. "I told you I've wanted to help people. That's the story I've promised to tell you another time. For now I'll just say that it always meant more than merely doing things for them."

Again I paused. I suddenly found myself in new territory with this Corrie Hollister. Until now she had been, as it were, my patient. All at once, the insides of *my* being were being opened up, and *she* was holding the surgeon's scalpel with the penetrating gaze of her eyes and her probing questions. I was not accustomed to anyone being interested in these deep places within me, and it was an altogether new kind of exchange for me.

"Because of what had happened in my own life some time earlier, I found growing within me an enormous hunger to help people really *be* complete. To help them become full people, to help them know their heavenly Father intimately and wonderfully. If that meant doing something for them, like nursing you back to health, then I was happy for such an opportunity. But there was also the side to it, which was even stronger, of wanting to help people see and know God and be his sons and daughters—wanting them to know his truth, and to know themselves, and to know how great was his love for them, and to know that he was not a faraway God Almighty and Omnipotent somewhere in the distant heavens, but that he was a close and present and tender and compassionate and loving Father to them! And it was this hunger in me that led me toward the ministry."

"How old were you?"

"I was in my teen years when God began to get deeply into me. I was twenty-one when I entered seminary."

"The bags of grain?"

"Right! Wheat by day, Bible and preaching and Church History by night!"

"Sounds like a lot of work."

"It was. But I desperately wanted to serve God's people, and the ministry was the only way I knew to go about it. I could envision no other place where such a hunger as mine could live itself out and express itself and exercise an impact in people's lives. So I worked hard and studied equally hard, preparing myself for a life in the church. That was the call I thought was on me, and I gave myself to it enthusiastically."

"And then?"

"I made it through the four years, obtained my degree of Divinity—"

"You are an actual certified minister!"

"In the flesh, a Doctor of Divinity."

"I'm impressed."

"Don't be. A few letters after my name means less to me now than I can possibly tell you."

"Still, it *is* something."

"No, it really isn't."

"No matter. Please . . . go on. I 'm sorry for interrupting you."

"Well, I was twenty-five, a newly ordained minister of the gospel of Jesus Christ, excited at last to be sent out into the harvest fields, so to speak, and to begin *doing* what I had prepared for and longed for. When I say 'harvest fields,' I do not mean the lost and unsaved, or the pagans in the jungle. I had long felt within my own heart such a desire and hunger to be part of the growth and nurturing process within the body of *God's* people—helping *Christians* know their Father better more than trying to bring unbelieving people into the church with salvation messages and hellfire sermons."

"Did you become pastor of a church?"

"Not immediately. But all the seminary graduates send out letters making themselves available. And there are notices of churches in need of pastors. It's the typical search of a new minister, fueled both by a great hope as well as a great dread."

"What dread?"

"The dread of no church wanting you, after you've prepared so long and so hard."

"That must have happened to you," said Corrie. "You're obviously not a pastor now, and it couldn't have been too long ago. I'm sorry."

"Why do you say it couldn't have been long ago?"

"Because you're so young. You don't look any older than I am."

"I'm thirty. By the way, Corrie, how old *are* you?"

She thought for a moment, trying hard to rummage through the parts of her brain still working to see if she could locate the answer.

"I don't know," she said finally with a sigh. "But I don't *think* I'm that old. I have the feeling I'm twenty-five or twenty-six . . . or maybe even twenty-seven. But I'm sure I'm not thirty."

"Well, I am. I graduated five years ago, in 1859—and I was full of optimism for the future. It did not take long for me to find a church that did indeed want me to be their pastor, and they issued me a formal call."

"You must have been thrilled."

"Of course. It was a decent-sized congregation too, in a section of the city where a young man just out of school would not expect to start. It was a prestigious way to make a beginning in what could well be a prominent career in the religious world."

"You sound . . . hmm—I don't know . . . I reckon a little cynical."

I could not help laughing, and I don't suppose I disguised the irony in my voice any too well.

"You're a very perceptive young lady, Corrie Hollister," I said. "I can see just what you said about yourself, that you are always looking underneath the surface of people, hunting for a story they can tell you. And you're exactly right. In retrospect I now see all too clearly that they wanted me for reasons I could not see then, would not have dared to admit."

"What kind of reasons?"

"It's humiliating even to suggest it," I answered, "but now I see that it wasn't for what life and truth they hoped I could bring them, but rather because—this is the difficult part to say!—I was a strong, able-bodied young man, whom they perhaps perceived as dynamic to a degree, and who would 'look good' in their pulpit and give their church a good name."

"Do churches really choose ministers that way?"

"Oh yes—all the time!"

"But you didn't see it?"

"No. I was unbelievably naive. I *was* dynamic in a way, I suppose—full of enthusiasm and ideas and, as I said, such an open-hearted desire to do good for people—spiritual good, to preach the truth and to talk about the Lord Jesus and to encourage my congregation to know him better and do more of what he said and to live as he told us to live."

"Why do you call that naive?"

"Because I assumed all Christians felt the same. I *assumed* that since they had heard me and investigated me, and had then called me, they *wanted* everything I had to offer. I assumed they were as hungry to grow and find the truth and live by it as I was."

"What did you do?"

"I jumped in with both feet!"

I couldn't help laughing. It all seemed so long ago now. "Oh, I *was* naive! I preached and visited with enthusiasm, and taught them what so burned in my heart about God's Fatherhood. And for a while I even flattered myself that my teaching and preaching was, what is called in religious circles, *well-received*. All the people were full of smiles and well-meaning comments and handshakes from Sunday to Sunday, and the church even began to grow somewhat. To say I wasn't aware would not be truthful. But I innocently concluded that it was the warm and inviting message of God's love that people were responding to, and that it was this message that was swelling the congregation from Sunday to Sunday."

"You don't think it was?"

"Among some few faithful and hungry souls, to be sure. But in general, no, it wasn't the message at all."

"What was it, then?"

"I am ashamed to have to say it, but your questions keep probing right to the center of the whole episode in my life."

"I'm sorry, I don't mean to pry."

"Please, don't apologize. It actually feels good to tell somebody. I never have told anyone the whole thing."

"I hope you will be able to tell me it all."

I looked away. Neither of us had eaten another bite since beginning to talk. A cold breeze hit me in the face and I was reminded of my patient's condition.

"Are you not too cold?" I asked, looking back upon her with concern. "Perhaps we should—"

"I am as cozy as a body could likely be under these blankets," Corrie answered without even giving me a chance to finish. "And I want to hear why your church was growing."

"Because of *me*," I said, almost blurting the words out. It already felt good to tell somebody. "I came to see that *I* was the attraction, not the gospel message I was trying to proclaim. I even learned later that—God help me, this is so mortifying to have to admit!—I learned that there were certain prominent men in the community who were bringing their daughters to my services because word had spread that the minister cut a dashing figure and there was scarce a better match to be found in the city. All the time I was in the pulpit preaching from my heart, there they were in the congregation trying to scheme their way into making a husband of me, while the rest were relishing in the church's growing 'reputation'!"

I sighed deeply at the painful memory and looked away again. I could not keep a tear or two from rising in my eye. A moment later I felt a gentle hand on my arm. I turned, and Corrie slowly pulled her hand away.

"Do you have any idea what a bitter blow it was to my spirit to realize all that?" I said quietly. "To feel that I was standing in the way, between my people and the message of God?"

She said nothing, just continued to look at me with eyes of compassion and, yes, understanding. I knew she *did* understand!

"It wasn't until later that everything began to dawn upon me. Things went so well at first that I was blinded to the truth. The church grew and the people were enthusiastic and I received invitations into many homes, hardly noticing that most were from the top rungs of society and most had eligible daughters in their early twenties. Where the poor and the downcast were—the kind of men and women Jesus had to do with—I did not stop at the beginning to inquire about. And thus it continued for two years."

"What happened then?"

"What else . . . the war came. For the country *and* for me."

"The *war* . . ." Corrie repeated softly, and immediately I could see a faraway gaze come into her eyes. Somehow we had not really spoken together of the war before that moment, and the mere mention of the word seemed to jar her brain into some new region of bewildered struggle to remember. I let her go, and said nothing, giving her time to reflect. Then slowly she seemed to come awake again to my presence.

"You were going to tell me what happened in your church when . . . when the *war* came," she said at length, though from the way she spoke I could tell there was still a haze floating about her consciousness.

"Yes," I said, "the war. Suddenly everything was about the war. No longer did people care about things of the spirit. Even the interest in finding a wife for me seemed to wane. Everything in the country was turned upside down. Yet I felt an obligation to continue to speak and preach and teach what I considered the *truth* without regard to political and national affiliation. Again, my naivete was profound! I was still, even after two years, under-girded by the assumption that the men and women of my congregation shared my vision and my hunger for truth and saw things as I saw them. I assumed we all had a similar desire to grow in all ways connected with the spiritual life. But I could not have been more wrong."

"What happened?"

"I discovered the bitter truth that most of the people I had thought were so with me were Southerners first, Republicans or Democrats second, and Christians last. I had somehow assumed their Christianity would take top position in their attitudes, not last."

"How did you discover that?"

"I made the mistake of beginning to preach openly from the pulpit against attitudes of judgment and rancor and criticism. A few cast skeptical eyes on me, but they kept mostly quiet at first. But then when my words about loyalty and submission hinted at opposition toward those over us, the criticism against me began to grow vocal and began to mount. Yet still the scales were not fully removed from my eyes. Still the naive assumption that most of the congregation *wanted* to hear such truth persisted. I deluded myself that it was only a small, discontented minority that was speaking out. And therefore I continued to take stronger and stronger stands concerning our sacred duty as God's people to raise forth a banner of truth and righteousness against the terrible divisiveness that was tearing the nation apart. I even was so bold as to declare that there could be only one nation, and that it was our scriptural duty as Christians to stand up and be heard.

"The final moment came late in 1861 when I preached a sermon denouncing slavery itself, speaking boldly about the equality of races according to the Bible, and declaring it our urgent calling to not let ourselves be swept into the political fray, that we had to remain firmly committed to the truths of Scripture. I called for us to stand up in unity with our brothers and sisters and fellow children of God in the North—to stand firmly *without* allying ourselves with the churches and church leaders who were finding spiritual justification for supporting the Confederacy."

"Did you say that your church ought to support the North?"

"No. I thought I was saying that we had to be God's people, *above* being Northerners *or* Southerners—that we could not try to justify a political position as Christians. But what they *heard* me say, and what was reported the next day in the newspapers throughout the city, was quite another matter. It was with swift and sickening realization that it finally dawned on me that my presence in the pulpit had had nothing to do with truth or the spiritual content of my words at all. I had been there merely to occupy a role which the church leaders perceived was fitting with the image they wanted for their church in the community. When my presence began to tarnish that image, everything changed with such suddenness that I still have not altogether recovered from it."

"What happened?"

"I never preached from that pulpit again. On the Tuesday following the sermon I spoke of, I was presented with a letter calling for my resignation. I would comply, I was told in no uncertain terms, before the following Sunday, or criminal charges of treason against the Confederacy would be filed against me."

"What did you do?"

"What choice did I have? What is a pulpit if no one is listening? That was not the ministry I had prepared and prayed for."

"So you did resign?"

"In absolute shock, I signed the paper they thrust before me. Overnight I was without a church. The men left in silence, and I laid my head down on my desk and wept bitterly for half an hour."

Again I turned away and fought back the tears that tried to recur every time I thought of the painful day.

"I know many men suffer the loss of something they have held dear. But the calling I felt was such a lofty one, and the descent so sudden and unexpected, I was absolutely devastated. The following days and weeks were of such anguish and a sense of loss, I can scarcely remember anything of them. Perhaps it makes me sensitive to your present plight. My brain and heart were singed as with a scorching fire, and there suddenly seemed nothing left to live for. Everything I had cared about had been swept away as by a hot desert wind—leaving nothing but the dry sands of the Sahara in its place. I felt worse than empty—emptier than empty.

I felt a void . . . a nothingness . . . a hot parching thirst but with no water to drink, no water anywhere."

"Did you lose your faith?"

"No, the void and emptiness weren't from that. It was that suddenly my faith had nowhere to lay its head, no place to rest, no place to exist within my being. The faith was still there, but I had nowhere to put it—if that makes the least bit of sense."

"Of course it makes sense," she replied earnestly. "What did you do? Did you look for another church?"

"Oh no, I was far too shipwrecked and desolate of soul for that. Nor do I think I would have been able to find one. The episode made most of the large southern papers. I was a traitor. Probably I might have sought my fortunes in the North, but my experience seriously wounded my desire to serve in the ministry. I still do not know whether such is a direction I will pursue ever again in the future. I have been wrestling it through ever since."

"But without an answer?"

"With many answers, but without *an* answer. There is no single direction I have for my future, if that is what you mean. And for every bit of light I think I receive about it, another dozen questions crop up to plague my spirit."

"So what have you done since?"

"Well, that was three years ago—a little more, actually. Once I left the pulpit, I thought I would be drafted into the army. I could never have fought, of course. I would not have carried a gun had they thrust it into my hands. They could have put me in prison or hanged or shot me for treason, but I would *never* pick up a gun. It is a vow I made when I was sixteen, and it has served me faithfully ever since, and I will never go back on it."

"But you weren't drafted?"

"In a way, I suppose, my ouster from the church kept me out of the army. When conscription was passed in April of 1862, had I still occupied such a visible position right there in Richmond, I have no doubt I'd have been wearing the Confederate gray within two months, perhaps as a medic or a chaplain. As it was, I had faded out of public view, and somehow I became one of those few able-bodied young white men who slipped through the planks. I was never summoned, and I never volunteered. I kept to myself, and not long afterward found this place here with Mrs. Timms. Her husband died just before the war began, so I have seen to the farm for her in exchange for my room and board. The war has been close many times—very close these last six months. When soldiers are in need, I do what I can. I have fed and patched together men with far worse wounds than yours, I can tell you that! But never have I felt a compulsion to join them. I do not believe in war and fighting under any circumstances, and to belong to the army, even as a chaplain, would be to go against everything I am as a man. I have been called a coward and a traitor. I have been spat upon by the very men whose lives I have saved when they discover I have remained a neutral civilian. But I have no choice but to put up with their insults. It is a matter of principle to me. I would be no true man were I not courageous enough to take such a stand. I do not *feel* altogether courageous. And many times I do not feel that I am much of a man. But I have done what I have done, and here I yet remain with the war—hopefully at last!—drawing to a close."

A long silence followed. As I told Corrie, I had never confided such things to anyone before. Mrs. Timms, although grateful for my presence, was, I think, always a bit uncertain about me and never asked. Now I had opened a door into myself that had been shut rather tightly for years. Corrie, too, seemed aware of the significance of all I had said, and reflected on it for several minutes. Neither of us spoke again for some time.

"I'm more curious about the inside part of you," Corrie said at length. "If you'd wanted to be a minister all those years, and worked so hard, it seems like it'd be a mite hard to just give up on it without maybe . . . I don't know exactly what I'm trying to say, but it seems like if you believed in it, that maybe you ought to fight for it more—whatever those people in that church thought of you. They might all have been wrong. You shouldn't quit just because they didn't like a sermon or two."

"If I didn't know better, I'd think you spoke from personal experience," I said with a smile.

"I don't know if I get your meaning," Corrie replied with a puzzled look.

"Oh, nothing really," I said. "It's just that you sound very convincing, as if *you've* had to go through something like that too—fighting to hang on to a dream you believe in even when it's not easy to do."

"Hmm . . . I don't know. What I said just kind of popped out."

"Well, there is a great deal of wisdom in what you say, Corrie. And perhaps the time will come when I will enter that so-called 'fight' and go back and pursue the ministry again. But now is not the time. I have to find out what I really believe and what God *really* wants of me first."

"I thought you said it didn't make you doubt."

"Doubt? That is a very complex word. Did I say I hadn't doubted? If so, I didn't speak truthfully. I haven't lost faith in God, if that's what you mean. But doubt—my life has been one of constant doubt ever since that fateful day when I was presented with my resignation paper to sign!"

"I always thought of doubt as the same thing as not believing."

"I don't think I've ever believed so strongly as during this three-year period of doubt. I suppose for many the word *doubt* implies doubt about God himself and his existence and his good-ness. But I never doubt *him*. When I speak of doubt, I speak of struggling to understand him more deeply, understand his ways, understand myself in relation to him, understand his truths. You see, for so long I now realize I took a great deal for granted about God and faith. With everything swept out from under me, I found I had to go back to the bedrock of God himself, not what I had been taught or had previously thought about him, and discover anew what I really believed. The doubt, so to speak, was not a doubt that took me *away* from God but which drove me all the deeper and more intimately *into* his presence. Where else could I go with my doubts and my questions and my hurts and my tears but to him? I had no one else. I could no longer even trust myself! My Father was the only possible solid rock in the midst of all my mental and emotional floundering. He was the one Presence I did *not* doubt, could never doubt."

"So explain to me what you mean by doubt. I still don't think I quite get what you're saying."

"That's as big a question as the one you asked before."

"Which one?"

"About what put in me the desire to help people."

"But you won't make me wait for this one . . . will you?"

"No," I laughed. "I've already told you more about myself than probably any other human being knows. I don't suppose there's any reason to stop now."

"Good," said Corrie. "I'm enjoying this fresh air more than I can tell you. I feel stronger than any day since . . . since I woke up with you sitting there on the side of the bed. So I want you to tell me, no matter how long it takes."

I let out a long breath. It felt so good to have such an honest interchange with one whose hungers seemed to point in the same direction as my own. Yet such things were not easy to relive!

"You're asking a difficult thing from me."

"I'm sorry, Christopher. If you don't want—"

"No, it's all right. I *want* to tell you about it. I'm only confessing that scratching a rake across the innermost ground of my soul, where there are still raw places exposed, is not an easy, or even a pleasant thing. But I think it is a *good* thing. Good does not always mean pleasant or enjoyable."

I paused briefly. "As I told you earlier, I was forced down to the bedrock of God's being itself, and was left with nothing much else to hang on to. I felt, as I told you, in the middle of a hot desert. I was alone and lonely, despondent, discouraged, broken. I cannot tell you how many tears I wept—some quietly, some with heaving anguish that racked my whole frame. I suppose there are many who consider it unmanly to shed tears, as a sign of weakness. But I *was* weak. Desperately weak! It is impossible to find the words to convey how stunning was the shock to be forced to realize that I had been alone in that church in my quest for deep truth about God. I saw my naivete, even my foolishness. I felt like such a sap, such a fool . . . so blind.

"And yet . . . I so deeply loved the church and God's people, and still wanted more than anything to be among them. So there was no bitterness *toward* anyone. But suddenly I was so alone and so isolated and cut off that I didn't know what to do.

"I spent hours walking these fields and hills, talking to God, crying out to him, falling on the ground in tears of confusion! I had to rethink everything I had ever believed. I suppose, in a sense, I had to reconstruct my very faith, as if I was building a whole new house. The foundation was still there all the time— God himself. But a hurricane had blown away everything else. Now I had to rebuild it all, board by board. And I wasn't able to use all the boards from the past. They were all new boards. I had to ask God anew about prayer, about faith, about obedience, even about his own Fatherhood. I had to wrestle through the relationship between the Father and the Son in a deeper way than I had ever studied about the Trinity in seminary. I had to grapple with heaven and hell from whole new vantage points of thought that had never occurred to me in all my wildest speculations when I was younger. I thought a great deal about unity and what it might mean, about what it *ought* to mean. I studied the passage of John 17 for countless hours—"

As I spoke I was unconsciously watching Corrie. At these last words, a sudden look swept across her face that I couldn't understand, a look as if she had been invisibly slapped in the face momentarily. I could see her gaze drift away and I stopped and waited. It lasted only two or three seconds. Then she seemed to shake it away, her eyes coming to rest upon me, and she said, "I'm sorry. Something about what you said . . . it just . . . sounded familiar somehow. But I don't know why. Go on . . . please."

"Mostly," I said, "I thought about the church itself, about Christians, about what growth really is supposed to be, about what the words *body of Christ* truly mean—mostly about what my place in it all ought to be. What was God leading me toward? What did God want of me? What was unity, what was the church, and what was I supposed to do? Was I supposed to be a minister as I had always thought . . . or did God have something else in his ordained plan that was still in my future where I could not yet see it?"

I stopped. I had been looking away as I spoke. Now I brought my eyes back to where Corrie was seated on the blanket across from me. She was gazing into my face intently.

"What did you find out through it all?" she asked. "Were all your questions answered?"

"Hardly!" I laughed. "I don't suppose that will *ever* happen.

As I told you, for every answer there are a dozen more questions!"

"Well, then, did you at least find enough boards to rebuild your house? You're not still in the desert?"

"Let me put it this way," I said. "The house is far from complete, and I still have no idea what it's going to look like when and if it ever gets done. But I think I do have walls enough for a room or two and a roof over my head. I'm dry and cozy and protected from the winds and hailstones and rains that were pelting me so fiercely a year or two ago. As I said, I don't know what the rest of this house of my faith and my life with God is going to look like. But I'm hopeful and optimistic once again. And I have more confidence in the solidness of the Foundation than ever before in my life."

"I don't mean to keep asking so much," said Corrie, "but I am so interested. I don't *remember* hearing anything like this before."

"Your curiosity is entirely forgiven!"

"Then would you mind telling me about the walls and roof you have built? I want to know about the boards you used. I want to know what the house looks like now, even *if* you don't know what it will look like five years from now."

"My, but you are inquisitive!"

This time Corrie didn't apologize but laughed along with me. And by now I found her questions wonderfully honest and refreshing. It was another two hours before we finally rose to return to the house, during which time I had learned some things about myself that even I hadn't known before.

By the time the day was over I was sure of her name! That she was a skilled reporter, I could no longer doubt.

CHAPTER 7

After supper that evening, while Corrie attempted to help Mrs. Timms and converse with her in the kitchen, I took my place at a little writing table I had been using since Corrie had been occupying my room. Fifteen or so minutes later, suddenly I was aware of her standing at my shoulder watching me. I gave a little jump.

I glanced up. "I didn't hear you approach," I said.

"I didn't mean to startle you," she said. "What are you working on?"

"Oh, nothing much," I replied. "It's my journal."

"*Journal* . . ." she repeated in a very curious tone. It was not a questioning tone, but I nevertheless took the opportunity to explain further.

"I write down most of what I do, especially things I am thinking about," I said. "My spiritual thoughts, prayers . . . sometimes I even talk to God on paper when I'm groping for light about something I'm puzzled about."

"*Journal*," she repeated again.

"After everything we talked about today, I wanted to begin getting it down before I forgot anything," I went on. "The thoughts of the human mind, especially when they are directed toward God and trying to learn more of his ways, are precious to me—even my own, if it's not too ridiculous a thing to say. It's almost something I feel I *have* to do, write down what I am thinking—even if no one but God himself ever reads it."

"I . . . I think I understand," said Corrie softly, her voice more pensive than I had ever heard it before. "Everything you say hits something deep in me. . . . I can feel your words going into a place in my mind, even in my heart . . . but it's a place I can't *see* with the eyes of my memory. I . . . I think I used to keep a journal too. . . ."

The look on her face was miles and miles away—perhaps thousands of miles away!

"Seeing your fingers . . . and the pen . . . and the words on the paper . . . it all reminds me of something far away . . . farther away than my mind can follow it. . . ."

"I told you in the beginning that I thought you were a writer."

"I'd hardly thought about it since, but now . . . I *feel* something tugging away inside me at the very sight of you sitting there . . . writing like that . . . and the word *journal*. . . ."

I rose and led her to a soft chair nearby.

"Sit down," I said. "There's something I've been waiting to show you. I think now the time has come."

She obeyed, still with the far-off gaze in her eye. I went into the bedroom where I still kept most of my scant possessions, and opened the second drawer of the bureau. I returned, then handed her the newspaper, already opened to the third page and folded back so that the article in question was plainly visible.

"I think it is time you read this," I said.

She looked at the paper, squinted her eyes momentarily, then glanced up at me with a questioning expression.

"It says . . ." Her voice trailed off softly.

"Yes, I know," I answered. "It says *Corrie Belle Hollister* there under the caption. If that is your name, it would appear you are more than a mere writer of letters or a keeper of a journal as I am."

A moment more she stared at me, then returned her attention to the paper and read the article in full. I sat patiently in an adjacent chair. At last she completed it, set the paper down on her lap, and looked over in my direction once more.

"Is this why you have called me Corrie Hollister without doubting it was my real name?" she asked.

"Along with the envelope, yes, I would say I am thoroughly satisfied. Don't you see how it all fits together—the ink stains on your fingers, your inquisitive nature, your responses about writing and journal keeping? But of course, all that I have seen and deduced is circumstantial. There is no proof that you are Corrie Hollister—not unless something comes to your mind from reading this article."

"It all . . . it all does have a bit of a familiar feel to it," she said, softly and thoughtfully, trying to understand her reaction even as she uttered the words. "I don't know how to rightly explain it . . . kinda like it was from a dream, or something that happened to somebody else."

"But you do recognize it?"

"I can't say it that strong . . . that plain-like . . . it's more something I *feel* when I read it, like I *ought* to know something more about it, but my mind can't quite lay hold of it—just like everything else."

Corrie looked away, and I knew she was crying softly. I rose, sought a handkerchief, took it to her and placed it in her hand, then departed from the room for a minute or two. When I returned she was in the midst of reading the article again, dabbing her eyes and nose occasionally, but reading with great intensity. I sat down beside her again and waited patiently. It took her longer to read it all this time. I could tell she was digesting every word. At length she put the paper down once more and looked at me. Her eyes, though still a little wet, were full of earnestness.

"This paper is from the North," she said. "But we are near Richmond. How did you get it?"

I smiled. "I hadn't thought that would occur to you. You have a very sharp and perceptive mind, Corrie."

"Never mind all that. How did you get it?"

"It's not important. I don't get papers from the Union regularly, but I have been interested in the election because I believe Mr. Lincoln is still the President of the entire country, and I wanted to hear about it without the negative Confederate bias of all the southern papers. So from time to time I manage to smuggle some papers in by mail. My means are devious," I added with a smile, "and there's no need to go into all that. The point is, I do get them from time to time, and here is one with your byline under a major article about the election campaign."

"The election . . . I hadn't given it so much as a thought since waking up here with you. I reckon in the back of my mind I have been aware of the war and the whole conflict about slavery, and you've mentioned it. But it's all seemed far away and dream-like. And Mr. Lincoln hadn't crossed my mind once. Now suddenly . . . it's all coming back to me . . . some feeling of . . . I can't rightly tell . . . something urgent, even dangerous. . . . I feel as if there's something I'm supposed to know or do or tell somebody. . . ."

She stopped, grabbed up the paper again, and with hasty fingers began unfolding it and turning the pages looking for a date. "When did you get this paper?" she said, not looking up but still sifting through the pages.

"I've had it probably three weeks. I think it came about the same time you did. Of course it was already more than a week old by then."

She stopped rummaging through the sheets. "Then when *is* the election?" she asked, looking toward me again.

"Corrie," I said, "the election was two weeks ago. It took place when you were unconscious."

"Two weeks ago!" she exclaimed in shock. "Then it's too late!"

"What's too late?" I said.

"Whatever I was supposed to do . . . the danger . . ."

She seemed to be thinking more clearly all at once, yet a confused, panicked expression was on her face.

"But . . . but what about the war? There's something I was doing . . ." she went on, struggling desperately to recall some vital piece of information that was eluding her. "And the President . . . there's some danger . . . I've got to tell him—"

Her words broke off in frustration.

"Corrie," I said softly after a moment, "wasn't the thing you needed to do, to tell people to vote for Mr. Lincoln?"

The words seemed to have a calming effect. Her forehead wrinkled in thought, then she slowly nodded. "Yes . . . I think you're right . . . that's what this article says, isn't it?"

"Wasn't that the danger? A danger to the country, to the Union, if he was defeated?"

Still she was thinking hard, and slowly nodding. "Yes . . . that must be it . . . that has to be what I was getting all stirred up about—"

"Don't you see then, everything is all right—the danger is past, and you *did* do what you needed to do."

She looked at me, bewildered.

"I don't . . . what do you mean? I haven't done anything."

"You wrote this article, didn't you? And apparently others before it."

"But how does that. . . ?"

She didn't have the words even to finish her question.

"Corrie, don't you hear what I'm telling you—the election is over. President Lincoln was reelected!"

Still her face was blank and confused, as if even this good news wasn't sufficient in itself to dispel her doubts and uncertainties. Then slowly the wrinkles on her forehead faded and she sat back in the chair and began to breathe deeply and more easily.

"Yes . . . that is good news . . . reelected. I'm glad to hear it . . . wonderful news . . ." Her voice, however, remained soft, just barely above a whisper. Reading the article and the ensuing exchange between us had clearly taxed her.

"But . . . but what about the war?" she asked after a moment. "Is it still going on?"

"I'm afraid so," I answered. "Terrible things are happening farther to the south. General Sherman's army has nearly destroyed Atlanta. Rumors have even been reported that he plans to burn the city to the ground. And closer by, General Lee continues to hold Richmond, while General Grant's siege of Petersburg continues. I don't know, Corrie, if the end is yet in sight, though I continue to pray."

But again, as I spoke, the faraway gaze returned to her eyes, and her voice was barely audible.

". . . Lee . . . *Grant* . . ." she murmured softly. ". . . Petersburg . . . where is that?"

"South of Richmond," I said. "Only about thirty miles. Both armies are encamped around it. They have been fighting in and around Richmond for five or six months."

". . . *Grant* . . . *General Grant* . . ." she whispered again.

I glanced away unconsciously for a moment. When I turned

toward her again I saw that she was fast asleep.

I rose from the chair, picked her up in my arms, and carried her to the bed, where I made her as comfortable as I could, keeping her wound well away from where she might accidentally roll over onto it.

CHAPTER 8

I had cherished the hope that reading the article, talking about the war and the election, and hearing about the election results would trigger the necessary mechanisms in Corrie's brain to stimulate her memory back into full operation. But it was not to be.

When she awoke the next morning, it was with a stupor-like gaze of unreality on her face. When I tried to question her about the things we had spoken of, her responses were vague, distant, and disjointed. She remembered the words only, but not the feel and emotional tug which had so gripped her before. We even discussed the article she had written about the country and President Lincoln, and she seemed willing to be called and even to consider herself Corrie Hollister in a more definite way.

Yet there was a matter-of-fact distance to it. It was as though she had ventured to the very precipice of her memory, and then, as she slept, retreated from it once more. I did not understand what had happened. I had felt the full return of her consciousness was at hand, only to find it suddenly gone.

Days passed . . . then another week . . . then two. They were pleasant days. We spoke of many things. The lump on her head was now gone. Her arm and shoulder were healing so nicely that I did not think it would be much longer before the sling could be removed. She was out of bed most of the day and followed me about a good many of my chores around the place. We became much more deeply acquainted in things spiritual than I had imagined it possible to be with another person. In that vein, there was certainly no diminishing of her mental acuity. She was as alive, ever probing, questioning, insightful, and full of what I can only

59

describe as the life of God. I continued to be marvelously refreshed and full of joy in her presence.

But when it came to her factual memory about her past, the void of amnesia continued and showed no sign of a change.

December came, Christmas approached, and slowly a deeper concern began to grow within me. What if the amnesia went on and on . . . indefinitely?

The question itself—once I summoned the courage to look it squarely in the face—was almost too enormous for me to consider. The implications were huge!

What if . . . what if she *never* remembered!

Here she was, obviously a Northerner—a Northerner of repute and importance—in the South, found wounded along the roadside with nothing on her person except a letter, whose return address I could not make out, from someplace in California I could hardly read and had never heard of, in the middle of a war . . .

What was I to do? Should I contact the newspaper whose copy we had been reading? Surely they would know something about her. Should I write a letter and make an attempt to reconstruct the whereabouts of this Almeda from the smudged ink on the outside of the envelope?

At first my duty had been plain enough—get her to safety, dress the wound, and do my best to save her life and nurse her back to health. Now that aspect of it seemed completed, or nearly so.

What now? I couldn't let her remain here forever. Surely she had family and responsibilities elsewhere. I *must* set some inquiries afoot—try to contact the lady in California and the newspaper. Yet I would have to be discreet. I could not put her at risk. Communications between North and South were unreliable just now. I could not let inquiries about her fall into the wrong hands. If she were found here by the wrong people, she could be put under guard as a spy.

I could not even ignore the possibility—though I could hardly make myself believe it after all I had heard from her own lips— that she *was* a spy. Why else would she be in the South? And the greatest mystery of all that constantly plagued me was the most obvious dilemma of all: Was the shooting an accident, or had someone actually attempted to kill this gentle, sensitive, thoroughly Christian young lady named Corrie Hollister? If so . . . what possible motive could they have had? *Unless* . . . she was indeed on some kind of secret mission for the Union behind the Confederate lines!

I could come to no immediate resolution of what to do.

To write letters concerning her to California and to a northern newspaper seemed too risky. I did *not* want to put her in the slightest jeopardy! Therefore, I decided to wait awhile longer.

If and when her memory returned and I could learn more of why she had been on a road outside Richmond, then I would do everything in my power to help her. Until then, I would be content to serve her as I had till now, looking to God to reveal any change I should make when the time was right.

CHAPTER 9

Christmas Day, 1864, was surely the most memorable and unusual Christmas I had ever spent!

Since deciding not to send out letters of inquiry just yet, I had been turning over another plan in my mind and had finally resolved upon what to do. Whether or not it would have any direct result I didn't know, but I wanted to do it regardless, even if just as a friend. It required a trip into Richmond a week before Christmas, and then many late-night hours of work by candlelight thereafter. But when the day came I was satisfied with my efforts and had managed to catch it almost completely up-to-date.

I found Corrie midway through the day on Christmas Eve, sitting with the newspaper from Richmond in her lap that had just come a day or two earlier. She again had an expression on her face that indicated a return to the perplexed and frustrating introspection of several weeks before. I approached. She glanced up at me, still with the same expression, then pointed to an article she had been reading.

"Do you know this man?" she asked me.

"You mean who wrote the article?"

She nodded.

I read the byline. "Not personally, of course," I answered. "But I know *of* him. He's a well-known reporter in Richmond. He's been covering the war and has been writing for the paper for years. Why?"

"The moment I saw his name, I felt that I ought to know him."

"You're both reporters, Corrie. It wouldn't surprise me for you to have heard of him."

"No, I mean really *know* him," she insisted.

"A friend?" I suggested.

"I don't think so. When I saw the name, a feeling came over me that I don't even know how to explain—that feeling of danger again, but different than before . . . not something close by but maybe from a long time ago . . . and with a little anger mixed in too. I felt myself getting kinda riled up without knowing why."

We were both silent a minute.

"You know," I said, "now that you've got me thinking about it, I seem to recall that he *did* spend some time out West quite a while back. I don't know where or what it was about. I think I was in seminary at the time. But something about it now begins to sound very familiar. You don't suppose. . . ?"

I let my tone indicate the question instead of finishing the words.

"Suppose what?" said Corrie, either not knowing what I meant, or else suspecting but wanting me to say it anyway.

"That . . . maybe you *are* from the West, and that your path did cross this fellow's, maybe that you wrote for the same newspaper even."

Corrie said nothing, but it was clear enough she was thinking hard. The confusion, however, remained on her face.

The next morning was Christmas. I had been up past midnight finishing my final entries, but was up at dawn regardless—stifling down a few yawns, it is true, yet eager and excited for the day. Whatever became of it, I had determined to make it special, memorable, and happy for my friend and sister Corrie Hollister, whom I had grown extremely fond of.

I was in the barn just finishing with the four cows when I heard the creak of the door. I looked up. There was Corrie walking toward me.

"Merry Christmas, Corrie!" I said. "You look very nice today. If I didn't know better, I would never know you had been wounded."

"Thank you, Christopher." Her smile was bright and showed not a trace of yesterday's inner turmoil. "My arm and shoulder feel wonderful. I am so glad to have the sling and bandages finally off."

"Does it feel well enough for a ride?" I asked, squeezing out the final drops from the cow's udder into the pail below.

"In the wagon?"

"No . . . horseback. I've been waiting until you were ready and I thought we could try it out for Christmas. You do ride, don't you?"

"I . . . I don't know."

"I've seen the way you eye the horses around here, Corrie. You have the look of one who knows them."

"Is it . . . I didn't realize. But now that you say it, something tells me you're right, that I *do* ride."

"There's a very special place I've been wanting to show you, but we can only get to it on horseback. I've been hoping today would be the day."

"You're my doctor. If you think I'm ready, then I'd love to go."

"After dinner then," I said, rising from the three-legged stool and giving the faithful milk cow a pat. "But before this day gets too far advanced, I've got to see to some hay and feed for these girls, as well as the others of the family. Christmas means nothing to them."

"Let me take care of the chickens and goats," offered Corrie.

"Not in your nice clean dress."

"I'll be careful. Please, I *want* to help. You've been doing nothing but waiting on me for too long."

"All right," I said, "but only if you put on that old overcoat of mine there—" I pointed to a hook beside the door where I kept my work coat. "And a pair of my boots."

"Agreed!" said Corrie with a smile, spinning around and bounding off. She snatched the coat from the hook and threw it around her shoulders, then disappeared out the door.

I cleaned up the cows' stalls, supplied Mrs. Timms' bovine ladies fresh straw for their beds, fresh hay for their feeding stall, then led them out to the pasture for the day. Returning to the barn, I saw to the pigs' breakfast, and met Corrie as she was latching the gate to the chicken coop.

"All done," she announced, holding up five fresh eggs in her hands.

"Mrs. Timms will be delighted. Could you use some help with the goats?"

"You're the boss, remember?" said Corrie playfully.

"Then we will feed them together!" I said. I offered Corrie my arm. She took it. And side by side we marched toward the pen where twenty hungry, rude, and insistent goats waited without an inkling of what happiness swelled my heart!

CHAPTER 10

Mrs. Timms had no family. She and I had forged a tolerable friendship under circumstances which had thrust us together when neither of us were at our best. She was struggling with the loss of her husband, I with the loss of my spiritual vision, and neither of us could offer the other what we needed most. Corrie's presence, therefore, had slowly enlivened the whole house. And as Christmas had approached I saw light and life in the eyes and face of my landlady that I had never before witnessed. Without her knowing it, Corrie Hollister was bringing fresh hope to both Mrs. Timms and me.

When the day came, it was no surprise to me that my landlady was up at dawn making preparations for a Christmas feast such as had not been seen on this farm since before the war. Provisions were scarce enough because of the war, but with eggs and milk and cheese and vegetables and fruit of our own from the farm, and with a few items she had asked me to pick up when I had gone into the city, and by virtue of the fact that there were only three mouths to feed rather than General Lee's entire army, she managed to put together what was nothing less, in my humble eyes, than a marvelously sumptuous holy day banquet. We had ham from a pig I had butchered and smoked back in September, topped with the delicacy of honey and molasses Mrs. Timms had been hoarding frugally, with yams on the side. We still possessed an abundant supply of potatoes in the root cellar from the fall harvest, baked to the perfect point where the pulpy white interior could be popped between the thumb and fingers, exploding out of their brown skins amid steam and a rich aroma. I had churned fresh butter only the day before for just this occasion, and a small pitcher of the purest cream stood ready, to be poured thickly over the melting butter, which made of the potatoes a luxurious treat indeed! Winter peas and carrots we still had too, in addition to plenty of wheat flour for steamy, thick-sliced brown bread, the recipe for which—though simple enough for list of ingredients, was yet unique in the proportions Mrs. Timms guarded with a jealousy of pride well-known among women of the old South. Apples were in the cellar if not exactly in abundance, yet in sufficient quantity for the two double-crusted pies—which came steaming and fragrant out of the cookstove just as Corrie and I were lamenting the last slice of ham we had talked each other into.

"You two young folks save some room for these!" said Mrs. Timms, at which we looked at each other and burst out laughing.

During the last two winters, I had experimented with means to preserve fresh apples all winter long and into the next spring. Though a few lingered on the trees into November, my methods had proved so successful that I kept Mrs. Timms in a steady supply of fruit. She, therefore, perfected her baking techniques as I perfected my storage methods, and I was an eager and willing practical source upon whom she could test various minor alterations in the quantity of cinnamon, sugar, flour, butter, or nutmeg. Notwithstanding my raves, when an hour later we sat down to the table again, to slices much too large of the still-warm pies, Mrs. Timms' eyes were aglow with anticipation, and resting entirely upon Corrie for whatever verdict she would pronounce after the first bite. A man may be enjoyable to cook for, but the palate of another woman is the truest measuring stick for success in any kitchen. So my own mother had once told me, and so Mrs. Timms' glowing eyes now confirmed.

"Oh, Mrs. Timms!" Corrie exclaimed, "you can't know how delicious this is. I've never tasted anything quite like it!"

It was all that was needed. Corrie now had a friend for life in the proud, lonely, quiet southern woman. And for the rest of the day her eyes shone with the light of happy contentment.

I let the two women clean up the table and kitchen alone. I would honestly have preferred to remain and help them. But by the time our slices of pie had been consumed, their talk had become so animated that I wanted to do nothing to intrude. I was so pleased for both of them, and knew how rich it must feel for the doors of their hearts to be unlocking each toward the other.

I quietly excused myself and went out to the stables.

There I groomed and fed the horses, then saddled the roan and the dark gray. No matter how long the women talked, I would not be diverted from my intent. I was glad for the time alone, for I didn't want Corrie to see me place in the saddlebag the package I had prepared.

There were also many things I had to pray about. The sense was growing within me that this important day was only just beginning.

CHAPTER 11

I was still in the stables, quietly sitting atop a bale of hay talking silently to the Father, when I heard Corrie enter.

"Is the invitation for a ride still there?" she asked.

I was having second thoughts about having encouraged her to ride. But since I usually went out myself at this time of day, I did not see what harm could come of it.

"It is," I answered. "How about your acceptance?"

"That's why I'm here," she replied.

"Good!" I said, jumping down from where I was sitting. "The horses are waiting for us. What is your preference—roan or gray?"

Corrie approached the two horses, standing nearly side by side in adjacent stalls, walked to them and stroked their long heads and noses one at a time. She had been here many times, but all at once she seemed to be taking in the individuality and personality of the two animals in a deeper way than before. The old gray had been in my family for years, and although an old horse, she was just as strong and trustworthy as the roan that I usually rode.

I watched as she looked them over. "I love to get out into the fresh morning air," I said. "It's a wonderful way to start a day alone—only you and your horse, with the cold morning air blowing in your face. This day is brisk enough that the afternoon will feel the same!"

"I hope my going with you doesn't intrude on your privacy," said Corrie with a questioning expression, suddenly looking at me anxiously.

"Quite the contrary," I said. "I have maintained the tradition of riding alone only because I had no one to ride with. Mrs.

Timms, you see, is not exactly what you would call a horse-woman."

I smiled, and it seemed to relieve Corrie's anxiety. "With you here, your company will make it all the more enjoyable."

Corrie grew thoughtful for a moment, one hand still absently stroking the long neck of one of the horses. "The smell of leather and hay is somehow familiar in my nose," she said, breathing in the aroma of the stable in long, deep breaths of air.

Corrie chose the dark gray mare. I offered her my assistance in climbing into the saddle, but found to my surprise that despite her injury she was quite capable of hoisting herself up into the saddle, and appeared as comfortable as if riding had been a regular routine. Ten minutes later we were heading west across the wide pasture. Now that we were actually in the saddle, I realized that there were a great many places I wanted to show Corrie. At the far end of the pasture grazed the four cows which made up our small herd. We rode slowly. I wanted to do nothing that might endanger Corrie's arm. But I knew her silence was not due to such a concern in her mind. The melancholy feeling of confusion and frustration had returned the moment she was in the saddle and had taken the leather reins in her hands. From the very way she sat, I knew in an instant that she was more than a moderately accomplished horsewoman.

I think she sensed it too. The smell of horseflesh, the squeak and feel and movement of the saddle and muscular equine body beneath her, the clomping sound of the hoofed feet on the ground, the occasional neigh or snort—all of it was familiar to Corrie, but she could not lay hold of it with her memory.

After leaving the pasture, we embarked on a gradual yet steady ascent up the slope of a small hill. The ridge of it extended for miles and miles as far as the eye could see toward the north.

I was thinking to myself that a short conversation about something unrelated to horses might pull Corrie out of the quiet mood that had come over her. When she spoke again, her very words gave me an idea with which to find out more, if I could, of what she thought about spiritual things.

"Where are we going?" she asked after several minutes, turning toward me.

"To a favorite spot of mine," I replied. "Up about another four miles, to the top of this ridge we are climbing, from which you can see for miles around in every direction. It's a wonderful view. I've wanted to show it to you for some time. I've ridden up here I don't know how many times to think and pray."

"What do you think about?" she asked.

"Oh, different things every time I come."

"Well, then, what are you thinking about *today?*"

"To tell you the truth, I was just mulling over in my brain what would make a great illustration for a sermon."

"Tell me."

"All right. I was thinking that this gradual hill we've been climbing reminds me of our acts of kindness and goodness that we do over a lifetime. In the same way that our horses' feet move up the hill at such an incremental small rate, by the time they have taken ten thousand small steps, we will indeed be on the very top of the hill up ahead. In the same way, good deeds, small and insignificant as each one may seem by itself, pile up one by one, as slowly as each single horse's step, but all taken together along with all the events of our lives will someday form a magnificent monument of testimony to a life with God. Just as we have been slowly and steadily climbing this gradual hill, so should be the acts of obedience and kindness toward others, so that in heaven, toward which we are climbing, the deeds will stack upon one another to form a mountain of eternal value."

I stopped. "Does that make sense?" I said. "I don't think it's quite ready for a sermon! I'm not sure I said it very clearly."

"I think I understand," replied Corrie. "It almost sounds familiar, as if I once knew someone else who explained things just like you do, with illustrations like that. Tell me more of what you were thinking."

"It's not only good *deeds,* so to speak, but the whole way we approach life, the way we approach everything. Besides *doing* things for others, there's the element of conquering selfish motives and attitudes within ourselves—they are like upward steps of the horses' feet too. Every time we squelch something that our soul or flesh might have wanted to say or do, that adds to the mountain of heavenly treasure too."

Now it was my turn to grow quiet. Corrie noticed, but did not interrupt it.

"My father used to say," I finally went on, "that every action, every thought, every decision that we did or thought or decided added a little piece of something to our future heavenly storehouse—either a tiny piece of straw, or a tiny flake of gold dust. And then, he said, someday, in the next life, it will all be set to blazing so that the fire can test to see what kind of things we were putting into the storehouse, straw that will burn up, or gold that will still be there even after the fire dies away. Then we will find out, just like with this hill we've been climbing, what all our words and deeds and attitudes and decisions have added up to."

The moment I mentioned the words *gold dust*, a funny look passed quickly over Corrie's face. But just as quickly it was gone. My words seemed to arouse Corrie's thoughts in new directions, but when she spoke again, it was to ask about what she'd detected on *my* face.

"You mentioned your father," she said. "What was he like?" Again I was silent for a while.

"I'm afraid it's too much to go into now," I said. "I would like to tell you about him," I said. "Very much, in fact. But when the time is right."

She was satisfied. We rode on for quite some time in silence.

As we climbed, gradually the panorama of the view widened. A massive sea of outstretched grasslands rolled off below us for miles and miles, containing many small hills here and there that reminded me of waves on the ocean. Although I had never seen the wideness of the sea, I had heard it described enough times to imagine that on a clear day the waves must look something like these rolling hills that sprang up unevenly out of the earth.

"I had no idea all this was here so close to the farm," said Corrie, clearly enjoying the view.

The sky stretched high above us with the usual cloud formations that children would call cotton-ball clouds. The sun shone brightly through the clouds despite the lingering winter's chill. It was indeed the perfect day to celebrate the Savior's birth, and for a long slow ride.

"How is your shoulder?" I asked. "Is it getting tired?"

"I seem to forget the pain altogether," Corrie replied. "I think it is going to be fine in no time. It is really a wonderful feeling to be on the back of a horse again."

"Again?" I questioned.

"Yes . . . I have the feeling I have been here before," she said, gazing out over the horse's uplifted head.

"Here?" I repeated.

"Not in this *place*," she said. "But on the back of a horse. I feel suddenly very much at home riding along like this, as strange as that may sound."

"It doesn't sound strange at all," I said.

"It's hard to describe. Although in my mind I can't remember that I've ever been riding before, my senses and even my body seem to remember."

"Like when you think of something during the day but can't remember where or when you heard the words before . . . or wonder if it was even from a dream."

"Yes. And I even feel," she went on, "almost like . . . oh, I can't quite lay hold of it!—like this is where I was—riding I mean—when whatever happened to me happened."

"That would account for the fall and the knock on your head."

"Somehow it's more than just that," she added. "I don't even know what it is I feel . . . it's . . . it's a feeling of . . . being at home—wherever that is . . . a feeling that goes down someplace inside me from a very long time ago. . . ."

I slowed my roan to a halt and signaled Corrie to follow my lead.

"I want you to hear something, Corrie," I said. "Just listen."

After a brief spell of silence she said, "I don't hear anything."

"That's just it," I said. "Have you ever heard such silence? Listen to the way our voices fade into the sea of quiet, like a raindrop into an ocean. However loud we may talk, how much louder is the silence. It is heard in very few places these days. When I was living in Richmond, although you could be all alone somewhere making no noise at all, there was always the background of the city. And even on the farm there are the chickens and pigs and cows. But out here, we have only silence as the background for our voices."

We started our horses forward again.

"I love riding through this wide open stretch of land," I said. "The land is so big and I am so small, it reminds me always of how huge God is."

"Does the beauty of this land always inspire you to think like this when you come out here in the mornings?"

"Hardly ever does my mind not think at least some kind of thought, Corrie, though rarely the same ones. The freshness of the air and the hard breathing on the back of a galloping horse not only gets the blood pumping in one's veins, but I find it pumps the energy into the mind that causes new mental surprises all the time. The measure with which we utilize the mind God gave us is also the measure with which our minds will grow and expand. Riding and breathing and exploring new places and thinking . . . it all mixes together for me. It is God's creation that inspires my thoughts, and so I feel he is part of the process, too, and is constantly putting new thoughts within me."

Corrie seemed to be thinking about all I'd said. But then without warning, suddenly she yelled at the gray, dug in her heels, and was off in a gallop. Before I could recover myself, she was thirty yards ahead.

I tore after her, caught up in the spirit of the race, even though I was fearful for what might happen should the horse stumble and fall.

But I needn't have worried. That she was at home on the back of a horse was abundantly clear. I knew the roan to be a faster animal than the gray, yet try as I might, I could make up none of the ground between us. Across the pasture we galloped, if anything the distance between us widening. I saw Corrie glance back, her hair flying wildly out in all directions, a huge smile of sheer delight on her face. Then she turned forward again, slapped the reins, and made for the trail in the distance which wound up the ridge I had pointed out to her.

I was terrified lest something happen to her. Yet on she rode, as I did my best to keep pace, as smooth and secure in the saddle as anyone I had ever seen—man or woman. When I finally did catch up with her about ten minutes later, it was only because she had reined in the gray to wait for me. I galloped up and pulled alongside.

"What's the idea?" I said, laughing.

"Oh, but that was wonderful!" she exclaimed. "I could have ridden and ridden like that forever!"

"Why didn't you?" I said.

"I didn't want to lose you."

"Lose *me*!" I rejoined in mock annoyance. "You're the stranger here, not me."

"I felt so at home, so complete, so free! I haven't felt like that in . . . in I don't know how long!"

"You must have ridden a lot."

"I . . . I think so," she replied. "It felt so *good* to run like that, as if it was something I've missed. How much farther to the top?"

"It's just there," I said, pointing. "Only six or eight hundred yards."

"Then let's go!" shouted Corrie, and again I found myself looking at the retreating tail of the gray.

"I'm right behind you!" I yelled as I lurched the roan to a gallop. Yet still I could do nothing to overtake her. She was fifty yards ahead by the time she crested the ridge. I slowed to a canter, and eased up beside her.

"Well, this is the spot," I said, dismounting. "Let's tie up the horses and go sit over there. I have a favorite rock where I sit and look down over the valley."

I led Corrie to a tree, where we tied up the two horses, and then to the large boulder. I jumped up and stretched down my hand to her. She took it, and I helped her to the top where we sat and gazed out over the green Virginia countryside stretching out westward in one direction and to Richmond in the other. We sat there for a long time.

"It's all so familiar," Corrie said at length. "The feel of a horse under me, the ride, climbing a hill like this, a wide view, even the rock. It's as if I've been here before too . . . or someplace just like this. Maybe I've *done* this before, ridden up a mountain to look out over a wide expanse. . . . I don't even know what I'm feeling, other than . . ."

She didn't finish. Her words drifted off, even as her gaze bore into the distance. Then suddenly she blurted out, as if to complete the sentence: "Oh, if only I could just *remember*!"

Leaving her where she was, I slowly climbed down from the rock and walked over to where the horses stood browsed in the low grass. I opened the saddlebag and pulled out the small wrapped package I had brought along. I walked back to the rock and sat down again beside her.

"I have a present for you," I said softly.

She turned away from where she'd been looking off into the distance, then first saw the small gift in my hand.

"Merry Christmas, Corrie," I said. "You are such a dear sister . . . may the Father *bless* you!"

I handed it to her.

She just stared into my eyes for a moment, speechless. Then she looked down, took the package, and tenderly began to remove the bow and white paper I had wrapped it in.

Slowly the paper fell from her hand onto the ground. For what must have been thirty or forty seconds she stared at the book in her hands, then looked up slowly to me again. "What is it?" she asked.

"Open it," I said.

She did so.

"It's not a regular book," she said. "It's got writing in it— *hand* writing."

"Open it farther," I said.

She turned more of the pages until she got past the writing.

"They're just blank pages," she said.

"It's a journal, Corrie," I said. "Blank pages . . . for *you* to write in, for you to keep your journal. Remember . . . like we talked about. You said you used to keep one."

"Yes . . . a *journal* . . . yes . . . I remember . . ." As she spoke, her voice became very soft, almost inaudible. She was no longer looking at me but down at the book in her hands. I searched her face to find her eyes, but they had glazed over. Then slowly I saw tears begin to rise in them.

". . . journal . . . horses . . . a long ride . . ."

Slowly and methodically her hands were turning the leaves of the book until she came again to the pages in front.

"That is my hand, Corrie," I said. "I hope you don't mind, or think it too bold of me, but when I bought the book for you, I decided to fill in the first part myself. I've been staying up nights to finish it before Christmas."

I don't know if she even heard my voice or not. Still she stared down, slowly turning the pages, but her tear-filled eyes seemed to focus on nothing.

". . . it's a beautiful journal," she said, still very softly, ". . . just like the one Almeda gave me . . ."

"Since you didn't remember and weren't able to write," I said, "I thought I would write down what happened to you since I found you. I know it won't be in your own hand and in your own words, but—"

Suddenly I realized what I'd just heard.

"What did you say!" I exclaimed.

But Corrie continued to murmur to herself, heedless of my question and my sudden mounting excitement.

". . . Almeda gave me one too," she repeated. ". . . Pa says I write too much . . . but I told Zack that you have to tell both what happens and what you're feeling . . . that's what a journal's for. Ma always told me I should keep a diary on account of not being the marrying sort. I don't know about that, but Uncle Nick said—"

Suddenly she stopped. The book fell from her hands. The next instant her head jerked straight up and looked me dead-on full in the face. Her mouth hung open, the tears had vanished, and her two eyes were as huge as the plates on Mrs. Timms' table.

All the glazed look of confusion was gone.

I knew she suddenly remembered everything!

PART TWO

CHAPTER 12

ME AGAIN!

When I opened my eyes and saw Christopher sitting there across the rock from me, the feelings and thoughts that passed through me were nothing like I could ever imagine! In two or three seconds, more flew through my brain than I could write about if it took ten years to do it!

To tell you that I "remembered" all of a sudden who I was and how I'd gotten there and what I was doing would only be the littlest part of it.

First I remembered my family and Miracle Springs and everything about California. For an instant I think I thought I *was* in California, up on top of Fall Creek Mountain where I'd ridden Raspberry on my twenty-first birthday. At first my brain confused this Christmas afternoon with that day six and a half years before. But that didn't last long either, because there was Christopher sitting beside me. For a slight second I couldn't figure out who *he* was. But then I remembered him too—how could I not!—and that it was Christmas.

Oh, it all suddenly came so fast! I felt as if I were standing in the way of a dam that had just burst, sending a huge river of water pouring over me.

In a way that's exactly what *was* happening. My memory had been dammed up, and now suddenly it had given way and here came twenty-seven years of memories crashing back through me. Yes . . . twenty-seven—I even remembered how old I was!

I can't imagine what I must have looked like! So many explosions were going off *inside*, I figured my face on the outside must have

83

seemed strange too. But Christopher didn't say a word, just sat there patiently, watching me trying to put all the missing pieces together.

It was like waking up, but different too. I've heard that before people die, their lives flash in front of them in just two or three seconds. That's just what happened! There were fleeting thoughts of Ma and the early growing-up years . . . then the wagon trip west . . . Ma dying . . . getting to California . . . Pa, Alkali Jones, Uncle Nick, Almeda . . . then such rapid images of faces—Katie and my brothers and sisters and Franklin Royce. My newspaper writing and the elections . . . the evening at the Montgomery Hotel . . . Pa's running for office . . .

It all flew through me, not like water from a dam but more like a wind blowing through my head. How can something seem to be in your brain for so long, when only an instant passes by in the real world? I felt as if I were reliving my whole life . . . but it took only a few seconds!

Then I remembered the letter from President Lincoln and my trip east . . . the stagecoach and boarding the train . . . meeting Sister Janette . . . the Convent of John Seventeen and the Sisters of Unity. Then suddenly the horrors of the Gettysburg battlefield came back to me, with more images and faces and awful sights and sounds and smells!

The war! Of course, the war was still on . . . and the election! My articles . . . President Lincoln!

"Mr. Lincoln . . . the election . . . what. . . ?" I stammered, suddenly very confused again.

"It's Christmas Day, Corrie," Christopher said, "you do remember that, don't you?"

"Yes . . . yes, but . . . but what about the election?"

"This is December 25. The election was last month. President Lincoln defeated McClellan and was reelected."

"Oh . . . oh, yes . . . I remember now . . . you told me that already. But . . . but the war?"

"The war is still going on. But it will not be much longer. Sherman has destroyed Atlanta and much of Georgia. He took Savannah just three days ago, yesterday's paper said. Only Lee is left for the Confederacy, and with Sherman now free to march north to join Grant, there is no doubt—"

"Grant!" I repeated. "General *Grant* . . . that's it . . . that's what I've been trying to remember! General Grant's in danger!"

Now I remembered everything—overhearing Cal and the others in Mrs. Surratt's boardinghouse . . . my flight out of Washington by train . . . riding south into Virginia . . . warning General Grant . . . and then our daring entry into Richmond to kidnap Cal!

"What kind of danger, Corrie?"

"They're trying to kill him . . . there's a spy in his own command, a Confederate spy . . . I've got to warn him!"

I jumped down off the rock and ran to where the two horses were still tied. When I reached them, I looked back. Christopher was stooping down at the base of the rock where we'd been sitting. He picked something up and slowly walked toward me.

"Hurry," I said. "We've got to get back . . . we've got to warn Mr. Grant!"

"Corrie," he said calmly, "please . . . wait just a minute."

"But you don't understand," I insisted. "There's not a second to lose!"

He approached and put his hand on the back of mine to stop me from untying the gray.

"Corrie . . . please. Sit down with me for just a moment more. You're still confused."

I turned and looked into his face. Every feature was so familiar to me, and yet in that instant it was as if he was also a complete stranger. Caught up in the danger to General Grant, I suddenly thought it was no longer Christmas Day but sometime back in October.

I stared into his face, almost not knowing who he was, confusing him with Cal and with John Hay and even with Zack and Pa! A huge, sickening sense of bewilderment swept over me, and I felt as if I was about to forget everything all over again.

"Corrie." I heard my name, but it sounded as if it were coming from so far away. "Corrie . . . that all happened over two months ago. You were shot, probably thrown from a horse, and left for dead. I don't know what the danger to General Grant was, or what you were trying to do. But he was *not* killed . . . and you have been with me here for two months."

I stared at him, still confused, trying to absorb the words and make them go into my ears in a way that made sense.

Then for the first time I felt a momentary twitch of pain in the back of my arm and shoulder. I moved my right arm and felt a slight tightening from the wound. With the pain came the remembrance of Winder Supply and Cal, of the anxious wagon ride out of Richmond, of being stopped by the Confederate soldiers, and then of John Surratt's charging toward us, of gunshots and shouts. I remembered galloping off ahead to try to escape . . . being chased . . . more shouts. I heard Cal's voice in the distance behind me . . . more shots . . . and then the sensation of drifting into a long and quiet dream. . . .

I sat staring into the face in front of me, my eyes wide open yet blank, still not able to take in the meaning of it all. *Where was I . . . who was this man . . . was I still dreaming. . . ?*

Slowly a recognition began to filter into my consciousness. The eyes of pale blue, the thick crop of light brown hair, the tanned cheeks, the wide expressive lips, the voice that spoke so gently and softly yet with command . . . gradually a feeling of *knowing* returned.

There he sat, patiently looking into my face with eyes of care and compassion. And then the day of my waking came into my memory, and I recalled opening my eyes, knowing I was lying in bed, to see this same man sitting at the bedside next to me.

The two moments blended into one. I blinked a few times, and came to myself just as I had two months before in bed. I had not known him then, nor where I was.

But now I knew. Gradually the continuous stream of events fit into an order and made sense—the day in Richmond . . . being wounded . . . falling . . . waking up. At last I remembered everything that had happened since I had been with Christopher . . . the farm . . . Mrs. Timms . . . Christmas dinner . . . and the ride up to this very ridge where we now sat.

The weight of relief was too overwhelming. I could not contain it. Tears filled my eyes as if a dam had been holding *them* back, and I began sobbing as I hadn't for years.

I hardly even realized it, but Christopher's strong arms encircled me. Careful of my wound, he pulled me close and then held me tight. Feeling it as natural as if it had been Almeda's bosom, I laid my head against his large chest, abandoning myself to my tears, and wept freely.

CHAPTER 13

FIRST PIECES OF COMMON GROUND

How much time thus passed while I cried in Christopher's arms, I have no idea. My sensations were so confused and mixed up, it could have been ten minutes since we had arrived on top of the ridge . . . or ten hours!

At last the reservoir of tears dried and I began coming to myself. I was half lying in Christopher's arms, my hair strewn about, my face drenched with tears. My first thought was embarrassment, yet he was so altogether sensitive and understanding that I felt no embarrassment in his presence again after those first few seconds.

I gave a little start and began to straighten up. He instantly released me, sat back a foot or two, then gave me a big smile.

"Hello!" he said.

"Hello," I said back, laughing sheepishly.

"I have the feeling you are fully awake at last."

"I think so," I replied. "I was a mite confused for a while."

"I know. I think I could read more or less what was going through that mind of yours just from watching your eyes, forehead, and mouth."

"Am I that transparent?" I said.

"Not always, but sometimes. You should be glad. It's a good quality, sadly lacking in most people these days."

"I'd never thought about it."

"Besides, I have made it my business to study people and to know what they are thinking and feeling."

"Oh yes, the ministry!" I said. "I'd forgotten for a minute."

"The *former* ministry," he reminded me. "But," he added, "before we go any further, now that memories are clear and the past is one straight line, don't you think we ought to formalize our introductions? You *are* Corrie Hollister, I take it? I have been correct all this time, have I not?"

"Yes, you have. Corrie Belle Hollister, that's me," I said with a smile.

"And I, for the record, remain your servant Christopher Braxton, itinerant farm laborer, minister of soiled reputation, but perhaps physician of sufficient note to have kept you alive."

I laughed, and took Christopher's outstretched hand of renewed introduction and greeting. It was a large hand, made rough from work, but it closed around mine with a firm tenderness that felt strong and safe. He shook my hand, then released it. We both laughed again.

"You did more than just 'keep' me alive," I said. "You *saved* my life!"

"Well, our Father is the only one who can do that, but I do consider myself honored that he used *my* hands to accomplish *his* work."

"You may be honored, but I am just grateful," I said, "to *both* of you!"

"Now I will give you your gift again," he said, pulling from behind him the book he had picked up from where it had fallen.

Again I took it in my hands. Suddenly it meant so much more!

"How can I ever thank you?" I said. "How could you possibly have known?"

"It was just a feeling I had."

"I've kept a journal ever since I was fifteen. I think by now I've got eight books filled."

"I suppose one who keeps a journal, as I do, can recognize that same instinct for communication in someone else. At least I was pretty sure I recognized it in you even though I didn't know much about you—which, by the way, I still don't! And now that you remember, I want to know *everything* about you! I want to find out about this young lady who has been my patient for nine weeks!"

"There's not that much special about me that you'd be needing to know," I said.

"Somehow I very much doubt that! And regardless of whether you think it special or interesting, I *will*. It has long been my conviction that within *every* human soul lie stories and dramas and adventures untold if only we could unlock them. I love people, Corrie—and that includes you!—people made in the image of our heavenly Father!"

I glanced through the journal again.

"I'm glad you wrote in it," I said. "It will make it all the more special for me."

"To be honest with you, I didn't know when your memory would return, or how it would, or whether when it did, perhaps all these weeks with me would instantly be blotted *out* in exchange for the return of the former. But if you were a writer, as I was fairly confident you were, then I knew one day you would want to know what had become of you during this time after your fall. And I thought having a journal of your own just might spark your brain back into action. So I wrote down what I thought you might like to know about these weeks, in case you didn't remember them well enough to write about it yourself."

"Thank you. Maybe sometime you'd let me read *your* journal of this same time. I'd like to know what *you* were thinking and feeling, too, while you were taking care of me."

Christopher laughed. "Why would you want to know that?"

"Because I am interested in people too! I just might want to write a newspaper story about you someday, you know! I don't want to know only what we *did* for these nine weeks. I think I can remember that well enough now. But what another person *thinks* and feels—those are the *real* treasures. That's why I love to write and find out about people . . . and why I keep a journal."

"Well, I shall think about it, Corrie. No one's ever read any of my journal before."

"I might even like to put some of it into mine," I said. "You know, to quote you. If there's anything that's true about these last nine weeks—it's that your life and mine were bound up together. So I want to know what you were thinking about it all."

He laughed again. "As I told you," he said, "I'll think about it. Opening myself up like that to the public gaze—even if it's just one person—is a new thought for me."

CHAPTER 14

WHAT TO DO . . . NEXT?

I was so happy to know who I was and where I'd come from and what I was doing in a farmhouse outside of Richmond, Virginia, that I hardly stopped to feel lonely about not being with my family on Christmas.

That evening I did think of them, but my thoughts were only happy ones. Later, after the three of us had enjoyed more of Mrs. Timms' apple pie, I sat down and began a long letter back to Miracle Springs. When I was done with that, I had plenty of catching up to do in my new journal!

I wrote until past midnight!

When I woke up the next morning, it was like waking from a long, long dream—yet a dream that had been real and that had actually happened. I felt like Rip Van Winkle!

I had not been up for long, however, when all my questions began to bang against my head. The main one was: What should I do now? This place wasn't my home. In fact, I suddenly felt very strange being in the South, remembering about the war, and how much I thought of Mr. Lincoln, and realizing that the Confederacy had set out to destroy him.

But where was my home now? With the election past, would Mr. Lincoln or Mr. Hay have any more use for me and my writing? Should I go see Mr. Hay? What about the war itself?

I thought of Clara Barton and all the other people I had known during the fighting. Might they still need my help?

Then my thoughts suddenly returned to Sister Janette and the other sisters, and I remembered how much I had wanted to be part of their lives. It had grown so distant, and now all at once my time at the convent came close again and seemed like only yesterday. Maybe I ought to go back there for a while to rekindle my friendships with the sisters and use the time to pray for direction about what I was supposed to do.

Oh, there were so many questions!

Then in the very midst of them, two faces rose up in my mind's eye. How could I have forgotten! If it hadn't been for the captain and his quick thinking, I would probably not have gotten away.

Captain Dyles and Jacob Crabtree! What had happened to them after I had galloped away from the check station?

They must have been captured, or . . .

I couldn't even force myself to think of anything worse!

If General Grant was still alive, had they gotten word to him? That could hardly be—they had been surrounded by Confederate soldiers. How might Cal have been further involved? And now that I was recalling the events of that day so clearly, why hadn't Surratt found me where I lay beside the road and finished the job? Why was I alone when Christopher happened along?

I might never know the answers to everything. Not unless I saw Cal again, and even if that were possible, I didn't know if I'd ever *want* to see him again!

Only one thing seemed clear: The captain and his huge black friend had probably been captured. And behind the Confederate lines like we were, I might be the only one who could help them.

Should I try to get back to the Union encampment, wherever that might be by now? Or should I see what I might be able to find out while I was still here, on the Confederate side of Richmond?

Even before I had finished asking myself the question, the answer was clear. How could I do anything other than see if there was some way to help them? It was my coming to General Grant with the plot against him that had gotten them into this fix. I felt responsible. I wasn't wearing the dark blue uniform of the Union. No one would suspect me. There must surely be a way for me to find out what had become of them!

I went out for a long walk while Christopher was tending to the animals. It was such an odd feeling! I'd walked around Mrs.

Timms' farm before, and taken walks and rides in the wagon with Christopher. But now that my *mind* was mine again and working in all the ways it was supposed to, it was like seeing everything all over again for the first time. Suddenly I felt like I did when I used to take walks to think and pray.

What a funny sensation, to have been awake all this time, but now to feel like I'd been asleep! So when I walked out through the field that morning and toward the small wood at the far end, it felt so good just to *think* again, and to talk to God again, and to know that I was . . . that I was *me*!

"Lord, I'm so glad you didn't forget me!" I said. "What would I have done? What would have become of me?"

But even as the words were out of my mouth, I felt as if God answered me right back. *You can trust me, Corrie. I wouldn't leave you alone and unprotected. Have you forgotten so soon that one of my sons happened by just after you fell? I take care of my people, Corrie, especially my daughters.*

"I was so alone," I said to myself.

You were as much in my thoughts as ever, he answered. *And when you are in my thoughts, Corrie, it is impossible for you to be alone. You are completely surrounded by my presence. My thinking about you brings you into the very center of my heart. There is no place in all the universe where you could be less alone.*

"But . . . but what if . . . what if I hadn't remembered?"

There are no what ifs for my children, Corrie. Haven't you learned by now that I use everything that happens to you—every encounter, every conversation, every event, every tiniest thing, every turn of what some people might call fate—to bring you closer toward my heart? Nothing happens by chance, Corrie. My hand is busy everywhere. There is no such thing as chance throughout the entire universe of my creation.

"I'm sorry, Lord. I guess I've forgotten some things about you too.

I would not let you truly forget. I was at work even when you were asleep. Christopher is my son too, and the ministry of his hands and voice and gentle spirit was my chosen way to bring life back to you.

"Oh, Lord, thank you! You are so good to me!"

Then, overcome with the joy of the moment, I set out running. It felt so good. My arm and shoulder were so nearly well I could even swing them freely without pain.

When I stopped I sat down on the grass, leaned down onto my back, and stared up into the blue sky. "Lord, what am I to do now?" I whispered. "I can remember again, but it seems as if everything that happened up until two months ago is from years back, another whole lifetime ago. It seems that everything has changed. I can't just . . . just *stay* here. I don't belong here, do I, Lord? But then I'm not sure *where* I belong? What am I supposed to do?"

All at once a sermon came into my mind that Rev. Rutledge had preached once. He'd said that the will of God for our lives was like a big thick book. He said that our natural tendency was always to want to grab the book and read the whole thing, especially to find out the ending of the story. But God, he said, isn't in such a hurry as we are. He lets us see only one page at a time. Then he turns the pages when he's ready, and never lets us go on to the next page until we have learned the lesson of the previous one. "Our heavenly Father is never in a hurry," he said. "He doesn't mind if it takes us a year to learn what he's written for us on a single page. He won't move on until the time is right for us to move on, because he's in no hurry to get to the end of the book. He wants to make sure we learn every lesson he's put in the book for us, and doesn't want us to skip a single one."

I breathed in deeply of the chilly air, letting many thoughts about the minister's words tumble through my brain. At last I felt I knew what the Lord had wanted to show me by bringing that sermon back into my memory.

"All right, Lord," I said, "perhaps it isn't best for me that you show me *everything*. What, then, do you want me to do now? I won't even try to think about the next page of your lesson book. But what is on the one you've opened before me *today*?"

Almost immediately I remembered something. It had happened just yesterday, on Christmas morning. It already seemed weeks ago!

Suddenly my body jolted up into a sitting position and my mouth and eyes opened wide in shock and amazement and surprise all at once. *It had to be him*, I thought! On its heels was the conviction that maybe *he* could help me find out what had happened to Jacob and the captain. Unless he had changed more than I expected, he would have all kinds of contacts and sources of information!

The next instant I was on my feet and running back toward the farmhouse.

CHAPTER 15

A NAME FROM THE PAST

I ran inside just as Christopher was coming from the barn.

"What is it?" he exclaimed.

"Where's the paper?" I asked out of breath.

"What paper?"

"The newspaper . . . you were showing it to me yesterday."

"Oh," he said, leading the way into the other room. "That's right, you had been looking at it as if you were trying to remember something."

"I think I just did," I said. "But I've got to make sure."

"It's still over here on the desk," he said, walking toward it.

Hurriedly I ran past him. I grabbed up the paper and immediately started fumbling through it.

"What page was it on?" I asked.

"If you'll just tell me what you're looking for—"

"The article I was looking at."

"It was on page two."

I tore back the first sheet and my eyes frantically scanned over the page.

There it was! I had *seen* it. I could hardly believe my eyes . . . but there the words were in plain sight.

Derrick Gregory! Reporter and correspondent for the Confederacy, read the byline under his name.

I sat down on the couch, slumped back, and let the paper fall to my lap. I must have had a glazed look in my eyes, and my mouth must have been hanging open, because Christopher walked toward me with a worried expression on his face.

"What *is* it, Corrie?" he asked.

Then I found myself unexpectedly starting to chuckle. It grew and grew, and pretty soon I was laughing outright. I couldn't stop! It was such a surprise, and yet in a way not a surprise at all, to see his name there staring back at me from the newspaper. Something about it hit me so humorously! I suppose it felt good, like running out in the field had, to let some of my emotions loose that had been trapped inside me for so long. I don't know what it was, but I laughed harder than I remember doing for a long time.

Finally I calmed down and took in two or three deep breaths. Christopher was still looking at me with a puzzled expression.

"He's somebody I knew briefly—a long time ago."

"How long . . . when?" he asked.

"Hmm . . . let me see," I thought. "What year is this?"

"Come now! You're supposed to be remembering these things now," said Christopher with a grin. "It's 1864."

"Oh yes, of course. Then, hmm . . . it was when John Fremont was running for President. That's eight years ago . . . 1856."

"And *where* did you know him?"

"Derrick was in California, trying to dig up some dirt on Mr. Fremont to keep him from being elected. I was on the trail of a story for my paper and tried to stop him. He was going to print lies."

"Did you?"

"No. His article made it into print, and Mr. Fremont was defeated."

The memory of it came back to me all so vividly that I no longer felt like laughing, that was for sure!

Christopher sat down in a chair opposite me, and the room was silent for a minute. At last I shook myself out of my reverie and looked up at him.

"Do you think you could take me into Richmond and help me find him?" I asked.

"I know where the newspaper office is," he answered. "Whether he'd be there is another question. I've seen reports he's filed from all over the South."

"That's something we can't know. But it's a place to start. And from the sound of this article, he *may* be in Richmond. I've got to try."

CHAPTER 16

ACQUAINTANCE RENEWED

The following morning, immediately after Christopher's chores around the farm were completed enough to allow for him being gone awhile, he cleaned up and then we rode off toward Richmond.

I was nervous. The last time I'd been in the Confederate capital, I'd been as good as a spy, and on a dangerous mission. I couldn't help feeling the same way now, thinking that everyone was looking at me and would know immediately that I was a Northerner. Christopher saw my anxiety and kept telling me to relax. I knew he was right, and that no one would think a thing out of the ordinary. But still I couldn't help myself.

He knew where the building of the Richmond *Star* was and led the horse and buggy straight to it, pulling up in front, then jumping out and tying the horse to the wooden rail.

"Do you want me to go in with you, or wait here?" he asked.

"I . . . I don't know," I answered. "Now that we're here, I hadn't really thought about what I ought to *do*."

"I'd be happy to accompany you in."

"Uh . . . no . . . now that I think about it, it's probably something I should do on my own."

"Then I'll be waiting right out here if you need me."

I hesitated before entering. The last time I had seen Derrick Gregory in Sonora, Robin and I had been running up into the forest with Derrick firing at us from below. Would he still be angry with me about taking his notes and ruining possibly the best story he would ever have? Would he look upon me with disdain, or forgive me for all I had done to him? I couldn't imagine why he would help me. What reason would he have to do something for me?

A great wave of doubt swept through me. "What am I doing here?" I asked myself. "Derrick Gregory is not the right man to ask for what I need to know. A stranger would have more reason to help me than he." He might even try to keep me from finding my friends! Yet . . . it was a chance I had to take. He was the only person in Richmond I had any connection with who could possibly have some contact within the Confederate army.

I took in a deep breath, tried to hold my head up, and strode onward and through the door.

I walked inside and timidly looked around. There was a long hallway with offices on each side. Nobody seemed to be around. It wasn't a very lively place. I made my way slowly down the hall. Most of the offices were closed, though there were a few open doors, but still I didn't see a soul.

Down at the end of the hall I could hear voices and the sounds of activity. The doors were open, and as I drew closer I saw a large room with some people bustling around inside. It was the layout room, and as I came to the doorway and stopped, I saw all the familiar sights and heard the sounds common to a newspaper room. There were voices and familiar clicking sounds, and I could smell the strong odors of ink and paper and machinery. It gave me such good memories of the *Alta* building in San Francisco. A large printing press stood at the far end, some men closer by were sitting hunched over desks, setting type, and here and there others occupied desks at various jobs, or clustered in small groups of two and three talking.

I took in the whole scene in a moment, then went inside. A man at a desk closest to the door glanced up and saw me. I quickly walked up to him before I should lose heart and retreat, and asked if he knew Derrick Gregory.

He nodded but didn't say anything, stood up, sent his eyes searching about the big room, then pointed toward the other end down toward the printing press and promptly sat back down without giving me another look.

I thanked him, to which he didn't respond, then walked on

through the desks and machines and people and presses in the direction he had pointed. As I drew nearer I saw a desk and a man's back, for I was approaching from the rear. I knew Derrick Gregory instantly, even without seeing his face.

As I drew closer I saw that he was sitting beside the opening to a designated area with walls only about four feet high that was like an office in the middle of the larger room. A tiny sign on the wall next to the desk read "Derrick Gregory."

Nervously I approached, looking at the papers on his desk. I wondered what sort of article he was working on.

I reached him and stopped. I tried to clear my throat and say something but couldn't. I must have stood there a minute or two, and then all at once Derrick realized someone was standing there. He turned his head and his eyes came to rest on my face.

For a second or two there was just a blank stare. Then a subtle glimmer began in his eyes, and the hint of a twitch about the corners of his mouth. The slightest sense of recognition had dawned on his face, but I knew it was not enough for him to remember where he knew me from.

It all happened in less than three or four seconds, but I knew his brain was racing frantically through all its corners trying to pin down something vague his eyes were telling him about having seen this person somewhere a long time before.

"Can I help you, miss?" A voice behind me startled me. I hadn't realized that I'd been mesmerized in a sort of trance for the few seconds too. I turned and saw two men approaching.

"I wanted to speak with Mr. Gregory," I answered toward the man who had asked the question. "Hello, Mr. Gregory," I said, now turning back toward him. "Remember me . . . Corrie Hollister?"

All it took was for Derrick to hear my voice. Suddenly the light dawned all over his face.

"Cornelia!" he exclaimed. "I can't believe my eyes!"

"Yes, it is, Mr. Gregory," I said. My nervousness must have shown.

"You don't need to be afraid of anything," he said.

"I . . . I thought you would be angry with me."

"Oh, Cornelia!" he exclaimed, though with a softness of tone

I had never heard from him. He rose from the desk and walked the few steps over to where I had been standing. "I have been hoping to see you again for the better part of these eight years."

"But why, Mr. Gregory?" I said. "I destroyed one of your best election stories ever."

"Come on, Cornelia . . . *Derrick*. We went through too much together to be so formal."

A shadow must have come over my face because he quickly added, "Besides, what's behind us is over and done with. I'm a reformed man now, Cornelia. You'd be proud of me!"

"How so?" I asked.

"I'm an honest newspaper reporter now, just like you. No more of that shady stuff I was involved in back then."

By now the other two men had gotten closer and had begun to listen to us. Derrick suddenly seemed to realize it and began to introduce me.

"Gentlemen, I want to introduce you to one of the finest reporters this side of the Mississippi . . . or the other side of it, for that matter too," he added, laughing. "Let me present Miss Cornelia Ho—"

But I interrupted him. It suddenly occurred to me that it might not be such a good idea for my name to be loudly voiced around the room.

"Please, Derrick," I said. "These men don't care in the least what my name is. But I am in a hurry. Is there a place we can go and talk?"

He gave me a funny look, not seeming to understand, but then answered, "Well . . . sure, Cornelia," he said. "We'll find an empty office somewhere and catch up on old times."

He glanced back at his desk, shuffled a few papers together into a stack, then led me away. I followed him back through the big room, into the hall where he led me to a small vacant office. He closed the door, offered me a chair, and then said, "It's really great to see you again, Cornelia. And I was serious a minute ago— I really have changed since all we went through together back then."

I could tell from the expression on his face and the softness of tone in his voice that he meant it.

"As I said, I have truly been hoping to see you for all these years," he added, "and *not* because I was angry with you."

"How do you mean?" I said.

"I mean all those things you said to me sank in," he replied. "You remember that day we rode out to Big Oak Flat?" he asked.

"Of course," I said. "That was a day I'd *never* forget."

"You asked me about honesty and right. You remember?" I nodded.

"Well, I have to admit I thought I had everything figured out back then. I thought the senator would make me a rich man, and I reckon I figured you were just a naive little kid."

"I guess in some ways I was," I laughed.

"No, Cornelia, you were far more than that. You had guts. You were—how old were you, anyway?"

"Let's see," I said. "I'm twenty-seven now . . . so I'd have been nineteen."

"There, you see what I mean! You were nineteen, but you had the guts to stand up to me, for the sake of what you believed, and that kid who was with you—what was his name?"

"Robin O'Flaridy."

"Flaridy, that's it. *He* didn't have much in the way of guts!"

"Robin's grown some since then, too."

"But what I was getting at is that you had what it took to stand up to me and not give me my papers in order to save that kid O'Flaridy's life—even though I had a gun on you. I tell you, Cornelia, I never forgot that night."

"You wouldn't really have shot me, would you, Derrick?" I said.

"Nah, heck no, I'm no murderer. I haven't even fought in this war. I managed to talk my way out of it every time they came after me to try to put a rifle in my hands!"

I laughed. "That I can believe," I said. "I knew you fired over our heads on purpose, though I was mighty scared at the time."

"I guess you were," he said, then stopped and grew real serious. It was quiet for a minute. I knew he was thinking and I didn't want to interrupt it. He was sitting in a chair opposite me and staring down at the floor. Finally, after what seemed like a long time, he looked up.

"I've been waiting eight years to tell you this, Cornelia," he said, "hoping the whole time that our paths might cross again. Even said a prayer about it a time or two. I wanted to lay eyes on you again to apologize for what I did—for almost getting you into a real bad situation, and for shooting at you like that . . . even if I did make sure I missed."

"It's okay, Derrick," I said. "I forgave you a long time ago."

"Well, I appreciate it," he replied, "but it *wasn't* right. It was a cowardly, selfish, unmanly thing to do. Not only were you a woman, you were practically just a kid, and I've been ashamed of myself ever since. So now I want to look you in the eye, like a man, and say it."

His eyes bore straight into mine and I almost thought he was going to start crying.

"So, Cornelia Hollister . . . I'm sorry. There—I said it, and it's from the bottom of my heart."

"And I forgive you, again," I answered, smiling at him and having to work to keep from crying myself!

"So, like I said," Derrick went on, "I thought a lot about you since back then in Sonora. But it was more than just what you said to me about a writer being truthful. It was that you had more guts and courage than I did to stand up for something you believed in. It got me thinking a lot about what I *did* believe in, and I can't say I found that I believed in anything but just myself. The more I thought about it, the more it struck me as none too noble a thing. I realized that what I was doing wasn't the way to get Buchanan elected. You were helping your man by building him up, not by tearing the other man down. Just that small realization helped change my whole outlook, Cornelia. And the long and the short of it is that the next time the senator offered me one of his dirty jobs, I turned him down. I decided if I couldn't learn to be an honest newspaperman, then I couldn't call myself much of any kind of man. By 1860 a total change had come over me. I wrote for the Democrats again, but I didn't write one article against Lincoln, even when I found something that might have really been able to hurt him."

"I'm happy to hear it, Derrick," I said.

"You ought to be, Cornelia Hollister, because you made an

honest man out of me! After the war started I landed this job with the *Star*, and that's where I've been ever since, covering the war. And that reminds me—you've been making quite a name for *yourself*, young lady! I've seen your name all over the papers from the North, whenever we can get them, and I had the feeling it was you."

"That's why I didn't want you to tell anyone my name in there," I said. "I didn't figure a Northerner like me would be any too welcome in the Confederate capital."

"Now that I think of it, what *are* you doing here anyhow, Cornelia?" As he asked the question, Derrick's expression grew serious. For a second it worried me.

"You're not going to turn me in, are you, Derrick?" I said.

"Turn you in?" he said, laughing. "Who would I turn you in to? There's no law against being *from* the North. And you're not even from the North at all, but from California. No, no, I'm not going to turn you in."

"You had an expression on your face I didn't know about."

"I just remembered about the war," he said. "I couldn't figure out what you were doing here right in the middle of Lee's and Grant's armies."

"I know it may sound strange, us being on opposite sides like we were back then," I said, "but I need your help."

"Listen, Cornelia, if you ever have anything you need from me, don't you even think twice about asking. Nothing I could do would *ever* repay what you did for me."

"Thank you, Derrick. I think now's that time, then."

"But how did you know where to find me?"

"I saw an article of yours in the *Star*, so I figured I'd try to see if you were here."

"Well, you found me. What's the favor?"

"It's got to do with the war, Derrick. It might get you into trouble if anyone was to know you were helping me."

"Aw, let me worry about that. I owe you, Cornelia, and now's as good a time as ever to pay you back. What is it you want?"

"I'm trying to locate two Union soldiers. They're probably being held prisoner around here someplace, if they're still alive."

"Northerners . . . and you want *me* to help! What makes you think I could find them?"

"I don't know. You're the only person I knew to ask. I know being a reporter's gotten me into a lot of unusual places. I figured you'd have connections, and—"

"I got a few among the troops," he said, then stopped and rubbed his chin thoughtfully.

"Why do you want to find them?" he asked after a moment.

"Do I have to tell you?"

A grin spread over his lips. "You are still just as cagey as ever, aren't you, Cornelia? No, I don't suppose it matters. I owe you more than I do the Confederacy. I'm not so convinced that slavery's a good thing, if you want to know the truth of it—just don't tell anyone around here you heard it from me!"

"I won't."

"All right, so you want to find two men. You don't want to tell me why. Fair enough. What are their names?"

"Geoffrey Dyles—he's a captain—and Jacob Crabtree, a Negro man who works for the army."

"Hmm, a darkie, you say . . . he's not likely to be faring too well, though if they are around that might make them easier to find."

Derrick thought a moment, then drew in a deep breath.

"Well, there might be something I can do, Cornelia," he said. "But I'm none too sure." He took a piece of paper and wrote the names down. "It may raise some suspicions, but I'll see what I can do. Where are you staying?"

"I'm a few miles out of town, in a little farmhouse."

"What are you doing there, Cornelia?"

"It's a long story. I'm not sure I want to tell you."

Derrick laughed. "Maybe it's best I don't know," he said.

"Could I come back in a few days to see if you have found out anything?" I asked him.

"You don't want to tell me where you're at?"

"No, I think it's best I come back."

We said goodbye, and I left the building.

CHAPTER 17

DIVINE APPOINTMENTS

Christopher still stood beside the wagon patiently waiting for me. My face must have said more than I realized because his next words were:

"It's easy enough to see you found Mr. Gregory."

"I don't know if I like that you can tell so much about me just from a look at my face," I said as we climbed back into the wagon. "That transparency again."

"I had a long time to learn when your sleeping face had to tell me things your mouth couldn't. Guile is the opposite of transparency, and Jesus gave one of the highest compliments in the Gospels when he said of Nathaniel that he was a man 'without guile.' So by saying I can read your face, I too am complimenting you."

"Then I will take it as you meant it."

"What did you find out?"

"Nothing about the captain and Jacob. But Derrick's going to see if he can learn anything. I have to come back in a few days."

We rode out of Richmond back toward the country. The fear of the city was gone now. I was hardly thinking about the war, in fact. Seeing Derrick Gregory again raised so many thoughts and feelings from so far back in the past that a quiet, almost melancholy mood gradually came over me, and we rode most of the way in silence. I think Christopher sensed it and didn't want to intrude.

Not only did seeing Derrick bring back everything that happened during my adventurous, frightening time in Sonora following the John Fremont story, it caused me to think about a lot of things I hadn't thought of in years. I suppose, most of all, Derrick's words lodged into me: *You had more guts and courage than I did to stand up for something you believed in. . . . I never forgot about that night . . . even said a prayer a time or two . . . wanted to see you again.*

I couldn't get out of my head that Derrick Gregory had been thinking about *me* all those eight years! I remember Almeda telling me that you could never know all the ways the Lord might put some small, insignificant incident in your life to use in some way and for something he was intending to do. But suddenly the huge meaning of her words rushed over me like she was just saying them to me right then.

It wasn't that I'd forgotten Derrick. I would never forget the incident. But for me it was just—I don't know how to explain it, exactly, but it was just something that *happened*. Then my life picked up and went on. But for him, the incident had made such an impression in his heart and mind that it wound up changing him. Really changing him for good! All this time he'd actually wanted to see me again, to apologize and to tell me that I'd had what I reckon you'd call an influence on his life.

It's pretty amazing when you stopped to think about it that I could have caused a difference in somebody's life without even knowing it!

Yet that's exactly what Almeda had said to me.

"Every person you meet, Corrie," I could hear her voice saying, *"even someone whose path crosses yours for the briefest moment, may be what Avery calls a 'divine appointment.'"*

"What's a divine appointment?" I asked her.

"A meeting, an encounter, a relationship, a situation that God has set up for some purpose we might not know about . . . might 'never' know about or be aware of."

"You mean God sets up 'appointments' for us with people, but never tells us about them?"

"That's exactly what he does. They're not 'earthly' appointments, but 'divine' appointments. They don't have a purpose that 'we' can see or even do anything about. But just like every earthly business meeting, or 'appointment,' has some purpose, some agenda, some reason for its taking place, so do God's heavenly appointments have pur-

poses he wants them to accomplish."

"But if we don't know what his purpose is, how can we do what he wants us to when the appointment comes?"

"We're not supposed to know. If we 'tried' to do something, we would be more likely to intrude upon and even get in the way of what his intention was."

"God doesn't want us to know his purpose?"

"Not always. Sometimes he does, I suppose. But not in the small moments of contact, what we could call 'chance' encounters, which is what I mean when I say divine appointment."

"So what are we supposed to do," I asked, "if we don't see them ahead of time and don't know God's purpose?"

"We're supposed to just be ourselves," replied Almeda. "But at the same time that means we have to be paying attention to God's voice in case he does prompt us to say something. And we have to behave as his children ought to, so that even if nothing is said, God's life is still able to rub off on the people around us. If we are walking as God's children, then God is able to accomplish any number of things around the edges of life and relationship—in the people we contact, in ways we may never know about."

"Are you saying that we may never know God is doing something, and may never realize he is at work, and yet a divine appointment can still be going on?"

"Exactly. I would even say that 'most' of the time it is that and we never realize a thing. You see, Corrie, if we knew what our heavenly Father was doing, or if we 'thought' we knew, we would probably try to say something that we considered appropriate or spiritual. We might even start talking about God himself, thinking we were helping, when actually we would be getting in the way. That's why God doesn't always let us in on all the divine appointments he has scheduled for us."

"Why would it be getting in the way for us to say something to someone about God?"

"Because the occasions are rare when God wants us to 'talk' about him. Sometimes he does, and at those times we'll find ourselves speaking almost in spite of ourselves. But more often than not, what God wants his people to do is simply 'live.' It's in the way we live our lives, and the way we speak about things that 'aren't' spiritual, and the way

we conduct ourselves, and how we handle problems, and how we treat people. It's all those kinds of things that tell most about our lives as children of the Father, far more than what we say. God schedules these 'divine appointments' all the time, every day, so that people who don't know him can watch his children 'live.' He isn't so much interested in scheduling these encounters that I'm calling divine appointments so that there can be a lot of talk about him, but just so that people can observe his children living their lives in a way that sets them apart 'because' they are his children."

For a minute I thought about everything Almeda had said.

"I reckon I see what you mean, I said slowly. God wants people to see how we behave when we're not thinking about him and are just kinda what you'd call acting normal."

"Precisely, Corrie."

"So the more we knew about all the divine appointments he was doing, we might mess up what he wanted to accomplish?"

"It's difficult to imagine us having the power to interfere with something God wanted to do, but I think we can do just that, especially when we 'try' to start acting and talking in a spiritual way."

It's funny how the whole conversation came back to me now. It must have been years ago that we talked about it. It all made so much sense all of a sudden.

Derrick Gregory . . . a divine appointment, Almeda would call it. I could see it all so clearly now. God had not even been on my mind that night so long ago when Derrick had held a gun on Robin and me. And yet, somehow I guess God had used the whole incident to show Derrick some things about himself that got down inside him and changed him—all unknown to me. There sure didn't seem to be much you could have called "spiritual" about the encounter! But it must have been a divine appointment nonetheless.

"What 'are' we to do about them then," I had asked Almeda again, "anything at all?"

"I always try to keep two things in mind," she had answered. "First of all, I try to just remember that God's appointment book is 'full' of situations and encounters for us, all day long, every day. I try

to remember that if you are a child of God, like you and I are, Corrie, then 'nothing' really is a chance encounter. God has divine appointments scheduled for us all the time. Everything that happens may be a divine appointment, for all we know. And just remembering that keeps me a little more on my toes as a Christian."

"What's the second thing?" I asked.

"I try to remember to pray for everyone I encounter, even if it seems like the tiniest and most insignificant interaction. You can just never tell what God may be doing in someone's life, behind the scenes out of our view. There are no chance encounters, like I said, God is always active and busy in the souls and hearts and minds of men and women. Our Father is always a busy, busy, energetic God in the affairs of men. Nothing happens by chance. So I try to remember to be in prayer for the people around me as much as I can. Sometimes I even find that he has been most busy in some situation that appeared to me 'least' likely to contain any evidence of his presence."

"How do you mean?" I asked.

"I mean sometimes God can be most diligently at work in the person who seems 'least' like someone who would be interested in God or responsive to his voice. That's why it's so important to pray for the people our paths cross, no matter what they seem like. God may have purposed for us to bump into them at that exact moment, and we may never realize all that's involved for them in the deep places within their heart."

That had sure been true with Derrick Gregory! I had no idea what he'd been thinking all this time! I'm not sure I'd ever prayed for him either, back then or in the years since. And yet his life had taken a different turn because of a chance encounter with me, of all people . . . a divine appointment.

It made me feel guilty in a way for not remembering to ever pray for him, and for being so unaware of the possibility of God's hand at work.

"God," I prayed silently, "I'm sorry for not thinking to pray for Derrick all this time. But I'm glad you were stirring things up in his life anyway. So I do pray for him now, and ask that you'd get into him in even greater ways and show yourself to him more and more all the time. And help me to recognize whatever other divine appointments you have for me, and to pray for the people who cross my path."

CHAPTER 18

THE RIDE BACK TO THE FARM

And speaking of divine appointments . . . what about this one sitting next to me in the wagon as we rode silently along!

What if Christopher Braxton hadn't come along when he did? Once I started thinking about how many little pieces of what most people would call "chance" fit together to cause things to happen, before long I began to realize how God's hand has to be in *everything* because of how connected it all is. Who could tell, maybe God had been scheduling hundreds of little "divine appointments" in my life, for eight years and getting me clear across the country, hundreds and hundreds of things, all leading up to that moment when my eyes happened to fall on the newspaper and see Derrick Gregory's name, which then led me to see him again, the very thing *he'd* prayed for himself.

It was such an enormous thing to consider, how interwoven and interconnected all the events of our lives might be in the purposes and "appointments" of God! I could hardly grasp it!

"I don't even know if I dare ask what you've been thinking about," Christopher's voice said suddenly in the midst of all my reflections. "You seem to have been a long ways away."

I glanced over at him and smiled.

"Seeing Derrick Gregory again gave me a lot to think about," I said. "Then I found myself remembering a conversation I'd had with Almeda. And then my mind filled with all kinds of things."

"I know what you mean," he said.

"Does that happen to you," I asked, "when your thoughts just take off so fast in two or three directions that you can hardly keep up with them?"

"Oh sure, all the time. So . . . what were you thinking about? Anything you care to share with a friend?"

I told him about my conversation with Almeda about divine appointments.

His face grew real thoughtful, then almost sad. When he spoke, which wasn't until after some time, it wasn't about anything I'd said at all, which is what it had seemed to me he'd been thinking about.

"Your stepmother Almeda sounds like quite a lady," he said. "I would love an opportunity to meet her."

"Oh, how I wish that were possible!" I exclaimed.

"It's a long ways to California," Christopher replied. "It's unlikely I'll ever have the chance."

"From what I hear, the two railroads are getting closer and closer all the time."

"You're right. I read an article on it just a few weeks ago—when you were asleep. The Central Pacific is planning to lay most of the rail across the Sierra Nevada when the weather turns later this year, and the Union Pacific is well begun across Nebraska toward Wyoming."

Just hearing the words *Sierra Nevada* sent a brief stab of homesickness through me, and reminded me of the Pony Express and Zack and all he'd been through.

"I've never told you, have I, that I worked for Leland Stanford for a while?" I said.

"The governor, one of the railroad Big Four?"

"Yes. I helped with his and Mr. Lincoln's campaigns in 1860."

"You are full of more surprises than anyone I've ever met, Corrie!" replied Christopher, laughing. "Every time I turn around I discover some new famous person who's your friend. You know Lincoln and General Grant, for heaven's sake, and John Fremont and—"

"You couldn't really say I *know* John Fremont," I put in.

"You worked on his campaign. And now it's Leland Stanford, and all you have to do is open up the newspaper, even three thousand miles from home, and there you find someone else you know, this Gregory fellow. Is there anybody you *don't* know?"

It was my turn to laugh. "It's not really at all like you make it sound," I said. "It's just that writing for the *Alta* has given me a few opportunities, that's all."

"I'm not at all convinced. I still think you're probably famous yourself and you're just not telling me."

"I am *not* famous," I insisted.

"You'll have to do a lot more than that to convince me! So anyway . . . tell me about Leland Stanford."

"It's a long story," I answered.

"You've said that before. Not only do you know more famous people than anyone I've ever met, you have more long stories to tell, too. But you haven't told me any of them yet. I want to hear them all!"

I fell silent. I *wanted* to tell Christopher everything. Here was someone I knew would be interested and who would understand whatever I did tell him. But we'd been together such a short time—how do you tell someone a whole lifetime's worth of experiences? I reckon it takes a lot of time. I wanted to know about what he'd been through as well.

As briefly as I could I told him about meeting Cal and how I'd become involved with him and Mr. Stanford and the election and the Sanitary Fund, and how that had led to the invitation from President Lincoln to come east.

"So it all ties in, you see, to what I was doing here when we came after Cal to see what we could learn about the plot against General Grant. But then Surratt came after us, I took off riding, he came after me shooting, and the next thing I knew I was lying in Mrs. Timms' bed and you were taking care of me."

"Pretty exciting adventures," Christopher said. "I can't say that anything like that has happened to me. Being a preacher is interesting in other ways, I suppose, but nothing like that!"

"For instance?" I said. "I want to know something about you."

Christopher thought a moment. "I can't keep from thinking about what you were telling me about your conversation with your stepmother," he said. "You just can't imagine how wonderful that sounds, just to have someone you can talk to like that."

"She is a special lady," I said.

"When I had my church, there were times I so desperately longed for someone I could pour my heart out to. But they were just looking at the external man, and had not much interest in my heart. I doubt they knew I even had one."

He sighed, and I could tell the memory was a painful one.

"And then in the time since, I've been essentially alone. It's been a good time. I know my Father is straightening around priorities deep within me in preparation—well, for *what* I haven't an idea, but for something. But through all that, you just can't possibly know how good it feels just to . . . to *talk* to someone your own age, someone who doesn't have motives or designs on you, who has no plan or agenda for you . . . someone who just listens, and understands, and who shares back in return. Do you see what I'm trying to tell you, Corrie? I consider you being here equally a godsend for *me* as much as whatever good I may have done you."

"Hardly the same," I said. "You saved my life."

"But I want you to know the depths of how I appreciate, as I said, just being able to talk and share with you. And hearing you talk about Almeda makes my hunger for it all the more. You mentioned your minister as if he was a friend, someone you all admired, and that you could talk to him too."

"Yes, that's exactly how he is, though it took a while for us to see those qualities in him—especially my pa."

"Oh, how I'd just like to be able to know them all—your family and your minister—what's his name?"

"Rev. Rutledge—Avery Rutledge."

"Well, I'd like to be able to know him, and Almeda. Listening to you talk, it sounds like you have such a refreshing communication between all of you, like you're always talking about everything."

"I reckon I never thought that much about it, but I suppose you are right. I guess I just took it for granted."

"Oh, don't do that, Corrie. It's very unusual, that depth of understanding and that sharing of ideas and thoughts. Not many families experience it. You should consider yourself abundantly blessed."

There was a longing in his voice that I could tell went deep and said more than his actual words.

"I wish you could meet my father," I said. "I know you would like him."

"Who knows . . . perhaps someday," he replied.

"You said it yourself, it won't be too many years before the two rail lines join California with the rest of the country. Then you could easily come out for a visit. Why would you even have to wait till then?" I added.

"It isn't that it would be impossible. But the Lord would have to initiate such a thing, don't you see, Corrie? You can't just charge off and go someplace or do something because maybe you want to. It's got to be what *he* wants you to do. And I'm still so uncertain about so many things regarding my future."

"I understand," I said. "I'm sorry, I reckon I got kinda carried away and—"

"No, no, think nothing of it," interrupted Christopher. "You were thinking of me, and I appreciate it, Corrie, truly I do. But there's one other element in what we were talking about that would make a visit difficult."

"What's that?" I asked.

"Just that it would be that . . . a visit."

"How do you mean?"

"What could it do but intensify my longing for such fellowship and relationships in my *own* life? When the time came for me to leave, where would I have to go, what would I have to come back to? This time at Mrs. Timms' place is only temporary. There's no *life* for me there, permanently. What will it be next? Another church someplace? Somehow that seems doubtful to me now. In other words, once the war is over, you have a home to go back to, people who are part of your life. But for me there just is no such place. After the experience in the church, I've been . . . well, alone."

"What about everything you told me before? Seems like I recall a conversation we had back before I remembered who I was, about your wanting to help people and being curious to know people."

"Yes. All that's there—it always will be. But you need someplace to *do* it, someplace where it can happen. Always before, I figured a church was the right setting. But now all that's changed. Here I am working for a lady on her farm, and how many opportunities do I get?"

"You got one," I said, smiling.

"And being here at the moment our Father knew you needed tending to is worth everything ten times over," rejoined Christopher quietly.

"I do understand what you are saying, though," I added. "You want to be in a place and situation where there are opportunities to give to people in need from what is inside you, from what God has given you to share, and yet you feel alone and isolated and unable to do the very thing you think he wants you to do."

"That's it exactly. You *do* understand!"

"I know what it's like to have something brewing and stirring inside you," I said. "Writing's that way for me. But I've been fortunate enough to be able to do it."

"And be very successful at it," added Christopher.

"I reckon that is so."

"I know the Lord will do whatever he has purposed to do with me," said Christopher. "I don't doubt that. Yet it is frustrating having no idea where I'm to go, what I'm to do. I know he will show me when the time is right for me to know."

We bumped along awhile longer. I knew from the now familiar surroundings that we had not far to go now.

"Oh, don't you just love the wide out-of-doors!" Christopher said all at once, breathing in deeply. "The grass on the hill over there, that grove of trees—they look just the same every day, and yet every day they offer some fresh opportunity for thought that might be totally different than the day before. I suppose people could say that God's creation is relatively unaltered on any given day—except for changes of weather—I would say that its beauty is not always in the thing itself, but rather in the heart of the one who chooses to receive it."

"Don't you think the world *is* full of beauty all by itself?" I asked.

"Yes, of course! But what I was attempting to say is that the person who does receive that beauty will receive great variation and variety in the same sight. We are, after all, not receiving messages of beauty and insights into the truths of creation from a mere attraction to some mountain or tree or animal, but a word from God himself. It is the heart of God who dwells within the essence of nature. He communicates pieces of himself in a very personal way through these things we look upon and say, 'I behold beauty therein.' God is everywhere, right in front of our eyes. The very people who go to church Sunday after Sunday, expecting there to get what they call closer to God, never suspect that he is perhaps even closer to them all the week long. And most of them rarely stop to spend a day alone in the woods or on a long ride on horseback, or sitting on top of a high hill, the very places where the Bible tells us the presence of God resides. I struggled to get the members of my former congregation to see this fundamental truth, and yet so often thought I was doing nothing but talking to myself."

He glanced ahead, then finished. "Well, that was the fastest wagon ride I've ever made back from Richmond. It would seem you've been spared any further sermons! Looks like we're home!"

CHAPTER 19

DERRICK AND CHRISTOPHER

The conversation riding back from Richmond seemed to act like a key opening up a locked door.

I suppose the locked door for me was the time I'd spent not remembering who I was, and for Christopher it was the time he'd spent alone since leaving his church. Over the next few days, both doors seemed to unlock and we spent hour after hour just talking together, about a hundred things that I can't even remember all of now. Even though we both kept journals, I hadn't realized how much I had missed having a real person, like Almeda, to talk to face-to-face. I'm sure it was even more that way for Christopher, because, like he said, he hadn't really ever had someone like that.

I waited four days. I hoped that would be long enough for Derrick to find out any information he would be able to.

"I could just ride into the city myself," I told Christopher. "My shoulder is fine."

"What!" he replied. "You think I'd miss an opportunity for another long ride for us to get to talk?"

I laughed.

"That is, unless you *want* to go alone?"

"No, no, that's not it at all," I insisted. "I'd much rather share the ride with you! I just didn't want to presume on your kindness."

"You presume all you want to, Corrie Hollister. I insist that you do. And it will be my pleasure to escort you into our fair capital city!"

"Thank you!" I laughed.

This time I asked Christopher to go into the *Star* building with

121

me. I'd told him all about what had happened with Derrick in '56, and then about our conversation of a few days earlier. We'd prayed for Derrick several times since and I wanted Christopher to meet him.

Curiously, the moment the two men met, I think I learned more about Christopher than anything he could have told me about himself. As they shook hands, I saw Christopher look deeply into Derrick's face with a gaze of such compassion that all I could think of was that such must have been how Jesus looked upon people. The Bible talks about him looking at people and *loving* them, and that's what instantly struck me as I saw the light in Christopher's eye. I knew that he hadn't just heard all I'd said about Derrick Gregory in a surface way, but that he'd realized God's hand to be actively at work, even though I hadn't seen it all this time, in preparing Derrick to see me again. Christopher took that as a sign that we needed to pray for Derrick. As we had prayed for him, I could feel a sense of expectation grow within me, just from Christopher's enthusiasm, that God really was up to something in the situation on a deeper level than just what met the eye. So when we saw Derrick, the meeting was so alive with meaning and purpose.

"I can't tell you what a privilege it is to meet you, Mr. Gregory," Christopher said with great sincerity. "Corrie has told me about you, and speaks quite highly of you."

Derrick immediately squirmed, as much from Christopher's penetrating look of kindness and the honest smile on his face as from the words themselves.

"Thank you, Braxton," replied Derrick, shaking Christopher's hand, "though I can't imagine Cornelia having much to say about a scum like me who'd shoot a gun at a young woman like her."

"She told me all about the incident," Christopher went on, still holding Derrick's gaze. "But she also said she didn't think you really meant her any harm. You can't imagine how great is her forgiveness toward you, Mr. Gregory. Corrie's a lady who takes the words of Jesus very seriously. Actually, she considers you a man of some fiber and integrity."

"Integrity . . . me!" exclaimed Derrick with a nervous laugh.

"Cornelia," he said, looking in my direction, "what did you tell him?"

"I just told him what I think of you, Derrick," I said. "And despite what happened, I do think highly of you. I told you before, didn't I, that I forgave you a long time ago?"

"Yes, but—"

"If it's worthy to be called by the name at all, Mr. Gregory," Christopher put in, "forgiveness is complete and total. There's nothing really so astounding about it. Corrie just happens to be a person who is under orders to a higher authority."

Derrick sort of shook his head. "Well, it beats anything I've ever heard of, and that's the truth. But I appreciate what you both say. I'm glad there's no hard feelings. Like I told Cornelia the other day, I've always thought a lot of her, too."

There was a pause. I didn't want Derrick to feel too awkward, and he had plenty to think about already!

"Did you find out anything about Captain Dyles and Jacob?" I asked.

"Matter of fact, I surprised even myself. I *did* find where they were taken."

"They're alive!" I asked excitedly.

"I didn't say that. I don't know. I didn't want to make the sergeant I was talking to suspicious, so I didn't ask too many questions. So I can't promise a thing. But the fellow owed me a favor, and I found out where—at least where he *thinks*—they were taken."

"Where is it?" I asked.

"Right here in the city. It's called Libby Prison."

"Used to be a ship's chandlery, didn't it?" asked Christopher.

"Yeah. A pitiful place, from what I hear," said Derrick. "More than thirteen hundred men in six dank little rooms. Chances of your finding who you're looking for, Cornelia, especially the darkie . . . I don't think they're too good."

CHAPTER 20

MORE MATURE BUT WITH MORE DOUBTS

This time the ride back from Richmond to Mrs. Timms' farm was quiet and somber. Part of me was happy to have found out what I had. Now at least I had something to pin my hopes on that Captain Dyles and Jacob were alive.

Yet I didn't even know what it was I was hoping for. And Derrick's words were none too encouraging. But somehow I had to try to do *something*. I couldn't help feeling responsible.

"You really want to try to find them, see them, talk to them, don't you, Corrie?" Christopher asked.

"Yes," I answered, "but I just don't see how."

"Well, don't give up. We'll think of something."

"But what?" I said in frustration.

"There may be a way. I know that part of Richmond pretty well."

We rode on farther in silence. I knew Christopher well enough by now to recognize the look of something turning over in his mind. But he was the kind of man who didn't like to say something until he had thought it through all the way from one end to the other. He wanted to make sure his words counted and that he didn't just fill up the air with them for the sake of making noise.

"It's hard to know where right and wrong fall in the middle of a war," he commented after a while.

"How do you mean?" I asked.

"Oh, nothing specific," he answered. "It's just more difficult to see the ethics of some things clearly when, in a way, you're

125

totally immersed in something—this war, for instance—that I would say is wrong by definition. Would it be *wrong* for us to stretch the truth in order to see or help your friends? It's just a question I can't quite see all the way to the bottom of. I believe in truth. Yet where might a small compromise of truth be justifiable for the greater truth of, for example, helping to set a man free?"

I thought immediately of my own struggle with that very question about truth in the episode that Derrick Gregory had been involved in so long ago. I never had thoroughly resolved it, there were so many factors involved.

"I'm sure it must be the very question Mr. Lincoln had to wrestle with, and perhaps even the leaders of the Confederacy, too," Christopher went on, "in weighing having to wage a war, clearly an evil thing, for the sake of upholding what they considered truth."

"If you're asking me," I laughed, "I don't have an answer."

"No, I don't suppose I'm asking you for an answer as such. These are just the kinds of things I find myself thinking about sometimes—the kinds of questions about spiritual matters that don't have clear answers. At least not that I can see."

"I've talked to Almeda about just that," I said, "—what's a Christian to do when right and wrong isn't as clear as black and white?"

"I must admit, I've struggled with more of them since leaving my church. There was a certain cocoon environment I now realize I was in—even during seminary, and before. For so long I saw everything through the filter of the church and its protective and encircling boundaries. But now so many things look different to me. It's funny though," he added, chuckling to himself.

"What's funny?" I asked.

"I feel like I'm twice the man I was a few years ago. I'm more mature, not nearly so naive as a Christian, more sensitive to the people around me, less prone to spiritualize things with rote responses, more practical."

"What's wrong with that?" I asked. "I don't see anything funny about it."

"Along with everything I just said, I seem to have twice as

many doubts, twice as many questions, and not nearly so much self-confidence as I did when I was in the church. Don't you find that humorous?"

"I don't know. Actually, maybe it's a good thing. Almeda and Rev. Rutledge have always told me that doubts were good."

"I know," said Christopher, laughing again, but thoughtfully. "I know they are. I know the kinds of things I wrestle through with the Lord now are the kinds of things that are necessary for spiritual maturity. But still, every once in a while it strikes me as funny—more mature, but less self-confident, more practical and knowledgeable about spiritual things, yet with more doubts and questions. It all just doesn't seem to go together very well."

We rattled along in the wagon, and were soon back to the farm.

I didn't see Christopher for several hours. He was busy with the animals. I ate with Mrs. Timms, and it was well after dark before he came in.

He walked straight into the sitting room, his face all lighted up.

"I've got it, Corrie," he said. "I know what we'll do!"

CHAPTER 21

LIBBY PRISON

It was a week and a half later, in the second week of January 1865, when I found myself walking alongside Christopher toward the door of Libby Prison in Richmond, Virginia.

I had been in many scary situations in my life. I don't know why I should have been trembling now, but I was. Maybe it was knowing that we were going *inside* the place and that the doors would close behind us, and that if they found out what we were *really* doing there, they might leave the doors closed and we might never get out!

We walked straight to the guard who stood there with a rifle.

"Rev. Braxton and Nurse Hollister to see two of your prisoners," said Christopher with a commanding voice. For someone who said he didn't feel very self-confident, he certainly could have fooled me! Immediately the guard turned and went inside. A couple minutes later he returned, an officer following him.

"What's this all about, Reverend?" asked the man.

"Like I told the corporal here," replied Christopher, "I'm Rev. Braxton and this is my assistant, Nurse Hollister. We've been sent by one of President Davis's assistants to examine two of your prisoners. It's all right here."

He handed the man a paper he'd been holding. The officer glanced over it.

"What's the trouble with these two?" he said, cocking his head toward the paper he still held in his hand. "We've got twelve, maybe thirteen hundred men here. We don't even know half their names."

129

"It's imperative we find these two—a Union captain and a big darkie fellow that was with him. Taken prisoner sometime in October, wasn't it, Nurse Hollister?"

"Yes, sir," I said.

"We don't have records on them," insisted the officer.

"We'll find them. You can leave it to us. We're under orders to remove them from the prison."

"Why?"

"Might be carrying cholera."

The man sucked in a breath of air but tried to conceal his alarm.

"What if they are? So a few prisoners die?"

"If they've got it, with the miserable conditions here, Lieutenant, the entire prison could be wiped out."

"They're only Yankees. It'll save us the trouble of shooting them."

"You think they're going to die and you and all your men are going to escape the plague, Lieutenant?" Christopher barked, sounding almost angry. "Don't you hear me, man? This is serious. The entire city could be infected! That's why the President sent us. We have to get these two men out of the prison. Now be quick about it, or I will have to report you to President Davis!"

"Yes . . . yes, Reverend," stammered the lieutenant.

"I'll take my orders back," said Christopher, grabbing the paper from him.

"Right this way, Reverend," said the lieutenant, leading us back the way he had come. As we walked inside, Christopher glanced over at me, took in a breath, and raised his eyebrows slightly. I could see just the hint of a smile come over his lips. It seemed to say, "Can you believe I got away with that!" Then the stern look came back over him, and his eyes went back to the shoulders of the lieutenant a stride ahead. The door thudded shut behind us, and I heard a loud clank of iron a second later.

We were inside now—completely inside!

It was just like Derrick had said—six large rooms, teeming with prisoners. I thought I'd seen the worst of it in the battlefield hospitals. But this was downright gruesome and morbid. I could hardly keep from gagging from the sights and smells and sounds!

There were men without arms and legs, many with open wounds. I don't know what they did for sanitation, but it smelled as if they didn't do anything! All the men were skin and bones. *So* skinny they didn't look as if they'd been fed in months, yet somehow they managed to stay alive. A few of them looked like skeletons that had just had some skin stretched tightly over the bones! Rats and mice scurried across the floor. It wouldn't have surprised me to know that half the prisoners were suffering from gangrene. So many of them had been taken prisoner during combat, it was hardly surprising that many were wounded, and their Confederate keepers did little or nothing to keep the wounds from festering and getting worse. They didn't care how many died. These poor Union boys were the enemy, whether on the battlefield or in a prison. Some of those lying on the hard, wet stone floor, I think *were* dead! But I didn't want to look a second time to know for sure. The less I knew of the horrors of this place, the better!

As we made our way out of one room and to another to see if we could find Jacob and Captain Dyles, we walked by a large open barrel. Such a horrid stench came up from it that it revolted my stomach. I gagged, then couldn't help asking the lieutenant, "What *is* that?"

"That's their drinking water, ma'am," he answered.

I gagged again, barely managing to keep my stomach down inside me.

We inspected a second room, then a third. There were probably two hundred men in each, but it didn't take longer than a minute or two to scan through the faces and know that I recognized none of them. About half the prisoners ignored us altogether. Others looked at us with pleading and longing in their eyes, probably knowing there was nothing we could do for them, yet still with enough of their wits about them to hope that the sight of a friendly stranger somehow might bode well for their horrible plight.

But alas, we couldn't take them all with us! Oh, this was an awful war!

In the fifth room, we found them.

I don't think I'd have even recognized Captain Dyles. And when my face first spotted his in the midst of a small group of men, I'm not sure he recognized me at first either in the nurse's attire I had on. He had more than two months' growth of beard on his cheeks and chin, but even without that, the hollow sunken eyes and emaciated frame hardly seemed like the same man. It was the voice I recognized first. Then a second later my eyes made sense of the face I had just seen.

It wasn't Captain Dyles' voice, though, but Jacob's.

Christopher and the lieutenant were at that moment a step or two in front of me and engaged in conversation. The whole time Christopher had been subtly keeping the lieutenant distracted and as far from me as possible, pretending to be looking for the two men but letting me keep as far back as possible. He must have known what could happen. So as I said, he and the lieutenant were talking and so heard nothing of what went on behind them.

"Miss Cor—" I heard Jacob's voice say.

I recognized it immediately, and the same instant realized that my eyes had just passed over Captain Dyles' face. I spun around toward the sound, my finger on my lips.

The look of urgency on my face must have instantly conveyed my message to Jacob because he stopped right in the middle of my name. I glanced ahead. Neither Christopher nor the lieutenant seemed to have heard him.

"Shh," I whispered, as loud as I dared, glancing at both men. "You don't know me! You've never seen me before. You are both very, very sick! Moan and act miserable!"

I prayed no one would hear my whispered message. Then I stood back from where I'd been stooped toward them and hurried after Christopher and the lieutenant.

"I think I've located them, Rev. Braxton," I said, running up from behind.

They stopped and turned toward me.

"These two men back here fit the description exactly."

I led them back to where Captain Dyles and Jacob sat together on the stone floor. They *did* look miserable! Poor Jacob! He must have lost half his weight! And it was clear he'd been beaten, probably in an attempt to find out what unit he'd escaped from. If he'd told them he was a free black man from the North, they'd probably have beaten him all the more. Southerners' hatred of black men was so extreme and irrational, I had to fight against hating the Southerners myself.

"What's your name?" Christopher asked the captain, rather sternly it seemed to me.

"Dyles, Reverend," he answered. "Geoffrey Dyles."

"And you?"

"Crabtree, Massah Reverrund, an' ah's feelin' real sick."

"That's them, Lieutenant," Christopher said.

I knelt down and pretended to feel about Jacob's midsection. "What does that feel like?" I said, then gave a little poke.

"Ow!" he yelled, and then the most pitiful wail imaginable followed.

"That's the cholera all right," said Christopher. Already the lieutenant had taken three or four steps backward and his face was pale. "We simply must get these men out of here without delay. It is imperative we get them out of the city before the worst of the infectious period comes. What do you think, Nurse? Are we already too late?"

"We may have found them just in time," I replied. "I can't be sure, Reverend, but it is my medical opinion that there is still twelve to twenty-four hours before the most dangerous time arrives."

"We must move quickly! On your feet, men!" ordered Christopher.

Jacob and the captain rose, a little too eagerly for the cholera, it seemed to me, but the lieutenant guard did not take much notice.

Already we were halfway out of the room. Christopher supported Jacob with one arm. Jacob, still moaning and staggering as if he could hardly keep his balance, entered into the charade with enthusiasm, although he probably was in reality very weak. I followed, helping Captain Dyles, though he seemed to genuinely need assistance. Cholera or not, he was only a shadow of his strong former self.

"What's to prevent the two of you from catching it?" asked the lieutenant, still keeping his distance but moving along with us.

"We've taken a little pill that is supposed to prevent it, if we're lucky," replied Christopher.

"And if you're not?"

"That's why they selected a minister and a nurse for the assignment, because we are in the business of giving our lives for others."

"Are there more of those . . . pills?" he asked. "Do you have one that I—"

"There are no more, Lieutenant," barked Christopher. "They're only experimental. If you're afraid, you can step back. The nurse and I will be happy to take it from here. You've been a great help."

Christopher increased his pace now, making it genuinely difficult for the rest of us to keep up.

We approached the door. It was still bolted.

"Get that door open!" yelled Christopher. "By order of President Jefferson Davis, we must get these two dangerously infected prisoners out of here immediately!"

A private and a corporal scurried toward the door. One threw up the iron bolt. The other unlatched the door and pulled it open. Beyond was the street and the blue sky of freedom!

"Thank you again, Lieutenant, for all your assistance!" Christopher called out behind him with just the slightest pause.

We were outside now, and, still supporting the two prisoners, who continued to moan, made for Christopher's wagon, which lay about fifty yards down the street where Christopher had tied the team.

Suddenly my stomach leaped into my throat!

Along the street came a detail of six mounted Confederate officers, straight toward us! The lead horse was mostly white, and the man on its back, sitting tall and straight and with dignity in the saddle, had a short crop of hair of nearly matching color.

The description fit perfectly! It could only be one man! The general's bars on both shoulders confirmed it. Robert E. Lee!

CHAPTER 22

SACRIFICE

I knew Christopher was eyeing the mounted officers out of the corner of his eye. Still he kept steadily on. I followed, not daring to look up. If those steely eyes of General Lee once caught mine, I knew I would wilt like a withered flower and he would see the guilt all over my face in a second!

We were close to the wagon now, and still walking slowly.

The horses moved slowly alongside us, then past. I could feel the intensity of six sets of inquisitive eyes following us.

We kept walking.

Then I heard the clomps of the horses' hooves come to a halt in the street. I didn't dare turn to look.

There was the wagon, only about ten yards ahead now.

"Stop, there . . . just a moment," at last came the dreaded words behind us. I knew the voice could be none other than General Lee's.

I saw Christopher flinch momentarily, but then he continued to walk straight ahead.

"Stop, I say," came the imperative voice again. "That's an order, be you a reverend or whoever you are!"

"Nurse Hollister," said Christopher, "continue on with these men and get them loaded into the wagon." As he said it, Christopher let go of Jacob. He looked deeply into my eyes for just a brief instant, then whispered, "Whatever happens to me, you get in that wagon and go. That is *my* order to *you*, Corrie! You get to safety . . . and then you wait for me. I will come to you. My life is in the Father's hands." Though his words were spoken so softly and rapidly so as not to arouse suspicion, never had words bored so deeply into me. There was such authority and command in them that though my heart was already failing me with fear, I knew I had to obey what he'd told me to do. "Now go . . . they will not stop you or harm you. I will not let them."

Then he turned to face the officers. "I'm afraid it's cholera, sir," said Christopher, sadly but confidently, and walking slowly toward the general.

"I have heard of no outbreak of cholera," I heard a voice behind me. But slowly I kept on.

Jacob and Captain Dyles and I reached the wagon. Slowly they climbed inside and lay down in the back, moaning. I untied the horses, then climbed up onto the seat and grasped the reins between my fingers.

"General, we really must investigate this. One of those two could be the man you are looking for," said another of the officers.

"I tell you there is no need of it," said Christopher, speaking with a calm assurance. "Any questions you have may be directed to me."

"It appears you have come from the prison with those two men, Reverend," said General Lee. "By what authority have you taken those men into your care?"

"By the authority of the one who sent me," I heard Christopher's calm and steady reply.

I urged the horses forward. The wagon lurched into motion. No words from any of the men shouted out for us to stop. Whatever was going on now, I could no longer make out the words.

I glanced back. Three of the men had now dismounted and were clustered about Christopher. It looked like one of them had pulled a gun from the holster at his side.

Tears came to my eyes. I spoke to the horses now. They increased their pace.

I looked back again. No one was even looking our direction. We were safe! They were not even pursuing us!

But in the distance I could see Christopher, surrounded now by the six gray-coated officers. It looked like his hands were in the air, and they were walking back toward the prison.

"No!" I cried. "This can't happen again!"

It was a terrible nightmare. I was reliving the awful moment when Jacob and the captain had been captured!

My mind blurred and began to get very confused. I could feel the leather reins still in my hands, but now suddenly I felt like I was riding . . . riding alone on horseback . . . riding like the wind . . . danger was behind me, but I could not escape it. Bullets flew faster than any horse.

A searing pain shot to my shoulder. I was still conscious, and I knew no one was behind us. Yet the very memory brought a renewal of the pain.

I whipped and lashed at the horses. "Faster . . . faster!" I screamed. "We have to escape . . . they're behind us!"

Bumping and jostling the wagon behind them, the two horses galloped under my strokes. I bounced up and down in the seat, nearly unaware of my two very sick passengers.

"Miss Corrie . . . Miss Corrie!" I heard from behind me. I turned and glanced over my shoulder.

"Miss Corrie," cried Jacob earnestly. "We be safe now. No one's behind us for miles. We'd be much obliged to you if you'd slow them two nags down a mite."

His words brought me to my senses. I blinked and shook myself awake. There still lay Captain Dyles and Jacob Crabtree in the back of the wagon, looking as if the last several miles had been as torturous as Libby Prison.

"I'm sorry," I said as I reined the horses in. I breathed in deeply, then took another, and then remembered everything clearly once more.

Then suddenly I remembered the vision of seeing Christopher being taken at gunpoint back toward the prison. Again I felt tears sting my eyes.

It wasn't fair! It was all wrong . . . all backward! *We* were the ones who were guilty, not Christopher. *We* had knowingly come into this enemy-occupied territory. He was the only one of the four of us who had done nothing wrong. Yet *he* turned and willingly walked straight into the hands of the enemy so that we could be free.

He had boldly walked straight up to Robert E. Lee, and just given himself up . . . while *we* rode out of the city to freedom!

He had already saved my life once. Now here he had saved it again!

By now I was sobbing so freely that hot tears were running down my cheeks. I could barely see ahead of me that we had already reached the road off to the right toward Mrs. Timms' farm.

CHAPTER 23

TWO LONELY DAYS

Under any other circumstances, the next two days would probably have been joyous ones.

I hadn't seen any way of being able to help Jacob and Captain Dyles. Then Christopher had come up with his plan. With Mrs. Timms' help we had fashioned what looked enough like a nurse's uniform for me, and with his old clerical collar and boldness, we had just walked straight into the prison and brought them right out!

Suddenly they were free men again! But what had become of Christopher?

All the rest of that afternoon and evening, we all kept watching the road for any sign of him. As quickly as we were able, Mrs. Timms and I got the two men fed and bathed and into warm beds. Once everything settled down some it became more than apparent that, in spite of not having cholera, both men were seriously weak and undernourished. They were still too stunned to question what we had done, and too weakly exultant in their newfound freedom to even worry about Christopher.

But Mrs. Timms and I were beside ourselves with worry. I kept wondering if I ought to go back into the city to look for him. But somehow the memory of his words as they came back reminded me that he wanted me to stay and wait. But it was excruciating not to *do* something.

That first evening passed, silently. Neither Mrs. Timms nor I were in much of a mood to talk, and the two men were in bed. Though there were four of us, all the *life* seemed to have been taken away now that Christopher was gone. The house was silent as a tomb.

How I got through the night I'm not sure. I must have been absolutely exhausted because I did manage to get some sleep. But whenever I found myself fitfully tossing and turning, all I could think of was Christopher, alone somewhere, probably in that horrid prison . . . or, what if . . . no—I wouldn't let myself think that! He *couldn't* be dead!

The following morning was Saturday. The two men arose in noticeably better spirits and condition. A sound night's sleep with nourishing food in their stomachs had already begun to work wonders.

We now had a chance to talk more. I told them what had happened to me since the fateful day we had been separated, and they told me more than I wanted to know about the prison where they'd been ever since. Once they knew everything, they realized just what a price had been paid for their freedom. Almost immediately they took upon themselves to pitch in and tend to as many of the chores about the place as they were able.

By then I had helped Christopher enough that I knew all the animals and their routines. So the four of us—two women who scarcely knew each other; a Union officer and a black man, both free now but still behind enemy lines—worked all day together. We probably worked harder than we needed to. But the work gave us something to do, and bound us together in our common indebtedness to the one who was not among us but about whom we all were thinking.

Every time I heard a noise, my head would jerk up and I'd look about. I don't know whether I expected to see Christopher or a detail of Confederate soldiers coming to take all of *us* to prison too!

By day's end, however, nothing had happened. I went to bed probably more downcast and disconsolate than at any time in my life. That there had been no word from Christopher in a day and a half meant there could be no doubt remaining that they were holding him . . . probably in prison!

The next morning dawned bright, but cold. Nothing the sun did could cheer my spirits.

We went through the motions of feeding the pigs and goats and chickens and milking the cows and taking them to pasture. Jacob was returning every now and then to hints of his former self and did his best to encourage me. But it was no use.

Mrs. Timms prepared a nice Sunday afternoon dinner for us. It was her way of trying to make the best of the situation and do what she could for everyone else. We all had our own ways of coping with it. But one thing we all had in common was that Christopher's absence seemed to put within each one of us a desire to serve and do things for one another. Mrs. Timms tried to make every mealtime homey for me and the two men, who were all away from our homes. Jacob and the captain did as much work around the place as they knew to do, and almost began to get annoying with their asking what they might do to help.

Even though it was a sad and lonely time, I suppose it brought out the best in us—the unselfish, the desire to put others first. I don't know if it's just something that happens at such times, or if Christopher's example had rubbed off on us all in different ways.

We sat down to eat early in the afternoon. But no one made a move to take any of the food. Even Mrs. Timms just sat there as if she was waiting for something, when it was usually her way to start passing around the dishes. We all sat and just looked at one another. Then I realized what we were all waiting for.

Slowly I held out my two hands and offered them to Mrs. Timms on my right and Jacob on my left. They took them, then each gave a hand in turn to Captain Dyles. Without even thinking whether I was the right one to do it, I began to pray.

"Father," I said, "we thank you for this provision, and for loving us like you do. But we ask especially right now for your protection and your hand to be upon your son Christopher Braxton. Wherever he is, and in whatever circumstance, Lord, we ask for you to—"

I never finished. The prayer had been answered even before I'd begun to pray it.

There was a sound at the door.

The next instant I was on my feet, running across the floor.

Without even realizing what I was doing, I threw my arms around him and held on to him as tight as I could

"Christopher!" I cried, then broke down sobbing for joy.

CHAPTER 24

CHRISTOPHER'S PLAN

"What's all this!" laughed Christopher as he entered, with more hugs and handshakes and slaps on the back following mine.

"We're just mighty happy to see you back in one piece, sir," said Captain Dyles. "I am Geoffrey Dyles. We didn't exactly have time for an introduction two days ago!"

"Happy to meet you, Dyles! And you must be Crabtree," he added to Jacob.

"Jacob Crabtree in your service, Mr. Braxton," said Jacob, taking Christopher's right hand in both of his and giving it a vigorous shake. "The captain and me's in your debt. Whatever we can do—"

"Forget it. Corrie was plenty fond of the two of you and seemed to have an idea it was her fault you both wound up in the pickle you did. This whole scheme was her idea!"

"You never told us that, Miss Corrie," said Jacob.

"It's only half-true," I said, laughing. "I told him all that happened and that I wished there was something we could do. But it was Christopher who thought up the plot to get you out of that prison."

"Well, however it came about, we're more grateful than you can know," said Captain Dyles. "You've both got more guts than half the Union army."

"The dinner's getting cold!" called out Mrs. Timms.

"Dinner? What dinner?" said Christopher.

"You're just in time, Mr. Braxton," said Mrs. Timms. "I made extra of everything because I knew you'd be back today!"

"I do have to admit . . . I am famished."

We all resumed our seats, though I scooted around to sit beside Mrs. Timms so Christopher could sit at the head of the table. Suddenly, spirits in the small farmhouse were noticeably brighter.

I had hardly taken a single bite before I could no longer contain my curiosity.

"Please, Christopher," I said, "aren't you going to tell us what happened?"

"Don't you want me to get some nourishment in my starving body first?"

"But I'm dying to know!"

"All right, all right. But you'll have to let me eat as I go, because I truly am hungry enough to eat *two* of Mrs. Timms' huge Sunday meals!"

He swallowed two mouthfuls of hot potatoes, then began. "Well, I walked toward General Lee."

"It *was* Robert Lee," I interrupted. "I was sure."

"The general and some of his top aides, all right. Believe it or not, they had just received word, after all this time, of your capture, Captain," he said, turning toward Mr. Dyles. "Hearing that you were part of General Grant's unit, I think he was planning to interrogate you."

"Lucky for us! You got us out just in time!"

"I am not a believer in luck, Captain, if you'll pardon my disagreement. You were being watched over, as were we all. Luck had nothing to do with it."

"Watched over? I don't understand . . . by whom?"

"By your Father of course, Captain. He is always watching over you."

"You mean . . . God?"

"Who else?"

"And do you mean to tell me God was watching over us even when we were in that foul, stinking prison?"

"Then more than ever."

"Bah, I don't believe a word of it."

Christopher smiled knowingly and patiently. "Tell me, Captain," he said, "was it so bad that you ever prayed when you didn't think you could stand it another minute?"

"Of course. Everybody prays like that."

"How about you, Jacob?"

"I prayed a heap, I can tell you! More'n I ever prayed in my whole life."

The captain looked over at his black friend.

"You never told me you were praying," he said.

"Ain't the kind of thing folks always goes around telling other people. Prayin's kind of a private thing. But I was prayin' all right. 'Sides, you didn't tell me you was praying neither."

"But don't you see," Christopher went on, "both of you *did* pray, and your Father was watching over you and answering your prayers in ways you could have had no idea of, watching over you the whole time in preparation for what happened two days ago. Why, he kept Corrie alive when some young women who weren't as strong would have died from a wound like hers. He sent me along just at the right moment to find her. He brought her memory back. He showed her the article in the paper by her friend. And Gregory just happened to be at the *Star* office when we went looking for him. He just happened to know someone who just happened to know where the two of you were. And then we just happened along an hour before Robert Lee was coming after you, and just happened to manage to get you out of that place."

He paused and looked at both Jacob and Captain Dyles seriously but with such a look of love and deep concern as I don't think I'd ever seen on a man's face toward another man. It was the same look he'd given Derrick Gregory.

"Don't you *see* it, men?" he said, with such entreaty and earnestness and conviction. "None of it just *happened*! It was all part of a divine plan. Every tiniest piece was a divine appointment—" and as he said the words he glanced at me with a smile. "There are no chance encounters for God's people," he went on. "I venture to say there are probably no chance encounters for *anyone*. But you see, we *are* God's people, Corrie and Mrs. Timms and I. And the two of you prayed prayers to your Father in heaven. And God, who is the Father of us all, was watching and he listened and heard and was making provision for answers far beyond the scope of what we can even grasp. You were praying in the prison and I was praying for Corrie as she lay in bed, and I know Mrs. Timms was praying for me, faithful lady that she is, because she knew of the hurts and doubts my heart was struggling with. Now here we all are, together, and God has answered all our prayers as he weaves a tapestry together. Each one of us is but one thread. But he is all the time interweaving the threads together to form a beautiful pattern that only he can see."

All of us around the table fell silent.

"Once you have eyes to see it, Captain, I would say there were probably twenty or thirty, or even a hundred different little pieces of what most people would call *chance* but I would call the sovereign hand of God, fitting events and circumstances together in such a way as led to your walking out of that prison two days ago—and you were unaware of it all. So yes, I say again, God was indeed watching over you far more carefully than you had any idea."

"I heard him ask you how you had authority to take them from the prison," I said, "and then you said that you'd been sent. That was the last thing I heard. Did you tell them Jefferson Davis sent you?"

Christopher smiled.

"No, I said nothing about Mr. Davis. By that time I was mostly praying myself."

He paused, and a look of deep thoughtfulness came over his face, like he was reliving the whole thing.

"From the very start such a conviction had come over me that the Lord was with us, that we were doing what he purposed for us to do, and that we would all be kept safe because we were in his hands, that I just felt no fear. That's not something I often feel. Actually, I don't consider myself a particularly courageous man at all. Sometimes the smallest things can frighten me. But on that day there was none of it. Even when I saw General Lee and the five other officers, I knew all was in God's hands.

"I should not say I felt nothing. My heart did skip a beat or two, but only for the safety of the rest of you, not for myself. Strange to say, that's what I felt. And so as I was praying silently in my heart throughout the whole thing, there was such a sense of asking exactly what God had purposed to do. Therefore, there was no doubt that he *was* going to answer everything I prayed, and I just acted accordingly. It's always a good thing to pray, of course. And prayer in the midst of our doubts is essential. Yet the kind of prayer that moves mountains, it seems to me, is prayer that lines up exactly with what God intends to do, and our only responsibility is to fall in line with his purpose.

"But anyway, to get back to what happened. After telling you to keep going, Corrie—"

"I've never heard your voice so commanding," I said. "You made me more afraid of disobeying you than I was of being captured!"

Christopher laughed. "I wanted to make sure you did as I said! I knew you would come to no harm. But I knew you didn't know it!"

"I did obey, but I hated it," I said. "I was so worried about you!"

"You needn't have been. I was in good hands. The moment I turned from you and began walking back toward the general, I began praying fervently that God would blind their eyes just enough from what was happening that they would focus their attention on me and pay none to you. 'Blind their sight, Lord,' I said under my breath as I approached. 'Give them eyes to see only me.' I walked straight toward General Lee, looked him firmly in the eye with a pleasant smile, for in all honesty even then I felt no antagonism toward the man, and continued to pray, 'Bring all of the weight of what is in these men's hearts to do—bring it all upon *me*, Father, and not upon whom I call my friends. Let the price of this war fall on my head, not theirs. Protect them, and protect me, Father, and keep us all in your care.'

"I was praying all that, over and over, on the inside, while outside I walked forward, smiled, and told them I was the man they wanted. By then they were off their horses and questioning me all at once, and before long you were all out of sight and safely on your way back here."

"But what did you *say*?" I insisted.

"Not much," chuckled Christopher. "Actually, that was the thing that drove the poor men more crazy than anything, that I was so pleasant and cooperative and unresistant, but wouldn't tell them anything. They literally barraged me with questions, and I kept praying that they would be distracted from seeing the rest of your complicity in the matter."

"You must have said *something*."

"When they asked about you, I simply said I had been sent on an errand of mercy, which was altogether true. I didn't go into it much more than that, and they didn't persist. The poor men were just very confused. I didn't behave anything like an enemy. My southern accent and my clerical collar verified to them that I was who I said I was. I made no attempt to hide my identity, and it turned out one of the men had heard of me and knew I was a minister. Fortunately, he wasn't aware of the stand I'd taken on the war! I kept praying, and when questioned about you and the incident, I continued to say that I *had* been sent and that my mission was one of compassion and that I was about the Father's business. I think I perhaps sounded like a kook to them. But I don't think they really wanted to punish or harm me, even though they couldn't get out of me what they were after. The Lord, I am convinced, sent a spirit of bewilderment upon them in answer to my prayers, and they simply didn't know what to do with me."

"So . . . what happened?" I asked.

"Finally, in frustration, General Lee left and one of his subordinates told them to throw me in the prison. The whole thing was extraordinary. They could have shot or hanged me. But within an hour or two, all the officers were gone, and there I was alone inside Libby Prison."

"I'm sorry you had to go through that for us, Rev. Braxton," said Jacob.

"It wasn't so bad, Jacob. I spoke with many of the men, prayed with those who would let me, gave comfort where I could. Actually, it was the most useful I've felt in the kingdom for a long time. I was there all that night, though I didn't get much sleep."

"The first nights are the worst," put in Captain Dyles. "The moans, the rats!"

"It was anything but pleasant. I sang a few hymns and it seemed to bring a calm to the room where they'd put me. I think a lot of the men were able to sleep a little better for it. Then the next morning—that would have been yesterday . . . it's amazing, already it seems like such a long time ago—two men came back to question me again. I'm not sure if they were the same men or not, though I may have recognized one of them. They bombarded me with question after question. But now that I was in prison and you were all safe, there was no need for me to defend myself. Finally one of them nearly exploded at me, 'Don't you realize that we have the power to take your life?' 'Only one has that power,' I answered him. 'You're right there, Reverend, and his name is General Robert E. Lee!' I didn't answer him. 'Still you've got nothing to say? You want me to turn you over to the firing squad for treason!' I felt sorry for the poor man. He just wasn't able to recognize the work of redemption that was going on right under his nose."

Again we all grew silent, each of us considering the implications of what Christopher had said for ourselves personally. Mrs. Timms made one more attempt to pass the platters of food around, but we had all eaten enough and were satisfied.

"After a while they threw their hands up in the air and just didn't know what to do with me. The rest of the day passed much like the first, and the night too.

"Then this morning, the lieutenant who had been on guard when we'd first arrived came to find me and said simply, 'Come with me, Reverend.' I stood and followed him out of the room and toward the entrance.

"The large door stood open wide even before I reached it.

" 'You're free to go,' said the lieutenant.

"I thanked him, shook his hand, and told him his Father in heaven cared for him, then turned and walked through the door into the bright sunlight of the morning. I so desperately longed to be able to bring all your fellow captives out with me. But I knew God himself would have to end this war in order to make that miracle possible."

"How did you get here?" I asked.

"I walked," replied Christopher with a laugh. "How else could I get home? You'd taken my team and wagon!"

"All the way from Richmond!"

"It took me only the morning. And after being in that prison for two days . . . I needed the exercise."

CHAPTER 25

"I'M NO SOUTHERNER"

It didn't take long before Captain Dyles and Jacob began to get jittery. Within a day or two their strength had revived considerably, and with Christopher now back, they were hardly necessary for chores or anything.

And of course the root of everything was the simple fact that Captain Dyles was a soldier and there was a war on. It was more than clear he was anxious to get back to his unit.

They asked Christopher a lot of questions about the war, but once it was clear that very little had changed in three months, the captain said the best plan seemed to be to just attempt to return the way the three of us had come in October, and make their way around to the south to where the Union army under General Grant was still laying siege to Petersburg.

"You got a couple a horses we could buy or have for the sake of the Union, Braxton?" the captain asked after they'd discussed what to do.

"I've only got the two," Christopher replied, "and I can't hardly part with them."

"We'd need three anyway," I put in. "You seem to have forgotten all about me, Captain Dyles."

"I never thought of it, Miss Hollister," he said. "I just figured—"

"Figured what? That I'd become a southern belle so soon? I gotta get back just as much as you do. I gotta get back to Washington."

"What's in Washington?"

151

His question caught me off guard.

"I . . . uh . . . well, the President," I said. "That's the capital of our country . . . everything I was doing is there—my work, the Sanitary Commission, writing for the President . . . Mr. Hay . . . I have to tell them I'm all right and find out what I should do now."

Everything kind of spilled out of my mouth at once. It made me realize that I *hadn't* really stopped to consider what I *would* do next.

"I don't belong here," I added. "I'm no Southerner."

Christopher was real quiet. I didn't realize it right then or I'd have apologized. I must have offended him by making it sound like an awful thing to be a Southerner. That wasn't exactly what I'd meant. But he didn't say anything for a while, and that must have been what he thought.

"We'll share you between me and Jacob," said Captain Dyles. "That is, we could if we had horses."

"I'll take you where you want to go," said Christopher, breaking the brief silence that followed.

"You've done enough for us already, Braxton," said the captain. "I don't want to see you getting yourself in any more danger. As it is, I'm going to put it to General Grant for you to receive a medal for bravery once this blamed war is over."

"I need no medal, Captain," laughed Christopher, his cheerful countenance returning once more. "Remember, I've been sent, just like I told them at the prison. That means I go and do whatever my Father puts before me. Besides, Captain, after what we went through at the prison, how difficult could it be to get you back to General Grant's army if we swing far enough to the south? We're surely not likely to run into Robert E. Lee down there!"

"I reckon you're right, Braxton. We're much obliged for everything. It's only that I don't like to put another man in danger for me."

So it was that three days later, the three men and I loaded into the wagon again.

"Goodbye, Mrs. Timms," I said. "How can I thank you for everything you have done? I owe you my life."

I suppose I expected the normally closed-mouthed woman to

reply with some ordinary pleasantry like, "Oh, it was no trouble." Instead, she just looked at me for a second, then her eyes filled with tears and she took me into her arms and hugged me tight.

"You dear, Corrie," she said, "it won't be the same without you here! Now you take good care of yourself!" she added in a motherly tone, trying to free one of her arms to brush back her tears.

I was so overcome I didn't know what to say. It was the first display of emotion like that she'd shown me, and now I was leaving and it was too late to find a way to return it.

I rode in silence as we left, bound away from the Confederate capital toward the west, and then southward, following the exact route Captain Dyles, Jacob, and I had on our way to Richmond to kidnap Cal. Christopher again was wearing the garb of a priest, hoping that might keep the rest of us out of danger. It was obvious enough by now that concern for his own safety was the least of the things he was thinking about.

CHAPTER 26

ONE LONE SENTRY

The ride that day was a quiet one.

As upbeat and cheerful as the atmosphere around the farm had been after Christopher's return, it had now grown very somber between us. Mrs. Timms had wept when I'd said goodbye to her, then embraced me. I was thinking about that, and I reckon the other three all had their own private thoughts too. Even though we'd been together only a few days, and the contrasts between us were great, somehow I think there was a sadness for all of us in realizing this peaceful brief interlude was coming to an end.

The war was still going. The divergent paths of our lives, after this moment of intersection, had to move forward in their own directions. Life never just sat still. This was one of those times when it kept moving, even though we might like to slow it down for a while longer.

We didn't expect to see any Confederate patrols out in the direction we were headed, away from where General Lee's forces were encamped between Richmond and Petersburg. Just in case, though, Christopher had thrown several bales of hay in the back of the wagon, along with two large tarpaulins. Try as we might, there was nothing much that could be done to disguise the two men's shirts and trousers as anything but Union issue. If we did happen to run into any soldiers wearing gray, Christopher said he'd talk his way through the encounter while the captain and Jacob hid underneath the hay in back.

The first day passed uneventfully. We rode on till dark, then made camp off the road in a small clump of trees. The men slept under the wagon, and I inside it. Even though it was January, the clear weather held. And the cold wasn't too bad since Mrs. Timms had made us bring along every blanket in the place.

We crossed the Appomattox River early the following morning, making our way southward in a wide arc, intending to come up toward the Union forces from the southwest of Petersburg.

We'd followed just the same route, in the opposite direction, in October. But what none of us realized was that the Confederate line just south of Petersburg had since then stretched much farther to the west, between Grant and the Appomattox. The line was thin, and only sparsely patrolled in spots, but held by southern troops nevertheless.

The first indication that we had not gone far enough west was when a Confederate sentry suddenly stopped us. We'd been going through a densely wooded area and hadn't seen him ahead. All at once there he was walking toward us, rifle poised. There was no time for Jacob and Captain Dyles to hide on the floor of the wagon.

"Good afternoon, Sergeant!" called out Christopher quickly, reining in the horses, then jumping down to the ground. "How far are we from the Union line?"

"About six hundred yards, Reverend," the man replied. "That's no-man's-land out there ahead. Say, what is this you're up to?" he asked, moving closer and eyeing the two men. "Those two look like Yankees."

"You've got sharp eyes, Sergeant," said Christopher, giving him a slap on the back. "They're Yankee prisoners, and I'm transporting them to the general."

"General who?"

"General Lee, of course. This here's Captain Dyles, Union army. Surely you heard that General Lee's been searching high and low for him."

"No, I ain't. Why ain't they tied up?" he asked. The man had a mean look and didn't seem the least bit swayed by Christopher's friendliness.

"I didn't think they needed it. I've had no trouble with them so far."

"What! That's the most fool thing I ever heard of! Prisoners need tying up. And what are you doing going that way if you're looking for General Lee?"

"Isn't that the direction of General Lee's headquarters?" asked Christopher innocently.

"No, you lame-brain priest! I told you, straight out there's the dad-blamed Union lines!"

"Rev. Braxton," I said, slowly getting down from the wagon, "perhaps it would be best for me to go on ahead with the two prisoners, while you finish explaining things to the nice sergeant here."

I approached with what I hoped was an equally innocent smile on my face. The sergeant was a seasoned veteran, however, and the charade didn't fool him for a minute.

"What kind of an idiot do you two take me for! You're talking gibberish and you expect me to let you walk right through here with a Union officer and some big black runaway slave!"

"I can assure you, Sergeant, that he is not a slave but a free man," said Christopher.

"I don't care if he's Abraham Lincoln's houseboy and you're the pope! None of you are getting through here unless you want a bullet from this rifle of mine in your head!"

"I assure you, there will be no need for such extreme measures. Nurse Hollister," Christopher said calmly to me, while still eyeing the sergeant with a steady gaze. "I think your suggestion was an excellent one. Why don't you get the two men and go on ahead. I will try to make everything clear to the sergeant."

I signaled Captain Dyles and Jacob to follow me, then began to walk slowly forward.

"Why you fools!" he cried, and I could hear the anger rising in his voice. Out of the corner of my eye I saw him swing his rifle up from his side and point its barrel in the direction of the wagon where Jacob was just jumping to the ground. "Once that darkie blood spills on the ground, you'll know I ain't nobody to think you can walk past with a pack of lies!"

I heard the gun cock.

"No!" I cried, leaping back toward him and knocking the barrel up into the air.

A sharp report of gunfire echoed through the trees.

"You miserable, perverse —" He shouted at me, grabbing my arm, giving it a painful twist, then knocking me to the ground.

It was the worst thing he could have done. Whatever evil name he was going to call me, no more words left his lips. The next instant he was lying unconscious on the ground from a punishing blow from Christopher's fist.

"I'm sorry you had to see that, Corrie," he said apologetically. "It's a cowardly thing to strike another man. But it's even more cowardly to strike a woman, and to call her names that mock the creation of God. It's something I will not tolerate."

"You're some fellow, Braxton!" said Captain Dyles, jumping to the ground and running forward. "Give yourself up to prison for two men you don't even know, won't utter a word to defend yourself, but you'd probably take on the whole Confederate army to protect Miss Hollister here. I can't say as I can quite figure you out. But once again I find myself obliged to you!"

"Get out of here, all of you!" yelled Christopher. "You heard him, you've just got six hundred yards to run." As he spoke he picked up the rifle and gave it a mighty heave into the woods.

"What about you?" I said.

"I will be fine. I intend to get the wagon turned around and move away from here as fast as I can without arousing suspicion. A minister, all alone in a wagon with a few bales of hay—no harm will come to me. Now go, you three! That shot will likely bring other men that you don't want to see!"

Captain Dyles and Jacob needed no more exhortation. They were already working their legs into a run in the direction we had been going.

But I couldn't move. I stood where I was. My eyes met Christopher's. He was standing about five yards away, one hand grasping the reins of his horses to lead them around.

Suddenly there was so much to say, yet neither of us could speak. It could only have been a second or two that we stood there, both of our faces so full with the sudden realization of what this moment meant. All my senses froze in that instant. Everything seemed to stretch out ahead and behind that dividing line of time. Yet within it, as I stood there, a giant moment of *now* consumed everything else, and I did not want to leave it.

Everything I thought I needed to get back to Washington for was all at once so distant and far away. What did any of that matter . . . now?

So many thoughts . . . so many words . . . so many unexpected feelings. Yet none could find escape. They just hung heavy
in the silent air between us, unsaid, but pounding as an unwelcome
weight of sudden grief in my chest.

"Miss Corrie, you gotta come . . . now!" came Jacob's urgent
voice, suddenly crashing through the dreamy moment of *now* that
was already fading into the past.

I turned. The big black man was imploring me with gestures,
yelling at me to come. "Miss Corrie, we gotta hightail it outta here
afore them Rebs shoot us good and dead!"

I took a step toward him, then two, then realized I was running. Behind me I heard the sound of Christopher turning his
wagon around.

I paused and glanced back one last time. Christopher must
have sensed it, for he was looking straight at me. I was just close
enough to see one of his eyes glisten with a tear. Again we held
each other's gaze, but this time only for a moment. Then he
smiled, spoke softly to his horses, turned, and was gone.

I spun around and sprinted after Jacob toward the bend in the
road around which he had already disappeared, blinking hard to
keep my vision from getting so blurry I might stumble.

CHAPTER 27

DINNER WITH GENERAL GRANT

Two nights later I found myself in a comfortable bed at General Grant's new headquarters up north at the mouth of the Appomattox at City Point. Captain Dyles had arranged for everything. When we returned, he made a full report, including about my being shot.

General Grant gave us all, if not exactly a hero's welcome, at least a warm one, and invited the three of us to have dinner with him. We were as relieved to see him alive as he was to see us again!

"I was worried about you, sir," I told him, "once I came back to myself and realized we hadn't done anything to stop the plot against you."

"Ah, but you did!" replied the general. "Seems you stirred things up so much in Richmond that your Burton fellow and that no good Surratt got worried. They tried to get word to their spy here to make a change in the plans. But by then I had men watching everything that came in, and we intercepted the message."

"Who was it, General?" asked Captain Dyles.

"Clary . . . Lieutenant Clary."

"Hmm . . . I suppose that might figure. From Missouri, isn't he?"

The general nodded. "Anyway, we locked him up and that was the end of it. So in a roundabout way, you three might have saved my life, after all, even though you paid a heavy price to do it. I want you to know, I'm in debt to each of you for the bravery you displayed, and I intend to see that you're all given medals for it by the President."

"There's someone else who deserves one as well, sir," said the captain. He then told General Grant about Christopher.

"A Southerner . . . hmm, though I don't suppose he's the first to help our cause. I'll see what I can do."

We talked awhile longer around the table. General Grant asked me what I wanted to do. I said I thought I ought to go back to Washington.

"Then I'll see to it directly," replied the general. "The *River Queen* is going north for supplies and repairs to the engine in a few days. That's my personal floating headquarters. Of course, I won't be on board because I have to remain here. But you will be my personal guest on the *River Queen*, Miss Hollister, all the way to Washington."

"Thank you, sir. You are very kind."

"Anyone who would risk her life for me, which you have done two or three times already as I understand it, deserves whatever an old war campaigner can do for her!"

And so it was that I reached Washington, D.C., the nation's capital, at the end of January, by water, some three and a half months after I had left it by rail—stowed away in a boxcar early one morning. Back then I had been desperate to reach General Grant to warn him of an attempt on his life. Now I returned on his personal riverboat as his guest and with a letter in my hand from him that he had instructed me to deliver to President Lincoln himself.

CHAPTER 28

BACK IN WASHINGTON

There had been only two fronts left where the South still fought on —in Georgia, and at Richmond under General Lee. But as the year 1865 opened, only Lee was left.

In the middle of November, General Sherman had burned a portion of the city of Atlanta, then sent his army on a march through Georgia to the sea, destroying everything that got in his way, determined to keep the rebel South from rising again against the Union. On December 22, 1864, Sherman sent President Lincoln a telegram that read: *I beg to present you, as a Christmas gift, the city of Savannah, with 150 heavy guns and plenty of ammunition; also, about 25,000 bales of cotton.*

President Lincoln was said to be delighted. Now all that was left was for Grant to take Richmond. Sherman was sent north, through South Carolina, to meet Grant's forces. Robert E. Lee was a stubborn adversary.

The winter turned more severe—freezing cold and much rain. I was so happy to be back in the capital before the worst of it. Yet from the reports reaching us, it didn't seem to slow down General Sherman's march northward.

At the same time, however, Lee's men were deserting in droves. All through the South refugees, slaves, former plantation owners, women, children fled from what had once been their homes. The entire Confederacy was collapsing, and yet General Lee's resistance meant that still many more men and boys had to die before the end would come. Robert E. Lee would not admit defeat while there was yet a single regiment left to fight.

Upon reaching Washington I went first to see Mrs. Richards. She was so happy to see me, and I was happy that she had a room available and had kept the few clothes and books I'd left there, though she'd had no idea what had become of me. Next, I went to the White House to see Mr. Hay and deliver the letter from Mr. Grant.

"Miss Hollister!" exclaimed Mr. Hay when I was shown in to him. "We have been anxious about you! We have had numerous requests—from the Sanitary people and several of the newspapers—everyone asking us what became of you. And we didn't know ourselves!"

I explained briefly about what I'd overheard at the boarding-house and why I had left town so suddenly.

"Surratt . . . hmm," he said. "I told you long ago that he was a bad apple. Haven't heard of the fellow Burton, though the name Booth is familiar too."

"He's an actor," I said.

"Oh yes, that's right. Now tell me what you heard them saying."

I repeated it as best I remembered.

"I don't like the sound of it," he said seriously. "But you say the general is safe?"

I told him what General Grant had said about apprehending the spy.

"What about Surratt? Is he in custody?"

"I don't know, sir. Not that I'm aware of. General Grant said nothing about him."

"With the election over and the war nearly won, security is not nearly so tight these days. Still, I worry about the President. There are too many people still about who hate him with a passion."

I handed him the letter from General Grant.

"Thank you, Miss Hollister. Will you be at Mrs. Richards' place should I need to contact you?"

"Yes, sir . . . that is, I don't have any definite plans. Will you be wanting me to do anything more . . . any writing?"

"Yes . . . yes, of course, Miss Hollister. The election is behind us, but the war is not over yet. There is yet a great deal to be done, money to be raised. I know the Sanitary people are most anxious to have you back. And even after the war, the country will need rebuilding. I know the President will be looking to people like you, people with a voice that is respected, to help bind the wounds and bring healing to this land of brave and free men and women.''

I walked back to Mrs. Richards', thinking about everything the President's secretary had said. I tried to tell myself that nothing had changed, and that I could enter back into my writing and my work with the Sanitary Commission just like before.

Yet I knew that somehow it *had* all changed. Was it that the election was past? Is that what made it seem different? When I reflected on writing newspaper articles or making speeches to raise money for the Commission now, it wasn't filled with the same kind of purposefulness as before. A year ago I was filled with an enthusiasm for what I was doing. I almost felt at home here in Washington, with the friends I had made and the work that kept me occupied. It didn't seem to matter as much anymore.

Now all the old thoughts and questions and doubts began to flood through me about where I really did belong, what I was supposed to be doing, what my writing meant . . . and where home truly was.

Sister Janette came to my mind again, and all the Sisters of Unity. Every time I thought of them, so many feelings came tugging at my heart because of the life they lived in dedication to Jesus—a kind of commitment that I truly wanted to make part of my life, too. Yet . . . did I belong there . . . with them . . . or someplace else . . . with someone else?

I could not even bring myself to face the questions squarely. I needed to get settled first. I had lots of writing to catch up on. I still had months to make up for in my new journal! And letters to my family! They would all be so worried. A pile of thirteen letters had been waiting for me at Mrs. Richards', all from Miracle Springs!

I would be busy writing for two weeks, and not a word of it would be for a newspaper to print!

I'd figure out what to do about my future later.

CHAPTER 29

HONORED BEYOND WORDS

I did write for the next two weeks, though I still didn't get caught up. I wrote individual letters to everyone at home, a letter to the sisters at the convent, a letter that I never finished and probably wouldn't send anyway, and on top of it all I did start an article about some of the things that had happened. I called it "Bravery in the Quiet Places," though it had nothing to do with me. And after all that, I had barely even begun to get caught up-to-date in my journal! I also renewed all my acquaintances at the Sanitary Commission, and tried to find where Clara Barton was. By the end of that time, some of the former busy schedule had begun to return because the Commission had grown steadily and was involved with more aspects of the war than ever.

Toward the end of February, I returned to Mrs. Richards' to find a message from John Hay waiting for me. *The President would like to see you* was all it said. *Tomorrow at 2 P.M.*

I arrived at the White House, eager and nervous.

Mr. Lincoln was already waiting when Mr. Hay showed me into the reception room.

The poor man looked so old and tired! He looked three or four years older than the last time I had seen him. I must have made some comment because he replied, "Yes, I *am* tired, Miss Hollister. You can't imagine how war tires a man, and how the presidency ages him. But the two together are bound to be the death of any but one with the constitution of a horse! Sometimes I think I am the tiredest man on earth."

"I'm sorry, sir," I said. It was such a lame reply, but I didn't know what to say.

"Don't worry about me, Miss Hollister. Any man who runs

for the presidency deserves what it gives him. But my reason for wanting to see you was to thank you for your courage in attempting to warn General Grant about the plot against him."

"It wasn't anything that—"

"Come, come, Miss Hollister," interrupted the President with a smile, "don't try to tell me it was really nothing. I happen to know a little about bravery. War separates brave men and women from cowards. Ulysses Grant happens to be a brave man, and so when he tells me you are braver than half the men under his command and deserve a medal for it, and that you were shot besides, well then, I listen to what a man like that tells me."

"Thank you, sir," I said. I could feel that I was blushing dreadfully.

"I decided to take the good general's advice," Mr. Lincoln went on. "John—" He motioned to Mr. Hay, who picked something up off the table and brought it forward. He handed it to Mr. Lincoln.

"This, Miss Cornelia Hollister," he said, "is a Medal of Valor. I want to present it to you on behalf of the United States of America, with the gratitude of her President."

He handed me the little silk-lined box with the medal lying in the middle of it, then shook my hand.

I was speechless.

"I . . . I . . . I don't know what . . . thank you, Mr. President . . ." I stammered, feeling so embarrassed but grateful at the same time.

"You may well be the youngest woman ever to receive this honor, Miss Hollister," said Mr. Hay, approaching me with a smile. "We are very proud of you."

"And now one more thing," added Mr. Lincoln. "I would be honored if you would like to attend my inauguration next week. I have arranged for an invitation for you."

"Thank you, Mr. President!" I said, finding my tongue at last. "I would *very* much like to attend!"

"Good. I'm delighted. You will be John Hay's special guest. John, you will see to all the arrangements?" he added to his secretary.

"It's already been done," answered Mr. Hay. "A carriage will pick you up at the boardinghouse, Miss Hollister, and bring you here to me. We will ride to the Capitol building together."

CHAPTER 30

A SURPRISE LETTER

The date was March 4, 1865.

The Capitol dome was at last completed, just in time for the inauguration—a huge, soaring new white dome with the crowning bronze Liberty statue on its peak, all looking down on the city of Washington.

The words of Mr. Lincoln's speech after taking the oath of office a second time held the same determination to make sure truth and freedom prevailed as if the war were only a month or two old. Yet at the same time they looked ahead to the peace and enormous job of reconstruction which everyone knew was now close at hand.

Here are some of Mr. Lincoln's words. I copied them down in my journal straight out of the next day's newspaper.

> Both sides read the same Bible, and pray to the same God; and each invokes His aid against the other. It may seem strange that any men should dare to ask a just God's assistance in wringing their bread from the sweat of other men's faces; but let us judge not that we be not judged. The prayers of both could not be answered. The Almighty has His own purposes. "Woe unto the world because of offences! for it must needs be that offences come; but woe to that man by whom the offence cometh!" If we shall suppose that American Slavery is one of those offenses which, in the providence of God, must needs come, but which, having continued through His appointed time, He now wills to remove, and that He gives to both North and South this terrible war as the woe due to those by whom the offense came, shall we discern therein any

169

departure from those divine attributes which the believers in a Living God always ascribe to Him?

Fondly do we hope—fervently do we pray—that this mighty scourge of war may speedily pass away. Yet if God wills that it continue until all the wealth piled by the bondman's two hundred and fifty years of unrequited toil shall be sunk, and until every drop of blood drawn with the lash, shall be paid by another drawn with the sword, as was said three thousand years ago, so still must be said, "The judgments of the Lord are true and righteous altogether."

With malice towards none; with charity for all; with firmness in the right as God gives us to see the right, let us strive on to finish the work we are in; to bind up the nation's wounds; to care for him who shall have borne the battle and for his widow, and his orphan—to do all which may achieve and cherish a just and lasting peace among ourselves, and with all nations.

The words of President Lincoln's inaugural address seemed to signal a new effort to make a final end to the war. Three weeks later he sailed down to City Point, where he met on the *River Queen* with Generals Grant and Sherman and Admiral Porter. Two days of meetings resulted in detailed plans for a final campaign against General Lee and the Confederacy.

By this time, General Grant's force had grown to 125,000, while Lee's had shrunk to only 35,000. As soon as the meetings with the President were completed, General Grant moved against the long Confederate line around Petersburg.

Two days after the President's return to Washington from his strategy meeting with General Grant and the others, I went to the White House to see Mr. Hay about something he had asked me to write. When our business was completed, he said, "Oh, and we received this letter yesterday—addressed to you, in care of the White House."

He handed me an envelope. I knew the handwriting immediately, but tried not to show my excitement. But seeing my name written in the familiar hand sent a tingle all the way up my spine!

I took it, thanked him, and left, fairly running all the way back to the boarding house. I could not read this anywhere except in the privacy of my own room, with the door closed.

Oh, but my heart beat wildly all the way . . . and not from the run! I ran into the house, flew up the stairs, threw the door of my room open, then shut it behind me a second later, sat down on my bed, and with trembling fingers ripped at the envelope.

DEAR CORRIE,

What a bold thing to do, is it not, to write you a letter in care of the White House! But I didn't know what else to do. Our parting was so sudden and ill-planned that we made no provision for correspondence. I hadn't an idea how to reach you.

And truthfully, Corrie, after the previous two months, the very idea of no longer being able to communicate and talk to and listen to one who I think has understood more the pulse of my spiritual heart than anyone previously encountered in my life was a thought to me unbearable. It has not, I grant, yet been a *long* life, for we are both young yet by standards of the three score and ten allotted to healthy men. But it has been long enough for me to recognize that unique form of relationship called "knowing," and to know that such knowing comes not many times across the path of any one individual's life. When it comes, therefore, it is to be cherished and not let go of without better reason than I now possess.

All the way back to the farm, without incident by the way—I know you will be worried for my safety—I chastised myself for the idiocy of saying nothing to you in that moment when our gazes locked. Honestly, words were the furthest thing from my mind just then, and my eyes were dancing with too much liquid to think clearly. Worse, however, when I came to myself halfway home, feeling such a heavy-hearted sense of aloneness at your departure, was the realization that you were as unreachable to me as the moon!

How I pray this letter finds you, though the very hope that it will seems tinged with absurdity. Yet I am hoping whatever your former association with President Lincoln was, that such will open the pathway for this letter to find its way into your hands.

Mrs. Timms is well and sends her regards. She misses you almost as much as I do, I think, though such is hardly possible. The cows and chickens and goats and pigs are also well . . . and all miss you too! Most of all, the house misses you.

Nothing is the same. A huge quiet has settled upon the place which neither Mrs. Timms nor I find pleasant.

I am enclosing my address here, so that at least you will be capable of locating and writing to me—should the inclination ever strike you to do so—even though your whereabouts remain a mystery to me.

They say the war is nearly done. Jefferson Davis continues to make outlandishly foolish remarks about "our certain triumph" and "our unquenchable resolve" and promising that "no peace will be made with the infamous invaders." But it is idle and hopeless prattle. The cause of the Confederacy was never a holy cause, but only a selfish and hopeless and vainly proud one. I am a Southerner, but the Confederacy causes me only shame. The disaster and destruction and death that has come has all been well-deserved. If judgment is to fall upon men for ills and torments they perpetrate upon others of their kind, then surely the self-righteous southern leaders who led this nation to split apart and then wage war with itself will have to bear an intolerable load of it upon their shoulders. Robert E. Lee is considered a great man, whose convictions were so strong he was honor bound to do what he has done. I find little within me capable of honoring him, when his refusal to lay down arms had caused such widespread suffering and death. The war was over a year ago. What has it benefited to prolong it?

Please forgive me. As the war ends, as Richmond prepares, by all indications, to crumble, I find myself rather caustically pensive about the worthlessness of it all. Does war ever resolve the conflicts that cause it? I doubt it. Though perhaps it does, if only by killing all those whose intransigence led to the hostilities in the first place.

You may think I am being rather candid for a Southerner. If this fell into the wrong hands, I would be lynched before dusk! Believe it or not, I rode into Richmond and paid your friend Mr. Gregory one more visit. I explained to him my dilemma and asked if he had any means whereby a letter might be gotten north to Washington safely. He said he had ways, and for Corrie he would do anything. He really did say just that! We had a pleasant visit. I believe the seeds have been well planted and watered. A new child of God is in the process of being birthed, I believe.

There is evidence that Lee's army is disintegrating. Soldiers on foot pass by here almost daily now. The end is days, not weeks, away. Why do you not return to us, even if for a short time? I promise you a quiet corner where you could write undisturbed. And I believe the opportunities for service and ministry to the crumbling armies may yet be great. I am sure you would be of great help and encouragement to the suffering.

In any case, please do write, if only to let me know this arrived safely into your hands.

I am, your servant and friend and fellow sojourner after truth,

CHRISTOPHER BRAXTON

Long before I had finished reading it, I was sobbing for joy and loneliness and longing to see him again. Reading his words was just like being with him, listening to him talk. I could hear his voice even as I read!

I was out of the house and on my way back to the White House even before my tears had dried. I hoped Mr. Hay would see me!

"Mr. Hay," I said, "I need to get back to Richmond."

"Richmond!" he said. "The city will be under siege in a day or two if Grant has his way with it."

"Not exactly *in* Richmond, just near it."

"Everything's perilous right now, Miss Hollister. This is it. We are on the eve of the final battle—that is, if Lee stays to fight."

"Is there no way, then?"

"If Grant is successful, the President himself may go down the Potomac and to Richmond. If the southern capital falls, he wants to be on hand personally as a symbol that the country is again one."

"If that happens, might there be space on the boat?"

"For you?"

I nodded. "I don't even need a seat," I added hopefully.

"I will see what I can do, Miss Hollister. I'm sure if there is space the President would be only too happy to accommodate you."

"Thank you, sir!"

Five days later, by April 1, the Confederate line between General Grant and the city of Petersburg had collapsed altogether. Union troops poured into the city, General Lee retreated across the Appomattox River, desperately searching for food for the starving and hopeless army which followed him, and the whole horde of Union forces at last marched freely to the Confederate capital of Richmond. Jefferson Davis and what was left of the rebel government fled.

The next day I was on board the President's boat, sailing down the Potomac, then down the Chesapeake Bay, and up the inlet of the James to Cold Harbor and Richmond.

The war was over. All that remained now was to find Lee and still the few guns that remained under his command.

CHAPTER 31

A DIFFERENT KIND OF
SILENCE

Smoke from the ruins of large sections of burning Richmond still lingered in the air as I galloped out of the city westward toward the Timms' farm.

Chaos was everywhere. Shattered buildings of brick were in ruins, women dressed in black mourned the death of the Confederacy, in some of the business sections of the city, mobs plundered what little was left in the shops.

The Confederate navy had blown up all that was left of its own fleet anchored in the James. Some ships sank outright, others lay on their sides, others still bellowed smoke. Even as I rode through, an occasional glass-shattering explosion could be heard. The land-fire had engulfed a Confederate arsenal filled with gunpowder and artillery shells, and the explosions from them had spread the fires even farther. The doors of Libby Prison were blown off their hinges and the rest of Captain Dyles' and Jacob's and Christopher's fellows at last gained their freedom, along with slaves, still at that late hour of history, walking the streets in chains behind diehard dealers in the horrid trade.

But though historic events and changes were going on all about me, there was only one destination toward which I pointed the nose of the army horse I had asked President Lincoln to have commandeered for me. It felt like home again to have a saddle and galloping horse underneath me, and I covered the ground in a fourth the time it had taken us to traverse it in the wagon.

I galloped straight for the house and was out of the saddle and

175

running to the door even before I had the exhausted beast well slowed to a canter. Not even stopping to tie him, nor to knock, I burst through the door.

Christopher had risen from his chair to see what the commotion was outside. A look of such stunned shock came over his face at the sight of me that he stood absolutely motionless for a second or two.

I suddenly realized what I'd done, and a wave of sheepish embarrassment swept over me. What if I had completely misconstrued his letter! What if he was only being polite? What if his letter hadn't been an invitation at all!

A mortified panic gripped me, and I felt my face go pale. What if he didn't *want* to see me?

But still I stood there. Our eyes met. But it was so different than last time. A huge uncertainty and fear filled me, and all at once I wanted to run away and hide. How could I have done such a foolish thing! Yet I was paralyzed in my tracks.

Then slowly his numbed expression melted. His eyes filled with light, and his cheeks flushed with color. His lips fumbled for words, but he seemed to be as incapable of finding them as I was.

"Corrie!" he breathed at last, half in question, half in quiet disbelieving exclamation.

Still I stood. Slowly the mortification gave way to sheepishness as I realized he was actually *happy* to see me, and the pallor in my cheeks was replaced by the blush I could feel rising up my neck and over my face.

"It *is* you!" he said, now slowly walking toward me. "I can hardly believe my eyes!"

"It's me," I whispered, but the voice I finally found sounded like the silly squeak of a mouse.

"But . . . but why . . . how did you get here . . . the war's—"

"You wrote and told me to come," I said.

"You got my letter!"

I nodded.

He burst out in the most magnificent and wonderful laugh of delight I had ever heard. "I can't believe it! It actually *got* to you!"

"Did you not really want me to come?" I said, fear trying to rise into my heart again.

"Oh no—of course I wanted you to, Corrie! But I dared not even hope you would!"

"I would die if I thought I had been a fool and—"

"Corrie, Corrie," he said, silencing my doubts with a tiny shake of his head and penetrating look of his eyes deep into mine. "Corrie . . . don't you yet know?"

He gently wrapped his arms around me and held me close.

Again neither of us had any words. But the agony I felt when last we had parted this time was a silence too full to require them.

There was no other place in the world I wanted to be, and it was enough.

CHAPTER 32

THE END . . . AT LAST

Even as his top general was pursuing General Lee's retreat westward toward Lynchburg, Abraham Lincoln arrived in Richmond by barge on the James River. As he stepped ashore, he said, "Thank God I have lived to see this. It seems to me that I have been dreaming a horrid nightmare for four years, and now the nightmare is over."

Negroes immediately mobbed him. In stark contrast with the desolate stillness of the ruins and devastation, they were laughing and singing for joy, and weeping with unabashed emotion. They knelt in his path, and strained and reached to touch him. One cried out, "I know I am free, for I have seen Father Abraham and felt him."

Mr. Lincoln was astonished at the outpouring over his presence. "Kneel only to God," he cautioned the crowd, "but not to me. It is God to whom you must give thanks for your freedom."

From the dock where he had left the barge, his destination lay about a mile distant, through the still-smoking city. For the last four years it had served as White House for the illegal Confederacy. For the past two days it had been the Union headquarters in Richmond. When President Lincoln sat down at the desk from which Jefferson Davis had conducted the war, a great cheer went up from the troops outside.

The Confederacy truly was no more. Abraham Lincoln now sat at the seat of power in both Washington *and* Richmond!

But still there was the matter of Robert E. Lee and his army. They were desperate for food, and pursued by Grant's well-supplied army of five times the size, yet Lee refused to surrender. Toward the mountains of the west they made their way, pursued by Grant. Everywhere they went, Lee's men searched and begged for food. On foot and by horseback they fanned out throughout the countryside, asking farmers for food.

We were farther north than the main flow of the retreat, yet at least a dozen came to Mrs. Timms' door, desperate and hungry. We fed what we could to those who came, and once we realized their plight, we began, all three of us, mixing and baking bread as quickly as possible. But our supplies were not unlimited either, and within two more days we were out of flour ourselves.

Famished and to the point that many of them were but staggering blindly forward, Lee continued to push his men, dropping guns and bedrolls from sheer exhaustion, many of them deserting along the way or leaving to surrender in hopes of being given food. On the sixth, in an attempt to force surrender, Federal forces attacked the beleaguered Confederates. Eight thousand more Southerners were killed.

Still Lee would not surrender.

By this time a steady flow of traffic moved along the road near the farm in both directions, bringing supplies for the Union troops, transporting prisoners back toward Richmond. From these we learned of the latest fighting at Sayler's Creek.

"Christopher, I've got to go out there," I said, "and see if I can help."

"We'll both go," he replied. "I'll hitch the wagon. You go inside and ask Mrs. Timms for anything we can use for bandages, cloth, blankets, even some food if we have anything left in the house."

"We'll need water," I added.

"I'll put several buckets in the wagon."

In an hour we were on our way, following behind the Union army, along the winding banks of the Appomattox River.

By the time we reached the scene of the battle, it was late in the day and there was little we could do. We fed and bandaged those we could, but our food and supplies were soon gone. There were not many casualties among the Union men, and we could not reach the Confederates without going beyond the front lines of General Grant's leading infantry divisions. The dead at Sayler's Creek were strewn out everywhere. The sickening revulsion I'd felt at Gettysburg returned to me all over again. Enough time had passed, however, that most of the wounded had been carried or dragged to the makeshift field hospitals that had sprung up immediately. The faithful workers of the Sanitary Commission were right behind the army's advance.

Christopher and I offered our willing hands at the white tents and were soon busy at the work I remembered well enough from the previous year. It was midnight before we lay down to sleep on the ground, he with the doctors and I with the nurses.

The following morning there was no sound of gunfire, no hint of movement. The air hung heavy with a sense of waiting. We continued to help as we could. Late in the day word came back that messages had gone back and forth between Grant and Lee. We didn't know of their contents at the time, but later they were all made public.

That day, the 7th of April, Grant had sent Lee a message that read:

> The result of last week must convince you of the hopelessness of further resistance. I regard it as my duty to shift from myself the responsibility of any further effusion of blood, by asking of you the surrender of that portion of the Confederate States Army known as the Army of Northern Virginia.

Though some of Lee's officers urged him to surrender immediately, Lee was angry. He had reason enough left, however, to send back the following word a short time later:

> Though not entertaining the opinion you express on the hopelessness of further resistance on the part of the Army of N. Va., I reciprocate your desire to avoid useless effusion of blood, and therefore, before considering your proposition, ask the terms you will offer on condition of its surrender.

The next morning came back Grant's reply:

> Peace being my great desire, there is but one condition I would insist upon, namely; that the men and officers surrendered shall be disqualified for taking up arms again against the Government of the United States.

All day long Lee considered his options with his small circle of closest officers. He was almost completely surrounded, both by long lines of dark blue and by the Appomattox and James rivers. Yet still the southern general held out hope for a miracle. He would strike a blow in the morning, he determined, and defeat Grant once and for all.

When word came, in scattered bits of news, of the messages passing between the generals, the reporter's instincts in me became aroused. All I could think of was writing one more great article for Mr. Kemble and the *Alta*—an eyewitness account of the end of the war!

Just let Robin O'Flaridy try to top this! I thought to myself. Why, maybe I'd ask Mr. Kemble for $20 or $30 for it!

"I've got to go to the front," I said to Christopher the moment I saw him the next morning. It was April 9.

"Corrie, that could be dangerous," he said. "I'm not sure I should let you."

"I have to, Christopher. I'll be safe. I'm sure there won't be any more fighting. Besides, it's Palm Sunday. Surely they'll respect that."

Christopher sighed. "I hope you're right, but I've not seen too much respect for sacred things thus far in this war—such as life itself. Do you want me to go with you?"

"No, you'll probably be of more use here. I'll be fine, and I'll move around better alone. Is it all right for me to take one of your horses?"

"Of course. But what are you planning to do?"

"Get the story of a lifetime for a reporter—I hope at least."

"I'll be here. Come back soon . . . and don't put yourself in any danger!"

CHAPTER 33

APPOMATTOX COURT HOUSE

It was not far from where we'd been camped to the front lines, just outside the tiny little town known as Appomattox Court House, right at the point where the James and Appomattox rivers met.

Already the Union troops had begun to move again that morning, readying themselves for an attack if Lee didn't surrender according to Grant's terms.

I worked my way through the line of blue uniforms of the Union Army of the James. A few heads turned my way, but nobody paid much heed. It had been a long war, and by now most of these soldiers were too sick of it to care if a young woman was riding through their ranks bareback. I made my way close to the point where I thought General Grant was. If anyone tried to stop me, I'd tell them I was a friend of the general's. And I suppose by now it was true enough.

It was just before noon when I approached what looked to be the supply wagons and makeshift tent of command. I stopped and dismounted, keeping my distance at the edge of a field in the middle of which there appeared to be some activity.

All of a sudden, from behind, I heard my name.

"Miss Corrie, what in tarnation are you doing in the middle of the war!"

I turned around.

"Jacob!" I cried, giving the big black man a hug. He had put back on nearly all the weight he'd lost in the prison, and my arms hardly stretched around him!

I stepped back. Jacob looked me over from head to toe with a big white-toothed grin spread all over his face.

"I had to come and make sure you were all right, Jacob," I said finally.

"Shoot, I know better than that! What are you *really* doing here—another plot you got wind of?"

"No, Jacob, nothing so sinister. But I do have the feeling this war's about to end, and I want to be there when it does. Always a reporter, you know!"

"You are some determined lady. Ha—just wait till Geoffrey sees you!"

"Is Captain Dyles here?" I asked.

"He's up with the general's staff. Been promoted to major, too."

"He has!"

"Yep, and they're waiting for word right now from General Grant, whether to keep laying back or attack."

"There might still be more fighting to come?"

"A message was intercepted this morning that said Bobbie Lee was fixin' to attack us. I can't imagine the fool trying it, but that's what they was saying earlier. But you wait here, I'll go see what I can find out."

Jacob turned and shuffled off quickly toward the tent out in the middle of the field.

He was only about halfway there when suddenly he turned back toward me, waving his hand like he was beckoning me.

"Miss Corrie, come . . . come quick!" he called.

I ran up to him.

"There's a horseman coming, he's riding this way fast—there, you see him?" He pointed.

"You see what he's waving over his head?"

"It . . . it looks like something white, Jacob."

"It's a white towel, Miss Corrie, and you know what that means! Come on, let's get over there!"

He started running again, though for his girth there ought to be some other word to call it.

The horseman was racing toward us in plain view now, bouncing along at full speed, waving his hat above his head and shouting at every jump. By now all the officers were on their feet, and in the distance as I approached I made out the familiar form of General Grant.

He strode up to the horseman as he galloped up and reined in the animal, and I saw him take an envelope from him. He looked at it for a second, then handed it to one of his men. He opened it, took out a single sheet of paper, then announced:

"It's a simple enough message," he said. "General Lee has accepted our general's terms. He has agreed to surrender."

Scarcely a sound followed. General Grant showed not a trace of emotion. Finally one man jumped up on a log.

"Three cheers for General Ulysses S. Grant!" he cried.

A few halfhearted hurrahs followed, but not many. More men were quietly weeping than cheering.

I watched it all in silent awe. I had come to see the end of the war, and this was it. I stood there trying to take everything in, not realizing that Jacob had left me. A few minutes later he returned.

"Miss Corrie," he said, "meet *Major* Geoffrey Dyles."

"It's so good to see you again, Capt—I mean *Major!*"

"After all we've been through, Corrie, don't you think it's about time you called me Geoff?"

"I'll try," I smiled.

"And with the war finally over, I hope to be a civilian again real soon!"

"What will happen next?" I asked.

"Arrangements are being made for the two generals to meet in town."

"When?"

"Soon, probably within the hour. Excuse me, it looks like I'm being summoned!"

"Is the major—*Geoffrey*—so close to the general that he's there for all the important decisions?" I asked.

"He's been with General Grant a long time," answered Jacob. "He may not be a colonel or a general, but General Grant trusts him like not too many others of his men."

We waited about another thirty or forty minutes, keeping our distance so as not to be conspicuous or in the way. At length the general and a contingent of thirty or forty men mounted their horses.

"I don't know about you," I said to Jacob, "but I'm going to follow them. I've come this far. What can they do but turn me back?"

"You always had guts, Miss Corrie!" he replied. "You'll come back by here and tell me what happened, won't you?"

"If I can, Jacob. If I don't, or if I get into trouble, it will be *your* turn to get *me* out of jail!"

He laughed, then boosted me up onto the back of Christopher's horse.

I followed at a distance of about a hundred yards.

When they entered the small town, the streets were nearly deserted. They stopped in front of a two-story brick house where several Confederate officers were standing. It wasn't until later that I learned it was the house of a Wilmer McLean, who had moved to this quiet little town from Manassas Junction in 1861 after the battle of Bull Run. Already sick of the war at that time, he had hoped never to see another soldier. Lee had sent a colonel into the town to find some suitable place to conduct the meeting with Grant, and the first man he encountered was McLean himself, who reluctantly agreed to let them use his house. Poor Mr. McLean later said, "The war began in my backyard and ended in my front parlor."

I approached the house very slowly. There were a few other riders around, probably other reporters like me—and some foot soldiers following out of curiosity. No one seemed to care much who saw what.

General Grant and about twelve men, including Major Dyles, went inside. The others stood at attention outside the house.

For probably forty minutes or an hour all was quiet. Then the door of the house opened and General Robert E. Lee walked out. I would have known him anywhere just from his description, even had it not been for the incident outside the prison. He mounted his white horse, then slowly started back toward his army, his head sunk low on his chest, the reins hanging loose in his hand.

I watched him go, and I couldn't help a deep feeling of melancholy coming over me. Glad as I was that the war was over, the downcast demeanor of this man, considered by so many to be one of the greatest generals of all time, made me feel sad.

I was standing beside my horse. Suddenly I decided to follow Mr. Lee. I jumped back on the horse's back and urged him to a slow trot after the white horse walking slowly back to the Confederate camp. I caught him in less than a minute. Two of the men riding beside him tried to stop me, but General Lee didn't even glance up.

"General Lee," I called out, "General Lee . . . I am a newspaper reporter. Would you mind if I asked you a question or two?"

Now at last the general looked up, waved off his two aides, then signaled me to join him. I rode up alongside.

He continued to stare straight ahead as his horse plodded along, not much interested in an interview but apparently feeling too defeated and despondent even to say no to someone wanting to ask him some questions. His eyes looked tired and sad, but such a stoic firmness was on his face too that I doubted he would shed tears over his defeat. Only the slightest wrinkle showed on his forehead, and eyebrows that looked like a remaining hint of resolve and subdued irritation over his surrender reflected the heartbreak of defeat. His white beard kept most of his other facial features from showing much, however. His mouth, surrounded by whiskers, betrayed not a hint of movement toward either a smile or a scowl.

"General Lee," I said tentatively, "I have read that you are a man with a strong Christian faith."

He nodded. "At this moment," he replied, "I would not claim my faith to be strong, but I *am* a Christian, and always will be grateful to God for my salvation." His voice was soft but firm, emotional but not wavering. I could feel the strength and dignity of the man just from his carriage and tone.

"Have you had the chance yet," I asked, "to ask yourself how this war, in which both sides prayed to God for victory and each felt morally justified for his stand . . . how the country will change as a result of it?"

The only sounds to be heard were the soft thudding of our horses' hooves along the dirt road. To all appearances General Lee had not heard a word I'd said. But though his face stared forward and revealed nothing, I knew he was thinking hard. At last he spoke.

"Yes, I have thought about what you ask," he said slowly. "But as to an answer, I have none. That the country will change there can be little doubt. But as to how, I am no prophet, only a soldier."

He paused, drew in a small breath, and for the first time I saw a hint of the inner turmoil he must have been going through.

"What a cruel thing is war," he went on softly, "to separate and destroy families and friends, and take from us the purest joys and happiness that God has granted us in this world. War fills our hearts with hatred instead of love for our neighbors, and devastates the fair face of this beautiful world."

"Is *your* heart filled with hatred, General?" I said, hardly realizing what a bold and pointed question I had asked. If I could have, I would have taken the words back instantly. But it was too late, and they hung there in the air for what seemed like forever.

I thought I detected a momentary wince in the proud face, but he continued to look forward. I felt like I had stabbed him in the very heart of his faith.

"I have fought against the people of the North," he finally answered, still not looking toward me, "because I believed they were seeking to wrest from the South its dearest rights. But I have never cherished toward them bitter or vindictive feelings."

He paused, and his next words, I could tell, came from his very depths. "And," he added, "I have never seen the day when I did not pray for them. So to answer your question, young lady— no, there is no hatred in my heart for any man of God's making, nor has there been throughout the years of this conflict."

So many more questions began to fill my mind. I wanted to ask the general what he thought about slavery, and why he had continued the fight against General Grant so long, at the cost of so many thousands of lives, even though there had been no possible way for his forces to win. I found myself wanting to know how his spiritual beliefs could allow him to consider so many lives expendable long after the cause he was fighting for was lost. It seemed so cruel, so stubborn, so proud. Yet this man beside me appeared none of those things, but rather a godly and upstanding man. I found myself wanting to know him and to understand him more deeply.

But there was no time. Already we were approaching the edges of the encampment of the Confederate troops. Seeing their general approach, foot soldiers began running toward him with cheers, some crying. Others just stood as he passed, grim and silent, or covered their face with their hands. A few officers merely saluted. I heard someone call out, "I love you just as much as ever, General!"

I knew my interview was over, and I wanted to get back to the town. I turned my horse and led it away. General Lee had already stopped to greet the troops who were running toward him. He had never once looked at me.

I slowly rode away in the opposite direction, but when I heard his voice addressing his men, I stopped one last time, turned around, and listened.

"Boys," he said, "I have done the best I could for you. Go home now, and if you make as good citizens as you have soldiers, you will do well, and I shall always be proud of you. Goodbye, and God bless you all."

That was all. I turned again and hurried back to Appomattox Court House. I had not been gone more than ten minutes. I dismounted, tied up the horse, and waited. Most of the Union officers still had not come out of the house, Jacob said.

A few minutes later General Grant emerged.

While they had been inside, quite a crowd of Union soldiers had assembled outside. At Grant's appearance they began to cheer. Then artillery fire began salutes of victory.

General Grant's hand went up.

"Stop . . . stop!" he cried. "We will not exult over the downfall of these Rebels," he said in a loud voice. "The war is over. They are our countrymen once again."

The outbursts subsided. General Grant mounted his horse, and without waiting for the rest of his detail, rode back to his tent.

I kept my eye peeled for Major Dyles. He came out of the house between Generals Sheridan and Custer, both carrying pieces of furniture they had bought as souvenirs from the owner of the house.

Major Dyles walked to his horse. I ran up to him. "Do you mind if I accompany you back?" I asked.

"Hollister, if you don't turn up everywhere!" he exclaimed.

"No, of course not. You got a mount?"

I said I did. I ran back, retrieved my horse, and soon was riding along at Geoffrey's side.

"Can you tell me what happened in there?" I asked.

"Back to being a newspaper lady, eh?" he grinned.

"Can't get good stories without asking questions."

"I don't suppose there's anything confidential about it," he said. "There's plenty of other fellows around interviewing all the generals. But you, Corrie Hollister, you got a *major* all your own to ask anything you want. I owe you, and I always pay my debts!"

"Then just tell me everything that went on inside that house," I said, "and we'll call it square for getting you out of Libby."

"A fair exchange!"

Major Dyles got serious for a moment, then started talking, like he was giving a speech.

"Well," he began, "Ol' Bobbie Lee was already there waiting. He was all decked out in his finest gray uniform and his polished boots and parade sword. And then when General Grant came in with just a dirty private's shirt and boots and trousers all splattered with mud, the two couldn't have looked more different.

"The two men shook hands. Grant said something about having met General Lee once before, during the Mexican war. Lee said he recalled it, but could not remember what Grant looked like."

"Could you tell what they were thinking?" I asked.

"Lee looked stoic and pained. He didn't let so much as a hair of his stern dignity down for a second. His face was impassible. It was obvious he didn't want to be there, but he held himself up."

"What about General Grant?"

"He was at ease. Not overly friendly, but tried to make pleasant conversation. He even seemed inclined to talk more about the Mexican campaign, but then General Lee reminded them what they were there for. General Grant got down to the business of the terms as he was prepared to offer them. As near as I can recall them, Corrie, he listed them something like this: Officers and soldiers of the Confederate army who owned their own horses could keep them. Officers could keep their pistols and personal possessions. All soldiers would be allowed to return to their homes, and would not be in any way prosecuted or disturbed by the authorities of the United States government.

" 'How many men do you have under your charge?' General Grant then asked. 'I understand they are in need of food.'

" 'I no longer know the number,' answered Lee, 'but I am sure they are all hungry.'

" 'Will rations for 25,000 men be sufficient?' asked Grant.

" 'That is more than generous,' replied Lee. 'It will have the best possible effect upon the morale of my men. It will be very gratifying and do much toward conciliating our people.' "

"Then a brief articles of surrender document was drawn up to indicate those things they had discussed. Both generals signed it. Then they shook hands again, and that was it."

We were nearly back to General Grant's headquarters by then. I thanked him, said goodbye to him and Jacob, then rode back to find Christopher where I had left him at one of the field hospitals.

CHAPTER 34

RETURNINGS

It was a time of returnings.

Soldiers everywhere returned home to try to piece together the broken fragments of shattered lives.

Robert E. Lee returned to his stately plantation outside Richmond, suddenly and forever after, a civilian again.

President Lincoln and his wife and son returned, after a week in Richmond and Petersburg, back to Washington. He had been fighting innumerable battles since first taking office. Now he could relax briefly before undertaking the enormous burdens ahead, socialize some, perhaps attend the theater.

Christopher and I returned from Appomattox Court House to Mrs. Timms' farm.

Even as we rode back, my brain was full of what I'd seen in the small town—especially the two men playing the lead roles on the stage that neither of them, had they been able to change the course of events, wished existed at all. Growing within me was the reporter's urge to find some larger meaning to the events I had witnessed. Most of all, I could not get out of my mind the significance and symbolism of Lee and Grant's peaceful meeting after four years of bloodshed.

Almost the moment we were back to the farm, I got out my things to try to begin working on the first article I had attempted in some time.

Two men from such different backgrounds—one of education, society, and gentlemanly stature, the other from more common roots, and whose military career had ended in ig-

nominy before the war—symbolize the two diverse person-
alities of the North and the South, and the great diversity
found in the United States of America.

Robert E. Lee, the stoic, proud, gentleman Southerner,
and Ulysses S. Grant, the practical, rugged, down-to-earth
Northerner, are like two brothers of very different tempera-
ments, yet from the same lineage. Brothers but enemies,
whose loyalties and strong wills inevitably would clash because of the intense pride of their convictions and loyalties.

Perhaps the face-to-face battle between these two great
generals for control of Richmond in the closing months of the
war was inevitable from the beginning. In the same way, perhaps this civil clash between North and South, between two
opposing views of freedom and what the Constitution means
when it grants its citizens freedom, was also inevitable, even
from the very beginnings of this nation and that Constitution.
As two brothers grow side by side, the time often comes when
conflict must resolve their differences in order to prepare them
for manhood. From the very beginning there was in the Constitution, and in the fabric of this country, a flaw, an unre-
solved corner where freedom did not exist. One of the brothers detected the flaw, the other denied it. And ultimately the
time had to come when they would come to blows over it. For
the country and the two brothers were growing and had to
mature sometime.

When the war began, Ulysses S. Grant was serving in total
obscurity in the distant west, while Robert E. Lee already
commanded the imposing Army of Northern Virginia. Their
posts, ranks, and power could not have been more different,
and the likelihood that the two would ever meet on the field
of battle seemed impossibly remote.

However, both proved themselves in battle, command,
and loyalty, and both moved steadily up in the ranks of their
respective armies. Grant rose from being an unknown whose
career had already been declared over, higher and higher in
the Union ranks, to become general, then lieutenant general.
Gradually destiny seemed to bring him ever eastward, ever
closer to the center of the conflict, ever higher toward the very
top of Abraham Lincoln's command.

Inexorably, they both climbed, moving closer together all
the time as if being drawn by fate toward a final face-to-face

confrontation that would decide the outcome of the entire war. In a fitting climax, by 1864, there they both were, the two great generals, Ulysses S. Grant and Robert E. Lee—the former in command of the entire Union army, the latter in command of the Confederate, and squaring off against each other between the two capitals, Washington and Richmond.

Had the end been scripted, it could not have come down to a more dramatic and appropriate conclusion. Grant vs. Lee, Washington vs. Richmond, the Union vs. the Confederacy. Only one would emerge victorious from the battle. Either Richmond or Washington would fall, and with it, only one—the Union or the Confederacy—would prevail.

When their armies met in the spring of 1864 in the wilderness of northern Virginia, indeed the battle between two giants had begun. All the war had, in a sense, prepared for this. And now, strategy and might and cunning and sheer determination and willpower would decide which of these two titans, these brother Americans, would be the greatest.

Far superior numbers were by that time on the side of the North. But the titan of the South did not give in without a fight. For a year the two armies battled to a stalemate, steel against steel, unflinching eye against unflinching eye, Grant against Lee, both determined—Grant about whom it was said, "He always wears an expression as if he had determined to drive his head through a brick wall and was about to do it," and Lee who seemed as if he would fight on without surrendering until his army was down to a dozen men . . . until at last the end, which had long been as inevitable as the clash, arrived in a quiet little Virginia town called Appomattox Court House.

When the black-bearded face of Ulysses Grant stared across the small table at the white-bearded face of Robert Lee, and the two determined sets of eyes met, and the two hands clasped at last in peace, it was the moment of brotherhood for which the nation—united now again—had so long struggled, when the brothers North and South, in spite of their conflict, and perhaps even because of them, were now ready to stand and become men . . . together . . . united as one to move ahead toward a future.

I put my pen down and drew in a long sigh.

I didn't know what I was trying to say. This would never be an article any newspaper would print! I hadn't written anything newsworthy for so long, maybe I had forgotten how.

I read over what I had done. *What* future? Where was the country moving . . . where was my *article* going! A rambling discussion of Lee and Grant, that's all it was. They had both been so on my mind, such forceful men . . . I could get the gaze of neither out of my memory.

But I still couldn't lay hold of what it all *meant*!

That's what I needed to find out if I was going to write an article on the war that had just ended—what was its purpose, what had it achieved . . . what did it mean?

The Wednesday following the Palm Sunday surrender, the Army of Northern Virginia formally laid down its arms. Twenty thousand men marched in formation toward the Union army to stack their rifles on the ground and surrender all their battle flags. The long Union lines of dark blue saluted their brother Americans clad in gray.

In Washington, fireworks and celebration and parades filled the air and the streets.

It was Good Friday, two days before Easter. "Listen to this," said Christopher, reading from Thursday's paper, which had come down by ship to Richmond and which he had just received the day after that. "There was a huge crowd about the White House, a band, fireworks, and they were all clamoring for the President to make a speech. He insisted he was too weary, but they wanted something from him in this moment of victory. Now listen to what he said, Corrie. What a diplomat! I can see why you are so fond of him. 'I have always thought "Dixie" one of the best tunes I ever heard. Our adversaries over the way attempted to appropriate it, but I insisted that we fairly captured it with the signing of the papers at Appomattox. I presented the question to the Attorney General and he gave it as his legal opinion that it is our lawful prize. I now request the band to favor me with its performance.' Imagine that, playing 'Dixie' to commemorate the end of the war!"

There was no way I could have known, but I would find out later, that even as the band was playing its rousing rendition of "Dixie" for the President, just a few blocks away John Surratt had gone in search of his friend, the actor, where the latter was drinking himself into a stupor at the National Hotel.

It was a dark time for the nation, he said, between swallows of brandy.

Surratt agreed.

Something must be done.

Would Booth like to come over to his mother's? All the others were there—Atzerodt, Powell, Herold. They had plenty of brandy.

Anything to drive away the blues of the terrible defeat, said Booth. He rose and accompanied him back to Mary Surratt's boardinghouse.

CHAPTER 35

GOOD FRIDAY, 1865

That same afternoon, Christopher, Mrs. Timms, and I read the Good Friday story and prayed together to remember the death of Jesus and what it signified to each of us.

"The willing, sacrificing death of Jesus is the foundation for the entire gospel message," Christopher said as we sat together after reading the biblical account. "Not merely the death he underwent on our behalf," he said, "but the *willing* death. It is the most overlooked aspect of the crucifixion by most Christians, it seems to me."

"I thought it was his dying, the shedding of his blood, that paid the price for our sin," I said.

"It was, of course. But the huge truth of Jesus' death is that he didn't *have* to die. The Father didn't force him onto the cross. He *chose* it. It was his God-nature that made atonement by the shedding of his blood. But it was his man-nature that *chose* to do it. And that is what is so wonderfully real and present about the crucifixion. That willing *choosing* is what makes us able likewise to enter into the death on the cross with him. Paul's words about us sharing the cross are such a puzzle to many. But once you grasp this willing choosing, this laying down of life, that is central to what Jesus did by allowing himself to be crucified, then it becomes clear that same *choice*, that same willing laying down of our own motives of self-interest, is open to us too. And thus we become partakers in the *divine* nature by sharing in the choice that Jesus made as a *man*."

"I'm sorry, Christopher," I said, "but you sound more like a preacher than I've ever heard you. And I'm afraid it's *still* a puzzle to me."

He laughed. "Forgive me. Sometimes I get carried away with an idea, and I have to follow it out wherever it leads me."

"But I do want to understand what you're saying."

"All right, then let me see if I can explain it this way." He stopped and thought for a moment. "What is the one way in which we can be just like Jesus?" he asked at length.

"I don't want to say the answer you're not thinking of," I replied with a smile, "so you tell me."

Christopher laughed. "I'm thinking of having the power to choose, as I said before. God gave us a *will*. It's our choosing mechanism. We can use it to choose good or bad. We can use it to exalt ourselves or exalt someone else. I can use it to put myself first, or to put you first."

"I see."

"Jesus shared all that completely. He had a *man's* will. In other words, he *could* have chosen to exalt himself. The Bible makes it clear that he had that very clear choice. He did not *have* to die. He was not coerced into it."

"And we have the same kind of will?"

"Exactly the same. And the choice we face is the same choice that Jesus did. We face it every day. I would even go so far as to say we face it almost every minute of every day."

"You are getting too far ahead of me on the path again, I'm afraid," I said.

"We do not face literal death. Yet every time—as I said it comes to us moment by moment throughout every day—we engage the decision-making part of us, and willingly *choose* to relinquish what *we* might want in and of ourselves, and choose instead to do what our Father wills, or choose instead to put the interests of another ahead of our own . . . in that moment we share, we appropriate, we partake in the very same part of Jesus' nature that led him to the cross. Jesus *wanted* to escape that death. That's what the Garden was all about, as we just read a little bit ago. I might even say that the world was redeemed in Gethsemane as much as it was on the cross, because there is where Jesus willingly chose to lay himself down, and to relinquish himself into the will of his Father."

"How do we face that same thing every minute, like you said? Jesus faced it only that one time."

"Every moment we live, our *selves* try to put themselves first . . . in *everything*! In the way we talk, how we behave, in our mannerisms, in every tiny aspect of how we think and go about all the multitude affairs of life. The question is—do we yield to that impulse to put our self first, and to do and say and think what pleases that self? *Or* do we by conscious effort of the will do the opposite of what it would have us do, say, and think?"

He paused, his face aglow. I could tell he was struggling to find just the right words to convey what he felt.

"Actually, Corrie," he said, "I believe that Jesus consciously willed his *self* to death a million times during his life. That moment in the Garden was the culmination of a lifetime of practice in yielding himself to the will of his Father instead of his own. Oh, it's so enormous in my mind I can hardly contain it! It's this that makes the prayer of asking God to make us like Jesus . . . this that makes it such a down-to-earth and practical prayer. If we pray it, and truly mean it, then God will confront us with millions of choices all the rest of our lives, giving us the opportunity in each one to do as Jesus did in the Garden—to yield ourselves to the will of the Father and to the good of others. And thus we allow God's Spirit to bring about that transformation of our characters that we have prayed for, and become the full sons and daughters of God we were created to be."

A long silence followed.

"I think I understand," I said finally. "I've talked to Almeda about this too, though it comes out differently from your mouth. I want to try to write down everything you said so I can read it over several times."

"Do you have room in that journal of yours?" grinned Christopher.

"I'm only writing very special things in the book you gave me," I answered. "I've decided that I want to go back through my old journals and find some of the things Almeda told me when I was younger, or bits of Avery's sermons I wrote down, and even thoughts I had of my own, and collect them all in one book of thoughts and ideas, things like what you've just been telling me.

I'm going to make the book you gave me a collection of truths and principles and things people have told me so I can read back over them and never forget. That's where I will write down everything you've just said about the crucifixion and choosing . . . if you will help me get it all down," I added.

"My pleasure."

Christopher sighed deeply.

He rose, walked slowly to where I sat on a wide divan. By this time Mrs. Timms had returned to the kitchen. Christopher sat down beside me and began to pray.

"Oh, Father," he said softly, "we *do* so want to be made like your Son Jesus, and we ask you to carry out that work in us."

It was not a long prayer, yet it was full of a depth of longing that I knew expressed the desire of Christopher's whole being.

"Help me to understand more about you, Father," I said aloud, my eyes now closed. "I want to know you and your Son Jesus more and more in my heart. And when all those times of choosing come, help me, God, to do what Jesus did and put your will first."

"Yes, oh yes, Father," said Christopher with a quiet and passionate sincerity. "Make the very nature of the redemption alive and practical in our mouths and in our characters by helping us to lay down and yield to your will and to the good of others, just as Jesus did. Help us, our Father, we pray, for we possess no power within ourselves to complete, nor even to begin this magnificent work you purpose to do within us. So help us, Lord . . . help us choose . . . help us to willingly yield to you. Amen."

We sat for a long time in silence.

"Well, that felt good!" he said after a while.

"What?" I asked.

"I haven't preached a sermon in I don't know how long. I'd begun to wonder if I still was able to."

"No fear of that."

He laughed. "No doubt you're right there. Once a preacher, always a preacher. But you can't imagine how nice it feels to engage in meaningful dialogue—even preaching!—with someone who is listening enough to ask questions instead of sitting in the pews falling asleep. I'd sooner preach to a congregation of one—if that one was you—than to any audience of ten thousand!"

I rose and went to see if I could help Mrs. Timms with the dinner. Christopher picked up the newspaper again.

"Hmm," he said as I was leaving the room, "it says here General Grant and his wife are in Washington as guests of Mr. and Mrs. Lincoln. They're going to the theater on Friday—that's tonight."

"What's playing?" I asked absently.

"Uh . . . let's see—*Our American Cousin.*"

"Who's in it?"

"An actress named Laura Keene, it says."

CHAPTER 36

HOLLOW WORDS OF PARTING

Just as the end of the war signaled a season of returnings for many people to their former homes and way of life, I could not help finding myself pensively reflecting on what course I myself should now follow.

I obviously could not stay here.

In his letter, Christopher had asked me to come . . . for a visit . . . to see if we could help and minister to those suffering from the fighting. I had visited, and we had done what we could.

But it was now past. The war was over. Everything had suddenly changed. It was time to look ahead. It was time for me to think what to do next, to find out the next chapter in the book of my life God had written for me. I didn't know what was in that chapter. But somehow I knew the first page had already turned and the new chapter begun.

It was time for me to follow to see where God was leading. Yet I could not see him ahead of me.

I was certain of only one thing: I could not think and pray clearly and rationally about my future here. Christopher was too much of a distraction right in the middle of everything. If God was going to speak to me and show me what was written in the new chapter which had begun, I strongly doubted he would be able to do it while I was *here*.

A time of returnings had come for me, too. Right now that clearly meant Washington. After that . . . who could tell? Back to California? Back to the Convent of John Seventeen in Pennsylvania? Right now I couldn't be sure. Perhaps I might remain in

Washington and continue to write and work for the Commission. Mr. Hay said there was still a great deal I could do for our country.

I decided to stay through Easter Sunday. Somehow it seemed right to spend that most special of days with Christopher. But the next day it would be time for me to leave again.

I told Christopher on Saturday.

He was quiet and unusually subdued. Oh, what I would have given for even the tiniest slice of his thoughts! But he said little, and I knew him well enough by now to know that when the time was right for sharing, he would tell me all. Until then he had to keep to himself and weigh his thoughts on prayer with his Father. It was so hard not to know what he was thinking. Yet how I admired him all the more for this cautious and measured part of his character.

"What will you do, Corrie?" he asked.

"I don't know, exactly," I replied. "Suddenly everything's changed. Four years, and all at once it's over. I suppose I have to think about what's next and where I really belong now that it's over."

He nodded in thoughtful understanding.

"And there's my writing, of course."

"Yes . . . you really like to write, don't you?"

"It's part of me," I said.

Again he nodded. "Women have to pursue their dreams just like men," he said.

"You're not against a woman having a career?"

"I see nothing about it to be against. God has plans for women just as he does for men."

"I don't suppose my career will ever be that brilliant. But I find fulfillment in writing. I do think God wants me to do it."

"As do I."

"You . . . want me to write?"

"Of course. If that's what God wants, then I want it too."

Again there was an awkward silence. I knew Christopher was thinking more than he was saying.

"I think I'll go on Monday," I said.

"I'll check the paper and see if there's a schedule of trains leaving for the Capital. I'm sure service has resumed to Fredericksburg."

"You don't need—"

"Nonsense. I'll take you into the city and see you off."

"Thank you," I said.

It was all I could do to keep back the tears. Everything sounded so cold and emotionless and final. The last time we'd parted, there had seemed so much to say and no chance to say it. Now we had two whole days ahead of us, but the only words that would come were thin and empty!

The conversation wound down to nothing. Christopher excused himself and went outside. It was time to feed the animals, he said.

I mumbled something about needing to get my things ready. I don't know why I said it. I hardly had anything to pack. I'd brought only a small carpetbag and two journals. All my possessions were at Mrs. Richards' boardinghouse.

CHAPTER 37

ASSASSINATION!

That whole Saturday was a quiet, downcast day.

If only we'd known. It would have been horrible, of course, but it would have jolted my mind out of the despondency of my own troubles.

As it was, we didn't learn of the horror until the following day.

Death was no way to celebrate Easter Sunday. Except for Jesus' words "Though you die, yet shall you live," I think I might have lost hope altogether. But ever after in my mind, the message of Good Friday and Easter fused into one. Never the rest of my life was I able to celebrate Easter without a heart-sickening sense of anguish at how awful was the death of the one innocent, sacrificed for the freedom of the many. To deify the President would not be right. Yet I could never escape the parallel that he, too, had given his life to free the slaves from their captivity.

Midway through the morning we heard the sound of urgent hooves galloping up the road.

The self-appointed messenger of evil tidings was riding from farm to farm.

"The President's been shot!" he cried as Christopher ran outside onto the porch.

The question from his bewildered listeners was the same at every stop, as was the hopeless finality of his reply. "Shot, Mister . . . I'm telling you the truth. It's all over the telegraph. Abraham Lincoln's dead!"

Then he was gone in a receding cloud of dust, as quickly as he had come. Mrs. Timms and I had followed him outside at the

209

shouts, and had clearly heard the last of the message. Christopher's arms closed about us both. We stood on the porch, weeping and holding one another, shaken with a depth of grief not even the war itself had caused.

Not a word was spoken for over two hours.

Mrs. Timms eventually returned to the preparation of Easter dinner.

Christopher had a few chores, and then later I saw him in the distance walking in the fields. Every once in a while one of his hands would gesture toward the heavens.

I sat for over an hour on the porch, staring straight ahead. The only sensation I can think of calling it was numbness. My brain had been seared by the news. I felt all color leave my body. It was as though my hands and feet and legs and arms all went dead. I felt nothing. All sensations stopped. I thought for a while that the amnesia was about to return, because I could not even force myself to think. I thought I was going into a waking sleep. After the initial shock, even the tears dried up. It was all beyond imagining.

Christopher saddled a horse and rode into the city.

He returned two hours later with a paper, an extra edition, only one folded sheet, that told of the assassination.

The instant my eyes fell on the name *Booth* my heart sank all the more.

I couldn't believe what I read! He'd been in the room right next to me back in October!

"Were there any others involved?" I asked Christopher, who was still reading through the report.

"There were several accomplices," he replied. "Some stage hand held the getaway horse. A fellow named Powell was with Booth and stabbed Secretary of State Seward. They suspect more, but don't give names."

"Was General Grant hurt?"

Christopher read on hurriedly. "No, the Grants decided not to attend at the last minute and weren't even there."

"Was Booth captured?"

"No . . . apparently he jumped down onto the stage, screamed something about avenging the South, and fled. He's still at large."

Christopher finished reading the account and handed it to me.

I read through it, crying again. It was too unbelievable . . . too awful . . . how could God allow such a thing . . . how could our country survive without him?

I read on, though I had to stop and wipe my eyes every few seconds.

Then I noticed a fact that hit me with stunning force. "Soldiers took the unconscious President from the theater," I read, "and to the street. A civilian directed them to a boardinghouse across Tenth Street, where Mr. Lincoln was laid out on a bed on the first floor. Surgeons were summoned from throughout the city, but they could do nothing."

Tenth Street! Of course . . . I had walked past Ford's Theater many times. President Lincoln had died in Mrs. Richards' boardinghouse, directly underneath my own room!

I don't know why, but the realization brought Mr. Lincoln's death all the closer and made me sick to my stomach. I went outside and gagged several times.

Later in the afternoon, Mrs. Timms served Easter dinner, but none of us ate much. Christopher prayed. We tried to focus on the Lord's resurrection, but all our thoughts were on Abraham Lincoln instead. I doubt if ten words were spoken between us throughout the meal.

How the rest of the day passed I hardly remember. Every minute seemed like an hour.

CHAPTER 38

RETURNINGS, DEPARTINGS

Christopher took me into Richmond the next morning.

It was not at all like I had hoped it would be. The ride was quiet. We had always had more to talk about than we could get said. Now it seemed everything had changed. There was the assassination, of course. But I knew it was more than that, though I didn't want to ask myself what it could be.

He waited with me until it was time for me to board the train.

"Well," he said when the time had come, "you have Mrs. Timms' address."

"And you have Mrs. Richards'," I returned.

"Right," he rejoined, forcing a smile.

An uncomfortable second or two passed. I picked up my bag, then turned toward the train. Christopher's gentle hand on my elbow stopped me.

"I . . . I wish you the best, Corrie," he said. "I really mean that! Truly may God go with you."

"Thank you," I said softly. As much as I know he meant them, the words just weren't enough. Tears stung my eyes again. But I didn't want to cry . . . not here . . . not now!

"Goodbye, Christopher," I said, choking, then quickly turned and climbed on board the train. I didn't look back. I knew if I saw his face again, I would break down sobbing and might not be able to stop. If I was going to cry today, I wanted it to be for Abraham Lincoln . . . not for Corrie Hollister.

I took a seat, tried desperately to draw in a few breaths of cleansing air, pulled out my handkerchief and dabbed my eyes, then drew in a long, slow draught into my lungs and exhaled.

"Well," I said to myself, "whatever the next chapter of the book holds from here on, I am *not* going to look back and feel sorry for myself!" I remembered again what Ma'd always said, and tried to remind myself that she was a wise lady, and that she wouldn't have said it if it weren't true. If God had wanted me to. . . . No, I wasn't going to say it, not even to myself! He *didn't* seem to want that for me, and I'd settled it a long time ago, and I was happy with my life as it was.

Once we were underway, I pulled out the letter I'd received from home just a few days earlier. There had been a steady, though not always regular correspondence between me and Almeda the whole time I'd been gone, though sometimes it made it easier *not* to write, so I wouldn't have to think about how much I missed everyone back in Miracle Springs. I think it was something like that for Almeda too, and she usually mostly just told me what was happening and didn't get as personal as she would have if we'd been talking face-to-face. She didn't want to make me any more homesick by something she might say.

Pa wasn't much of a letter writer. I'd had only a few words from him the whole two years I'd been gone. But then in this letter, down at the bottom after Almeda had signed her name, he added just a line: "It's been two years since you left, Corrie Belle. Ain't that about long enough for you to be away? We'd all like to see your face again. Especially your pa."

I must have read over his hand-scrawled words twenty times. And just like after every one before, I cried again today. A change was coming, I could feel it. Pa was right. It had been a long time.

Back in Washington, Mrs. Richards was beside herself with grief. She let me have my room back as always. There were people about for some time. There was blood to be cleaned off the carpet. Photographers came and took pictures of the room and the house. The entire city lay under a cloud of silence. The whole capital, the whole nation mourned.

I went to pay my last respects to the man I had loved and whose invitation had brought me east in the first place. President Lincoln's casket lay in state, first in the White House, and then in the rotunda of the Capitol building. After that it was loaded onto a special funeral train and borne to Philadelphia, where the coffin lay in Independence Hall. A double line of mourners stretched three miles to see it. It was there he had earlier declared that he would "rather be assassinated" than surrender the principles of the Declaration of Independence.

From Philadelphia the funeral train went to New York, then east toward Springfield, Illinois, the President's final resting place, where it would arrive on May 4.

Along with thousands of others, I stood in the silent weeping crowd saying and waving farewell to our beloved President as the black funeral train pulled out of the Washington station that 20th day of April, 1865. As the sound of the slow-moving cars faded from hearing, gradually the crowd dispersed. It was time to look ahead. We had won a war and lost a President—all within two short weeks.

I walked back toward the boardinghouse.

Even before I arrived there, I knew I could remain in Washington no longer. There was nothing for me here now. All the work that had kept me so occupied had been bound up in Mr. Lincoln and the war. What purpose could there be in my remaining in the capital any longer?

I needed to find someplace to think and pray and collect myself, to write in my journal, and to ask God what he wanted me to do. So many possibilities and thoughts had flooded my mind, but now with the war over and Mr. Lincoln gone, suddenly everything was changed. Two years ago I had been strongly drawn to the life Sister Janette had shown me. Since then I had been swept into so many things! I had served as a nurse, as a writer, as a political campaigner, as a fund raiser . . . even as a spy!

But now . . . all that was past.

What did God want from me now? What did he want me to do? Where did he want me to go?

Three faces kept returning to my mind—Christopher, Sister Janette, and Pa. And every time I thought of Pa, I could hear his words: *Ain't that about long enough . . . see your face again. Especially your pa.*

He was probably right; it was about long enough that I'd been away. But before I could go back, I still had a few questions to resolve. There was only one place I knew I'd be able to think, to pray, and to work hard in the meantime, a place where I knew I'd find a ready welcome. And it still could be, I thought, that God would have me live there permanently. But whatever he had in mind for me, that was surely the best place for me to seek it.

I turned around, went back to the station, and checked the departure schedules.

Then I returned to the boardinghouse to gather my things, to tell Mrs. Richards I would be leaving her, to thank her for everything, and to make sure she had my forwarding address . . . just in case.

CHAPTER 39

THE CONVENT

Sister Janette and all the other nuns at the convent were so delighted to see me, and welcomed me so warmly, I immediately felt one of their fellowship again. If I hadn't known better I would have thought only a week had passed since my first visit, not just two months short of two full years.

"You look wonderfully well, Sister Janette," I said. "I would never know you had been wounded."

"I've never felt better, Corrie. The Lord has been good to us here. But what of you?"

"It would take a week to tell you everything," I replied.

"Then we shall take a week! How long will you be able to stay with us?"

I shrugged. "Maybe as long as you'll have me," I said. I explained that I needed some time to pray and think and write.

"I'm so happy you wanted to come here to seek and inquire of the Lord," she said. "You will be welcome for as long as you like. Come, I'll show you where to put your things."

For the next week I did nothing but enter into the life of the convent with the sisters—working, tending the animals, helping with the food and dishes, joining in prayer times and Mass, going to visit people in the community. I can't say I stopped thinking altogether, but I consciously did my best just to enter into the life around me and not dwell on the uncertainties that lay in front of me.

Whenever I prayed, which was many, many times every day in the midst of other duties or work or activities, I simply said,

"Lord, show me what you want me to do now. Show me what to write, where you want me to go, and however much of the next chapter of my life you want me to know."

Ever since the day when General Lee and General Grant had met at Appomattox Court House, I had been thinking a lot about the war and what it all might mean years from now. I suppose seeing General Lee up close had stuck with me even more than had my association with General Grant before that. I thought I understood General Grant. He seemed to be a soldier and not much more. But Mr. Lee struck me as more complex. He was a brilliant general, everyone said that, but he was also a southern gentleman and an outspoken Christian. I had heard that he read his Bible every day, even through most of the war, and prayed frequently with his men. And I just could not understand all that. From everything I'd heard and read in the newspapers during the whole last year of the war, thousands and thousands of lives— maybe even a hundred thousand!—would have been saved if Robert Lee had given in sooner. I had a hard time seeing much other than stubbornness and pride in his fighting on and on against the North after everyone knew the war was over. He must have known it too, yet he kept right on fighting, causing more and more young men to die.

And yet when I rode beside him for those few minutes that day, he didn't *seem* like a cruel man who would take death lightly. But all the way back from that short interview, I couldn't help but think of how much less destruction and killing there would have been, and Atlanta and Savannah and Richmond and other cities wouldn't have had to be destroyed, if only he and Jefferson Davis and the other southern leaders hadn't been so stubborn and kept fighting for so long. I suppose I was seeing it from the side of the North. I'm sure Southerners didn't look at it that way.

Then my mind turned to wondering why the war had had to be fought at all. It seemed it had to do with pride and stubbornness as much as slavery. And now the South was practically destroyed, President Lincoln was dead, the war was over, three million young men had taken up arms against each other, and six hundred thousand of those were now dead. Could anything be worth such a huge price? And judging from what I'd seen on Robert E. Lee's face, and from what John Wilkes Booth had done, the pride and stubbornness still remained.

For some reason I found myself thinking about Pa and Zack. They'd known each other for a long time. But then there'd come that moment of conflict and separation and breaking between them when Zack had left and spent a year away. It was a heartbreaking time for Pa, but once it was over, he and Zack knew each other even better, in deeper ways. In the last letter I'd had from Almeda, which had been waiting for me at Mrs. Richards', she told me about some new project Zack and Pa were working on to dig a new mine where they thought there might be a fresh vein of gold. Maybe the pain of that time when Zack was gone had accomplished something between them that might not have been able to happen any other way.

I didn't know if that was true. It didn't seem right that pain and conflict and fighting had to be the thing that brought two people closer together, but I reckon it sometimes did work that way. Maybe it would be the same with our country, like if the North and South were two brothers who had to fight each other as teenagers to get to know each other well enough to grow up into adults who cared about each other and could work together.

After I'd been at the convent for five days, I knew that something was bubbling and stewing inside me about all I'd been thinking. Whether it would turn out to be a new article about the war, or the completion of the one I'd attempted about Grant and Lee, I didn't know. But I had to try to write down my thoughts and make some further sense out of what had happened. I scratched down some ideas for a day or two, then decided to rewrite it all as well as I could, even if only to help me organize the ideas that were coming to me. I went to the writing desk the sisters let me use, got several sheets of paper, took the lid off my bottle of ink, dipped in my pen, and began to write. After reworking some of it several times, trying to get the words just right, this is what I wrote.

What should we call this war just past? It has already been called many things: the War of the Rebellion, the War Between the States, the Brothers' War, the Late Unpleasantness, the War Against Northern Aggression, the Second American

Revolution, the Lost Cause, the War Against the States, or the War of Attempted Succession.

Whatever label we give it, any civil strife such as this is full of hurtful and bitter ironies.

Now that we have faced the sternest battle we will likely ever face, in the adolescence of our nationhood we have encountered a foe that we least expected—the mirror of our own self, our very brother. Thus, for reasons mysterious, the conflict was more bitter and hateful than the Mexican War or the English War of 1812. Why this should be so is a puzzle. Why have we so despised our own flesh and blood? Did it in truth take the death of more than half a million to free four million Negro slaves? Perhaps we will never know if the price was worth it.

But we do know that we are but *one* nation. We have found out that about ourselves, even at a tragic cost. We have looked within ourselves, man into man, woman into woman, brother into the heart of brother. Perhaps in so doing we will grow stronger, and take our place as a nation of higher stature.

Writing about brother looking into the heart of brother reminded me again of General Grant and General Lee and what I had said about how they stood for the North and South settling the last squabbles of their youth.

Was this war a good thing, a healthy thing, in the life of our nation? Will it lead to stronger bonds and a greater unity of national purpose? Or was it fueled by nothing more than stubborn sectional pride and a bitter hatred that grew more and more determined with every passing week the war dragged on? How will it serve to make us all—Northerners and Southerners—better Americans?

As I wrote, so much was going on inside me. Not only did it apply to our country, it all had to do with *me* too, and with some things I was beginning to look inside to find out about myself.

How might it have been different had Robert E. Lee accepted the command offered him by President Lincoln over the entire Union army? Most families lost young men on both sides of Mason-Dixon. Four of Mrs. Lincoln's brothers fought in gray uniforms against her husband. At Cold Harbor, seven thousand young men met their death in twenty minutes. In two days at Shiloh, more Americans fell than in all previous American wars added together. So great was this epic conflict that all of us who lived through it, who watched it, who read of it, and who endured it will forever be changed. And in the end, the finale of the war brought no triumph, only an anguishing deepening of the heartache with the disgrace of assassination.

We all have been changed. We will all continue to be changed by this national tragedy, by this four-year-long moment when we as a nation focused all our energies and efforts inward upon ourselves to ask ourselves what kind of people we are, and what price are we willing to place on our mixed, confused, and conflicting convictions.

What are we made of?

I had been changed by the years away from home as much as from the war itself. Yes, so many changes had taken place. And now the last question I'd posed stared back at me from the page. I hadn't intended it, but it was as though I'd asked it of myself.

That there was greed and selfishness exposed in our beings there can be little doubt, yes, and a great evil pride. But we found courage in far greater supply, and dignity and bravery and heroism, and selflessness in a thousand unseen ways in a thousand quiet out-of-the-way corners on every one of the ten thousand places where conflict took place during the last four years of this war.

Perhaps we learned that hatred resides in us, and that is a painful thing to learn. But perhaps most of all we learned that we are brothers, after all. And that freedom, though it is hard won at a bitter cost, is something we believe in though it cost the blood of our national family to preserve it.

I stopped.

My thoughts were getting jumbled and I didn't feel like I was accomplishing anything. The article wasn't focused and I couldn't come to any conclusion.

By now I had begun to turn my introspective questions onto myself. I started by looking at the country and talking about mirrors and asking what kind of people we were as a nation. Now I was wondering what I was made of as an individual. Inexplicably, I found myself thinking about the small town of Bridgeville, New York. What did it have to do with the war?

I rose from the chair and walked about the room, stretching my arms and legs. I couldn't do any more writing now. By this time I had learned that when the thoughts stopped flowing, there was no use forcing them. When more perspective on the war was ready to occur to me, it would wander out of the depths and into the front of my brain.

Sister Janette was in the kitchen preparing vegetables for dinner. I joined her, rolled up my sleeves, took a knife, sat down on a stool beside a large pot of potatoes, and began helping her peel them.

"Why is it called the Convent of John Seventeen?" I asked.

"Because we are the Sisters of Unity," she replied.

"What does that have to do with John Seventeen?"

"John Seventeen is the chapter where Jesus' prayer for unity is found."

I had heard Almeda and Rev. Rutledge mention it, but I asked Sister Janette what special meaning it had to her.

"What do you think, Corrie?" she asked. "Do you think Jesus could pray for something his Father didn't want to do for him?"

"I don't suppose," I answered. "For him to pray in opposition to God's will would be . . . I don't know, it just doesn't seem like it could even be, could it?"

"I don't think so," Sister Janette said. "I can't imagine Jesus praying in opposition to God's will. That would put a dividing line straight between the Father and the Son, and I simply don't think that is possible."

"There is Jesus' prayer in the garden," I said.

"That used to trouble me somewhat," Sister Janette said slowly, "until I looked very closely at it."

"And what did you see then?"

"I looked at the words of Jesus' prayer very carefully. He didn't pray that the cup, that is, the crucifixion, *would* be taken away. He only said that *if it was possible,* he would like it to be taken away. But his true heart's prayer, the thing he specifically requested the Father to accomplish, was to do his, the Father's, will.

And *that* prayer the Father did answer perfectly."

"So all of Jesus' prayers were answered," I said.

"No, there's one important prayer that *hasn't* been answered yet—but not because it wasn't prayed according to the will of the Father. Jesus prayed it because his Father wants to do it, but it just hasn't taken place yet."

"Jesus' prayer for unity?"

"Yes. He prays that all his followers will someday be one in the same way that he and the Father are one. It hasn't happened yet, that is clear, because his people are far from united. But we believe it *will* happen one day. It *has* to happen. God's people *have* to be one because Jesus prayed for it, and he couldn't pray for anything that God the Father did not purpose to do. He prayed for unity, therefore someday there *will be* unity among the children of God. And that is why this is called the Convent of John Seventeen, because we are the sisters who have committed ourselves to working for unity among God's people."

We peeled away at the potatoes in silence for a while. I couldn't help thinking about what I'd been trying to write before. Maybe that's what had prompted me to ask about the name of the convent.

"This country sure hasn't been unified," I said after a while.

Sister Janette shook her head sadly. "I would like to think that it may again become what could be truthfully called the *United* States of America, but after the devastation and killing, it is difficult to see how it could be."

I recalled the words I'd just written—*brotherhood . . . united as one.*

"Our nation is not so much different than the church that calls itself Christ's body," Sister Janette went on. "People on all sides of every argument like to think that God is with *them*. Southerners and Northerners alike all prayed to the same God, and all invoked his blessings to help them prevail."

"Will there ever be unity?" I asked.

"In the church, or in this land?"

"Both, I guess."

Sister Janette smiled, but again her countenance was sad. "I don't know, Corrie. The war is over, so I suppose I should be optimistic about the country. Yet I confess to many questions.

Unity would seem to have come back to our nation. But I cannot help wondering if it is really worthy of the name unity, or if it is only defeat. Was there ever unity before the war? It is not likely. The states never were united, and it took a dreadful war for us to find out just how disunited we were all along."

"How about in the church?"

"I hope it will not take such a conflict among God's people for us to awaken to the truth of Jesus' prayer in John seventeen. I am hopeful. All of us here at the convent are hopeful. Of course there *will* be unity among God's people. Jesus prayed for it. But when . . . that is not an easy question to answer."

We were silent again, and after peeling the rest of that evening's potatoes and putting them on the cookstove to boil, we went outside. By then we were talking about other things and did not return to the subject of unity, either in the church or the country.

But all the rest of that afternoon and evening, my mind was filled with the two images of Robert E. Lee and Ulysses S. Grant—what it must have been like the moment their eyes met in the house in Appomattox, and what it must have felt like as their hands clasped.

Was that unity?

Did that handshake symbolize, perhaps for the first time—even more than what had happened when the founding fathers had written the Declaration of Independence and the Constitution—the true *uniting* of the northern and southern factions of this great land?

Was that moment the *true* beginning of what could rightfully now be called the *United* States of America?

I drifted off to sleep that night pondering the question and wondering what Jesus thought of it all.

CHAPTER 40

THE LETTER

When the letter came I didn't even look at the postmark. I first stared at it with disbelief. My reaction was so unlike when Mr. Hay had given me the one addressed to the White House. This time I was so calm that I almost put it away until later. I hadn't thought I would hear from him again . . . at all! I suppose I'd already prepared my emotions to stay in place and not rise up with unpredictable femininity.

But it was no use! The moment I saw the handwriting, a quiet urge—small at first, but steadily rising—began to take hold of me to rip the envelope apart and get to the letter inside. I didn't stop to analyze why the writing looked so different. I recognized it, wasn't that enough? I knew I'd seen my name in that familiar hand before. I knew the particular curl at the top of the *C* and the wide graceful *H*.

I did my best to keep up a sedate outward demeanor. But inside, my heart was starting to pound. At the first opportunity I excused myself. I wanted to take a long walk outside and be alone as I read.

DEAR CORRIE,

With the war now over, it is time, in my opinion, for us to make amends and put the past behind us. We both went our separate ways for a time, doing what events compelled us to do. You will perhaps be gratified to hear me admit, which I freely do now to you, that I was wrong about the North and the South. It would certainly seem that I indeed put my money on the wrong horse, as it were, and that you were on

225

the side of the winner, after all.

Experience is a cruel teacher sometimes, but a necessary one. And even though the events of this last year have gone very badly for me, your own Mr. Lincoln has met with his demise as well. Thus it would seem that we both, you and I, Corrie, must face the future with a sad realism that life does not always yield the bright visions we dream of.

There have been things we both said and did in days past, in the heat of the moment. But one thing I sincerely meant was that I found you a remarkable young lady whom I was capable of admiring greatly. I still feel the same.

I would like to suggest that we let bygones be bygones, as the expression goes. If you can find it in your heart to forgive me standing you up in Sacramento, I will likewise forgive you for that nasty business in Richmond. We can both chalk it up to the war, which makes us all villains for a season.

Those times are past. I have carefully watched and read about you and all you have done. I have kept track of you, Corrie, and through a couple of the northern papers you wrote for last year have managed to track you to this address in Washington. I am hopeful you will find it within you to open your heart a crack again to one whom I venture to say once meant something rather more than a mere friendship to you.

The war ruined most in the South. But not all. For those able to see the handwriting on the wall, and read between the lines of what it said, there were great opportunities in the final months. Not many Southerners were shrewd enough to use the South's loss to their advantage. But I was one of those who was able to come away untarnished. *Opportunity*, Corrie, remember! It's all about being in the right place to strike when opportunity presents itself!

All this is by way of saying that I happen to have become quite a wealthy man, and it is my hope you will want to share in that wealth with me. I am presently in New York, where I maintain a suite of rooms at the Matador Palace. You are indisputably a woman of the world by now, Corrie, sufficiently so, I would think, not to be taken aback by an invitation to join me here in the city for a few days. I will wine and dine you and show you a time such as you have never had before in your life.

I do admire you, and know you are one who could go far

in the right circles, especially if you were to share your career with mine. Your visit here will enable us to talk at leisure about our future together.

I am, yours fondly,

CAL BURTON

I could barely finish reading it, I was so furious!

Furious at Cal for even *suggesting* such a thing! How dare he! Didn't he know me any better than that?

Furious at Christopher, too, as irrational at it sounds, for not being the one to have written me. Didn't he know how desperately I was longing to have even a single word from him?

Furious at myself I suppose, too. Furious for being such a stupid, emotional woman who was acting like a teenager in love! How could I have let myself be duped? It had obviously not been Christopher's writing on the envelope! Why didn't I notice?

Woman of the world! Ha!

That's the last thing I want to be, Cal! *Wine and dine* me in New York at a posh hotel! What makes him think I would care a straw for all that!

But all my ranting and fuming over Cal's letter couldn't keep the bitter tears of disappointment away, and eventually they came in a flood. I was so glad to be alone. I walked on, crying with abandon, my face wet. I wasn't really mad at all, just so hurt and disappointed and confused . . . and feeling so very lonely all of a sudden.

I didn't want to admit that my expectations had been dashed in hoping for a letter from Christopher, only to open it and be stung with a bitter memory from the past. Oh, I *did* long to hear from him! And now I couldn't help thinking of his face. I thought about what he would say to me if he were here. How I wished I could go back to the convent and then see him come walking through the door just like that Easter Sunday at Mrs. Timms'. By then I couldn't stop myself, and I dreamed of what it would be like to run to him, just like I had on that day, and feel him holding me in his arms for several moments as all the loneliness I had been feeling melted away.

But then the daydreams dissolved, and I again felt the warm tears on my face, and all the loneliness returned even worse, and

with it the unwelcome image of another face I *didn't* want to see—
Cal Burton's!

I wondered how the war could have made Cal a rich man.
Certainly not in an honest way, if I knew him as I thought I did!
The collapse of the South had probably left thousands of people
just ripe to being taken advantage of, and I was sure that's exactly
what Cal had done. He was the kind of person who could take
any situation and turn it to his advantage. And he would call it
opportunity!

That's what he was trying to do with me! Was I too just another
of his so-called *opportunities*!

Villains, Cal? I thought to myself. The war didn't make everyone a villain! I happen to know one that it made a man of, Cal!
Ten times the man you'll ever be, though if you saw him, you'd
probably laugh to hear me say so, because your kind can never
see the true manhood he walks in. God forgive me for what I may
have done wrong, but I hope it didn't make a villain of me either,
Cal—though from the sound of it that seems exactly what it made
of you.

With tears flowing again, I ripped Cal's letter into tiny shreds,
threw them down on the ground and stamped the pieces into the
grass and dirt, all spongy and wet from last night's rain.

Then I ran toward the woods. If I couldn't cry the loneliness
out of my heart, maybe I could drive it out by sheer exhaustion.

CHAPTER 41

TIDINGS . . . OF JOY!

Three days later the other letter arrived.

Numerous comments immediately circulated about the doubling of the convent's mail service since my arrival.

"Don't you all know what an important young lady Corrie is?" said Sister Janette. "She writes for all the biggest newspapers and was on special assignment from the White House. Why shouldn't she be getting important mail?"

The mention of the White House quickly brought an end to the conversation. It was still too soon even to think about President Lincoln's death without a sudden horrifying reminder of loss.

Again I sought the fields with the unopened letter in my hand. This time I truly was hesitant to open it. An indescribable fear seized me. I didn't know if I could endure any more pain without my heart crumbling to pieces altogether.

As I walked away from the convent buildings, the envelope burned in my hands, even as the fear burned in my heart. What could I do *but* read it? Even though it be the worst . . . I *had* to know!

I glanced down at the address again, over which Mrs. Richards had written the box number of the convent. But my eyes weren't looking at her writing but the hand that had penned my name underneath. This time there was no mistake. I looked at the postmark. The word *Richmond* was clearly visible.

At last I tore open the envelope and pulled out the papers inside. There were two pages. I breathed in deeply, then started to read. The first two words were the same as the letter from Cal, but after that they were as different as night and day. I savored every word, trying not to read too quickly.

DEAR CORRIE,

First let me humbly ask your forgiveness for my distant silence during your final two days here. I am so sorry! I know it was difficult and burdensome to you, and you no doubt have been fretting ever since over what it could have meant. Many things were on my mind, some of which were capable, even as they can do to a woman at times, of causing a man not to act himself.

I am unable to explain myself further at present. If the time should ever come when it is appropriate, I will make a full confession of my mental state at the time. Please, only forgive me and think of it no more, and be not anxious that in any way whatever you did anything to annoy or offend me. I doubt such could ever be the case! The emotional and mental turmoil prompting the quietude of my countenance all originated with me and not in any way in yourself. I thank you, even from this distance, for your kindness in granting this request for forgiveness.

My cheeks were already drenched with tears of happiness and relief. "Forgive you! Oh, Christopher," I whispered, "don't *you* know!" I dashed the back of my hand across my face, then read on.

Here all is the same . . . yet nothing is the same. An emptiness fills all the silent spaces. As I said to you before, Mrs. Timms misses you, the cows and chickens and goats and house all miss you . . . as do I most of all. But beyond that, there is a silent emptiness that the war's end has brought to the South. This war was never a noble one. Yet as long as it endured, there persisted a vain proud hope within the southern consciousness that somehow a day of prevailing would come when glory would belong to the Confederacy in something of a dreamlike memory of the 1840s and 1850s. I daresay those were not such pleasant times for the slaves. And yet the illusion persisted, right up until a few months ago, that happy days would come back to all of us again. The southern pride has slipped away as the Confederacy comes to an end. There is devastation everywhere, especially of the spirit.

The happy days are gone, the South is quiet, and its women mourn in black. Not so much for the loss of their sons and husbands and fathers as for the loss of their pride. I do not understand it myself. My *pride* is the *first* thing I should wish to lose, and the *last* thing in all the world I should ever wish to come near me again. Alas, for me! They of the South have lost theirs, but I, who hate the thing, still find clinging with stubbornness to me!

I'm sure you've heard of Mary Chesnut, wife of the southern senator, and, like you, a journal writer. She is often quoted in our papers these days. She wrote on the first of April: "Richmond has fallen—and I have no heart to write about it. . . . They are too many for us. Everything lost in Richmond." Her words reflect the sad, depressing air that is everywhere and over everything.

And I read in the New York *World*—perhaps you have already seen it: "There is a stillness, in the midst of which Richmond, with her ruins, her spectral roofs . . . and her unchanging spires, rests beneath a ghastly, fitful glare. . . . We are under the shadow of ruins. From the pavements where we walk . . . stretch a vista of devastation. . . . The wreck, the loneliness, seem interminable. . . . There is no sound of life, but the stillness of the catacomb, only as our footsteps fall dull on the deserted sidewalk, and a funeral troop of echoes bump . . . against the dead walls and closed shutters in reply, and this is Richmond. Says a melancholy voice: 'And this is Richmond.' "

Such it is, Corrie. I have been twice into the city since you left. I have walked her desolate streets, praying for God to rebuild this nation and to give the South back her life. Alas, I hated the Confederacy, but I love the South, and I loved Richmond. I have heard my own footsteps echo through the hollow alleys. I have climbed through the fallen rubble of bricks where once were buildings of commerce and business and life. I sought my old church to see if anyone was about, anyone who needed comfort or help. But it was shut up tight and silent as a tomb. The only people about drifted aimlessly and silently along the brick-strewn streets. There were no smiles, no eye contact, no shared humanity. They all want to wallow in their misery.

Adding to the desolation, though none here would admit

to such a heresy, is the loss of Abraham Lincoln, a great man by any estimation. Grant and Lee are both great men, it is said. But greatness reveals itself at many levels through the course of history, and men of Lincoln's stature come but once in a generation or two. By my perception he was the one man who, having guided us through the war, the reunited nation might have looked to for the strong leadership necessary at such an urgent and critical time. But now he is gone.

By his one desperate act, the actor Booth achieved the larger stage he sought, and thinking to avenge the South, in fact, did it more harm and damage than anything any man could have done. I fear now that the process of reconstruction will be long, tedious, and bitterly painful for the South. Lincoln was probably the best friend the South could have had at this moment in her cloudy history.

I am kept busy these days, not only with the farm, but with doing what I can to help the huge flow of persons suddenly roaming the byways of the South—freed Negroes, soldiers trying to get back to their homes—wounded, shoeless, starving. Oh, the grief that is all around, and how weak I feel to help! I have even encountered two or three men who were in Libby Prison and who remember me from there. Mrs. Timms' barn some nights resembles a hospital ward and rescue mission all in one!

I know I am going on and on. Forgive me . . . again! You cannot know how pleasurable it was to have someone with whom to share my thoughts. I fear I grew addicted to it altogether. My journal thus now seems a very uninteresting and impersonal companion alongside someone with a face and a mouth that moves and eyes that light up when she reads the words I write, as I flatter myself yours are doing at this moment.

If you should do me the honor of returning the communication of these sheets with some of your own penned to me, I promise my eyes shall dance and my mouth laugh over your words, too, if you find such a proposal more interesting than *your* journal.

You left your medal from the President here. You had shown it to us and it was sitting on the mantel when the dreadful news came to us about Mr. Lincoln. I will, however, guard it with my very life, and keep it safe for you.

With regards kinder than you can know,

CHRISTOPHER BRAXTON

CHAPTER 42

TWO FACES

I just had to stop crying! Every time I turned around I was in tears again!

By the time I got to Christopher's signature I could hardly see the letter on the page from my wet eyes! And how I did laugh with his quaint ways of expressing himself with such dry wit. He knew I would laugh too, and I could hear his voice chuckling as he set his pen down. He probably knew I would cry too! If not, then he didn't know me yet as well as I suspected he did.

I hadn't even thought about the medal. My mind had been too occupied with other things.

What a weight was lifted from my shoulders with his letter. I had been so worried that he was angry, that something had changed, or that I might never hear from him again.

My tears and laughter and smiles gradually subsided. I continued to walk along, out of sight from the convent now, over a little hill toward the north.

I had received two letters this week. And there could not have been any stronger contrast between the two, nor between the two men who had written them. How could I ever have been so blind to the realities of his nature and character as to be fascinated, even in love, with Cal? The very thought both embarrassed and baffled me.

I suppose that a man's or a woman's true nature doesn't always show itself until life's successes and strains knock it around some to see how strong the stuff is that it's made of. When a man deliberately tries to flatter a young woman, as Cal did, if she doesn't

233

keep her wits about her, she'll get her head turned in just the opposite direction from where she ought to be looking.

And I hadn't always had the benefit of knowing a man like Christopher with whom to compare men like Cal. If you've never known the real thing, then the counterfeit looks real enough. Somebody told me that's the way it is with diamonds. The cheap, flawed gems look dazzling to the untrained eye. But once you've seen a pure, flawless, brilliantly cut stone, all at once your eyes are open to all the marks and scars and dark or dull spots in those of less value.

Until you've known people who walk confidently and truthfully and without compromise in their relationship with their Father, you just don't know that so many others—to all external appearances whole and mature—are in reality far less complete. It's easy to take one look at an apple or a pumpkin or a cabbage or a horse or a house and tell right away if it's complete. If it's dwarfed or stinted, or only half-grown, or if the dog is missing a leg, or if the house doesn't have a roof, anybody can tell that something's wrong.

It's different with people. Wholeness in people isn't that easy to see.

Maturity isn't the kind of thing you can see from the outside. Neither is wisdom, although there are hints of it in the eyes. But it takes mature eyes to discern mature eyes, and wise eyes to see them in another. They're not the kinds of things you can detect just from hearing somebody talk either. Even Cal's smooth words fooled me into thinking he was a more complete person than he really was.

I don't know if I can exactly put my finger just on *what* makes a man mature and wise, or a woman too for that matter. How they make decisions . . . how they carry themselves . . . what things are important to them . . . how unselfish they are . . . whether they *do* the things they know, or are content just to know them . . . I reckon there's all sorts of things you could look at.

After reading Christopher's letter, I found myself thinking a lot about the faces of the two men—Cal Burton and Christopher Braxton. Images of both of them filled my memory, looks I remembered, things they'd said, hearing them talk and laugh, listening to their serious sides, recalling things each had said to me about his passions and dreams—for they both had a passionate side that desperately hungered to reach certain objectives.

But how different were the two men, and the directions they were going in life!

Cal's passion was *opportunity* . . . Christopher's passion was *truth*.

Cal lost no chance to do anything that would help advance *him* . . . Christopher lost no opportunity to help *others*.

Cal's goal was to *get and achieve* all he could . . . Christopher's goal was to *serve*.

Cal looked at people in terms of what he could *get* from them . . . Christopher looked at people and asked what he could *do* for them.

Cal was a *taker* . . . Christopher was a *helper*.

Cal's life was *himself* . . . Christopher's life was *God's*.

It was becoming more and more obvious to me every day that I had indeed met the real thing, the valued diamond, the eyes reflecting the depths of maturity and wisdom behind them, not a perfect man but a *whole* man, whose purpose in life was established.

By now whatever remaining images lingered from the memory of Cal's face faded altogether. Only the quiet, smiling mouth, penetrating but sparkling eyes, and light brown hair of Christopher's countenance remained to fill my imagination out to the very edges of my brain.

I *had* to talk to him, touch him, communicate to him, respond with my heart to the words out of his heart that he had given to me! If paper and pen were the only way to reach across the miles and touch him, then I would use them.

But I would still have his bright face in my mind's eye to light up every word!

CHAPTER 43

CORRESPONDENCE

DEAR CHRISTOPHER,

I received your letter. But as you will see I am no longer in Washington. Mrs. Richards forwarded it to me in Pennsylvania. I am with the Sisters of Unity at the Convent of John Seventeen that I told you about.

After the funeral train bearing the President's body left the station, to take him to his burial in Springfield, I realized that there was nothing remaining to keep me in the Capital. There were many, many things on my mind, one of which, I have to admit, was the silence and awkwardness that you mentioned in your letter. I forgive you for anything, as you asked, though it seems a mite strange to say it. But even without that, suddenly Washington felt to me a little like you described Richmond—a place without much life. I needed to find some time to pray and think with God about what's to become of me next, and the first place I thought of was the convent. So I came here, and here I am, and you can see the post box number if you care to write me again. I would like it if you did.

When I met Sister Janette on the train, I wondered what it was like to be a nun—many young girls do, I think. I'd never thought of it much before that. But once I was here, and I saw what lives of dedication the Sisters live to the Lord and to one another and to their friends and neighbors and other Christians, something deep in my soul hungered to give myself that completely to Jesus, too. I don't know if I'm supposed to stay here. But I knew I had to come back and at least

237

tell the Lord I'm willing to if he wants me to.

So that's what I'm doing here, and that's what I'm telling God. And I am also asking about writing, and, well . . . lots of others things that are on my mind, too. I feel as if I'm going through a tunnel and I can't see to the other side. The light at the other end of the tunnel is my future, and the place where I entered the tunnel is everything that happened up to the end of the war. Now I'm walking from one end to the other. But I can't see too much of what's ahead.

This is a short letter. I kind of ran out of things to say. I'll try to write you again. Please write.

Yours sincerely,
CORNELIA BELLE HOLLISTER

What an uninteresting letter, I thought to myself as I laid down my pen. He'll never write back if I send him that!

It sat for two days. Finally I hurriedly stuffed it into an envelope and gave it to Sister Mary to mail before I had the chance to have any second thoughts.

Eight days later another letter came for me. My trembling fingers were back!

DEAR CORRIE,

Should I address you, as you so formally signed your letter, as "Cornelia"?

I too know something about tunnels. There are certain aspects of tunnel darkness surrounding my vision of things ahead now also. It is not the first time such darkness has occurred in my life, however, and I have learned that God has appointed such times for our maturing. That is not to say that I enjoy the process, only that I recognize the spiritual benefit to be derived from our human eyes being unseeing for certain seasons, enabling us to learn—if we will—to trust to the sight of the Father, who sees even when all to us is darkness and who *always* sees what is for our best. I have also learned that if we see too much with the eyes of our flesh, we often mistake what we may want for a higher "best" that we cannot then see. By taking away our sight for a time, the Father forces us to stretch out our hands and place them in his. Then he leads us, even in our sightlessness, to the best he has purposed for us from the beginning.

So in my own tunnel, I wait quietly for the Father's guidance, and trust his step to go before mine. I encourage you to do likewise. For light will surely dawn in time, and the very *best* always comes to those who trust him.

I do not mind a short letter. To hear from you is a delight. I imagine your voice speaking your words, and see your face as well. I thus receive a threefold blessing—through my eyes and ears, and into my heart.

I understand what you say about the convent, although it was my impression that most young women wanted to get married and have a family. I was always fascinated with the thought of the monastery when I was young, and I thought more than once about being a monk. The solitude appealed to me. But I am not Catholic. And as much as I relish being alone, still I crave the company of people too. There must be someone to serve! So I became a minister of the gospel instead. And yet now I curiously find myself almost living the solitary life of a monk!

And so we are back to the subject of tunnels and not being able to see the far end of God's design. In the matter of my ministry too, therefore, I wait, and all will be well.

Did you read that Booth was located and shot? The fellow named Herold surrendered at the same time. They have apparently taken some others into custody and set a large investigation underway to round up the entire conspiracy. I have heard nothing about the two fellows you mentioned, however, in connection with it—Burton and Surratt, weren't they?

This too is short . . . for me at any rate. As you know from looking over my journal, I can be a long-winded preacher when the right bee gets trapped inside my bonnet.

> Cordially,
> CHRISTOPHER

This time I didn't even wait a minute. I pulled out a sheet of paper and my pen and bottle of ink and began my reply immediately.

DEAR CHRISTOPHER,

No, don't call me Cornelia.

I will take encouragement from your words about tunnels as you told me to. Sometimes you sound like Almeda and

Rev. Rutledge put together. But you being just about my own age makes it easier to remember you are still learning about the things you talk about, just as I am.

Maybe our tunnels will cross in the dark and we'll be able to help each other out if we stumble over the rocks.

I'm glad you became a minister instead of a monk. Otherwise you wouldn't have been there to save my life. I'd be dead. And worse, I'd have never met you. Now that I think about it, I suppose it's even good they made you leave that church. Good for me, that is, because if they hadn't, you wouldn't have been at Mrs. Timms', and there I'd be—dead again. Is that what you mean, about everything always turning out for the best?

About being a nun . . . I don't know about other girls when they start getting old enough to think about such things. I reckon you're right about most of them wanting to find a man to take care of them and be married and have a family. But I think many girls are afraid no man will want to marry them, so they secretly figure that if they join a convent, then that'll keep them from having to worry about it. If you're a nun you won't get married, but it protects you from the humiliation of waiting and waiting and then finding out no man wants you. Then you're an old maid and people talk about you behind your back and wonder why you never found a husband. Girls who become nuns choose the lesser of two bad things that can become of them, and at least they have a place to live and belong and some friends who aren't married either.

For me, thinking of joining the convent here had nothing to do with marrying or not marrying. I figured that had already been sort of decided for me a long time ago. One of the first things I remember my ma saying to me was that I wasn't likely to fetch a husband so I ought to take up writing or teaching so I'd be able to take care of myself. I think she meant I wasn't comely enough, and I always accepted that as the way it was meant to be, because my ma was a pretty smart lady. And that's how I got started writing.

Speaking of my ma, an idea came into my head just two days ago and I haven't been able to stop thinking about it. I'm not so very far from where we used to live with my ma and pa, before Pa left and we went to California. I might take a trip up to New York to see if I can find our old farm and see who's there now. I may never have the chance again.

The sisters here don't know you, but they see me getting letters from you and writing back, and they send you greetings in Jesus. I wish you could know them. They are such wonderful ladies! I want to be a servant like they are, wherever the other end of my tunnel leads.

Bless you. Write!
CORRIE

I signed the letter, put it in an envelope, sealed it, and wrote Christopher's address on the front, then laid it on the table by the door. I went out for a walk.

It always felt so *good* to communicate, to say things from deep down, to put on paper what you really felt. How could anybody not want to be a writer, I thought, or at least keep a journal!

I walked and walked, far across the fields, through a wood, along a little stream. I felt good, free, contented. I hadn't felt this way for a long time. Maybe I couldn't see what was out there ahead in my future, but the feeling was gradually coming back to me that there *was* light ahead, and that the Father saw, and that he *was* guiding and leading me, just as Christopher had said.

Christopher had told me to take encouragement from his words. And I did. I suppose it felt good, too, just to know someone was there to care about me and to tell me something like that to do. It was a little thing, for him to give me that advice. But it made me feel a little less alone, as if there were people—friends, brothers and sisters in the community of believers—who were sharing life, even the tunnel, with me.

Suddenly I stopped dead in my tracks.

All at once I realized what I'd done.

I can't send that letter talking about marriage and what Ma said and the fear of being an old maid to Christopher! I thought with a sudden sense of panic.

What could I have been thinking to have let myself get so free and open with my words! I had no intention of saying all that!

A dread feeling swept over me. The next instant I was running as fast as I could back to the convent. It took me fifteen minutes to get there. I'd been out well over an hour, lazily walking all over the place.

I burst panting through the door and glanced down at the table.

"What is it, Corrie?" asked Sister Janette.

"The letter . . . I had a letter here," I gasped.

"Yes, I put it with the other mail. The postal carriage was here thirty or forty minutes ago."

CHAPTER 44

A FRANTIC TELEGRAM

The thought of Christopher reading what I'd written was mortifying!

The rest of the day I tried to enter into some of the work around the convent. But I was too distracted to do anybody much good.

If I had any intention of being a nun, I chastised myself, I'd better figure out some way to quit being so preoccupied with a man! Nuns didn't act like I was behaving.

The next morning I had an idea.

I asked if I could borrow a horse. I saddled one of the riding mares and took her into Lancaster as fast as I dared but without galloping her the whole way.

I located the Western Union office, tied the horse outside, and walked in. I already knew exactly what I wanted to say.

"I'd like to send a telegram," I told the fellow behind the counter.

"Where to, ma'am?"

"Richmond."

"Virginia?"

I nodded.

"Lots of lines down in the South. Might take a few days."

"How many days?" I said.

"Oh, some places been running three, four—"

"How about Richmond?"

"I'd guess two, three at the most."

"And mail?"

"Mail's usually three or four days."

243

I swallowed. I didn't have much choice. "I'll go ahead with the telegram," I said.

"Write it down there," said the man.

I took the paper and pencil on the counter and wrote out: *To Christopher Braxton. Urgently request you to not read next letter. Corrie.*

I handed it to the man and gave him the address. He counted the words while I stood there dying of embarrassment, hoping he could somehow send it without reading what I'd said, then told me how much it was.

I paid him, watched him send it over the wire, then left.

Lancaster was a long way to come for a five-minute errand, but now I found myself breathing a little easier.

All the way home I thought about what I'd told Christopher in the letter about going up to New York. I had been thinking about the war and the article about the two generals I had started. More and more it had come to me that maybe what the war *meant* had to do with the country coming of age, growing up out of the infancy of the Revolutionary War and the early 1800s into young adulthood, and then finally adulthood itself. Maybe this war we'd just fought with ourselves was the country's way of doing just that—coming into adulthood, having to fight, like I had said about Lee and Grant, as brothers who eventually learned to put the conflict behind them, shake hands, and become men. Maybe it was necessary as part of that process for a nation to look at itself, even to look *inside* itself, to find out some things about itself that it didn't know before—adult things, the kinds of things without which you can't become fully mature unless you know about yourself.

And maybe the process was the same in people—that process of looking inside yourself to find out what's there, maybe looking into corners of yourself you've never looked at before, looking at them in a new way, and asking yourself what it all means, and what kind of person you are. It seemed like maybe there wasn't any other way to really know yourself all the way down to the roots without that kind of self-examination. Maybe that's part of what growing up was all about.

How could I know what God wanted me to do now, for the

rest of my life, or at least for the next chapter of it, if there were still things about myself I didn't know fully.

The more I thought about it, the more I came to the conclusion that there couldn't be any better place to ask the Lord about myself, and about what he wanted me to do, than the very place where my life had begun. I remembered thinking a lot about New York on the stagecoach two years before, and looking backward toward the past with different and more mature eyes. I'd even thought of a visit back then, but had become so busy with everything that had happened since that I'd forgotten. But now at last the time seemed right. It was time to "look back with different eyes" and see what I could see. I reflected on it all the way back from Lancaster. And by the time I arrived back at the convent late that afternoon, I'd decided to do it. Ever since the idea had come to me, a sense had grown steadily stronger that more than idle curiosity was behind it, that it was something I needed to do, that the Lord had urged it upon me in answer to my prayers, and that perhaps the clarity that would light my path toward the future would come as I went back and took another look at the past where I'd come from.

Back at the convent I wrote to Christopher again. I would make sure I said nothing this time that I couldn't send!

DEAR CHRISTOPHER,

I apologize for the letter which I hope you received but did not read, and for the telegram. I am sometimes far more emotional than I want to admit, and I feel very foolish. So this will probably be very short.

I have decided to travel north, to New York State, to visit the place of my early childhood where we lived before going to California. We left exactly thirteen years ago. Most memories have grown dim, but I will know the old farm, and something tells me I need to go there.

I have sensed for a few days that this is something God may be telling me to do. There are still many questions, and I am still praying about what to do, but I think this may be part of the answer, or perhaps some guidance or answer will come when I am there.

I don't know how long I will be. Probably not longer than a week, maybe less. I will then return to the convent. After that . . . hopefully the tunnel will have shortened some so as to see the light at the other end.

Yours,
CORRIE

CHAPTER 45

THOUGHTS OF BELONGING

All the way north to New York on the train, I thought about my past, my future, Bridgeville, and Miracle Springs . . . and of course about Christopher.

How could he not be in my thoughts as much as all the rest? In a way, I suppose he filled more places in my mind than all the rest put together, though I was afraid to look straight at it and admit it. It was too fearsome a thing to admit, because then I'd have to admit that I cared about him a whole lot more than I'd let myself think, and admit that I was just like he'd said all young women were . . . that I *wanted* a man to love me and take care of me and protect me.

I didn't want to admit that.

I'd always wanted to think I didn't need anyone—even a man. I could do just fine on my own. I could write, I could do things, I could earn money, I even had a pretty decent career as a newspaper writer. I could take care of myself, with or without a pretty face.

There it was again . . . what Ma'd said to me when I was ten or twelve. I didn't hold it against Ma for saying it. I'd known before then that I wasn't pretty. Comely or not, I wasn't dumb, and I knew what a mirror was for as well as anyone, though I'd never found much pleasure in standing in front of one.

Maybe that letter I didn't want Christopher to read had more to do with what *I* thought of myself than embarrassment over what *he* might think. Maybe my words to him had scraped the scab off my own doubts about why the convent appealed to me, and opened up the sore spot that had been there underneath all this time, all these years since Ma had told me I wasn't the marrying sort.

Had her words hurt more than I'd realized?

I recall Miss Stansberry quoting Shakespeare, saying that when you protest too much about something and say it *doesn't* matter to you, that's really a way of showing it *does*. I think I may have said something like that. I'd gone on and on in that letter about the convent not mattering to me in the same way most young ladies might think of becoming a nun. I *did* admire Sister Janette and the others, and I *did* want to dedicate myself to Jesus with the same abandonment and fervor they had. But now I wondered if deep down in another place within me there lay some of that very fear I denied I felt—fear of being alone, fear of being an old maid, fear of being talked and snickered about . . . the fear that no one would want me or care about me.

I loved to write, to express myself, to communicate what I was thinking and feeling. But was part of my desire to be a newspaper writer just a roundabout way—like joining a convent might be for someone else—of making sure I had something to protect myself with so that people wouldn't look at me and think me strange for not being married?

Realizing how much I cared for Christopher, and how much I cared what he thought of me, made me vulnerable to all these fears and questions about myself in a whole new way.

But it was hard to admit you cared what someone thought! The minute you did, the carefully constructed house of self-protection collapsed, and in rushed fears and anxieties and self-doubts and dilemmas of self-worth that you never knew were lurking down beneath the surface!

It was as if I didn't know who I was anymore, just like during those first weeks under Christopher's care. Now, I knew the name *Corrie Hollister*. I knew my history. I was on my way to the very place where I was born, where I had lived half my life. I could see all the events of my twenty-eight years stretching out from this place, all the way to California and then back again . . . all the way right up to this moment. I knew the *events* that had gone together to make up what is called my "life."

Yet I found myself wondering if I really knew what is most important of all—did I know *myself*?

Was I afraid to face that one, that deepest, that most personal truth about one's *self*—the horrible fear that maybe no one really *does* care about you all the way down into the deepest places of your being where no one sees?

Is that why I hadn't wanted Christopher to read the letter—because I was afraid it might expose what he thought about me? And just the possibility of discovering that he didn't care for me in the same way I found myself caring for him was simply too painful a thought to face!

Yes . . . I was afraid. Not with the kind of fear that a wild bear strikes into you when you're out walking alone in the forest, but a deep, quiet, lonely sense of dread that no one is there to hear the silent cries of your heart.

I *wanted* somebody to hear, to care! I *wanted* somebody to know me! I wanted to talk and know that I was heard. I wanted to laugh and cry and know that it mattered to someone.

I wanted somewhere to *belong*.

Was it in Washington with my friends and fellow workers with the Sanitary Commission? No. The war was over and all that would change now. That had been something for me to *do*, but not a place to belong.

Was it at the Convent of John Seventeen with the Sisters of Unity? Perhaps it could be. But in my deepest heart I did not think so. There were tight bonds of unity *with* the sisters. I would never forget them and would always consider them among my dearest friends. But I was not one *of* them. Not because I wasn't Catholic, but that I didn't feel called by God to set myself apart in the same way they had.

Could it be here, in this town toward which I was riding? There had at one time been a home there, a place to live and grow with my family. But it could not be so again. Pa had left before we had. Ma was dead. No kin of ours were left—that I knew of anyhow—no friends, not even a handful of acquaintances who might remember Ma or Pa or us kids. No, this place had stopped being a place for the Hollister and Belle clans to belong when we'd pulled up stakes and left thirteen years ago.

Then why was I going there?

Maybe I needed to go to the very spot where life had begun for me in order to find out once and for all just where I *did* belong. Was it for this time, these next days, that God had prompted me to leave Washington and to pray and reflect about my life and future? Is this where the *rest* of my life was to begin—now, from here, where the first half of my life had begun twenty-eight years ago?

What was God getting ready to show me?

CHAPTER 46

THE TOWN OF MY CHILDHOOD

It was two days later when I walked out of the boardinghouse in Bridgeville where we'd lived so long ago, and began to make my way through the town.

The northbound train had arrived late in the afternoon. I purposely didn't try to look around after arriving, but made my way straight to one of the two boardinghouses in town. I wanted to save my impressions for the next morning.

That evening I'd thought a lot about what I was doing, and I'd prayed and asked God to use this time to bring things back to my memory that he wanted me to think about. I asked him to make a daughter of me he would be proud of. I asked him to wash and cleanse away any last pieces of my childhood that were still clinging to me like a bit of dirt that he didn't want soiling my clothes anymore. I asked him to give me a grown-up's eyes about my whole life—about what had happened here so long ago, and about all that my life had been since. I asked him to give me *his* eyes to see, not only my life, but inside my deepest self.

So when I went out early the next morning, I was full of a sense of anticipation and expectancy, wondering how God might be going to answer all those prayers, and how he was going to use this time full of memories to put my youth behind me.

Bridgeville wasn't a large town, then or now, but it had changed some and I could tell it was growing. There'd been no rail line back then, of course. There were new buildings and stores and homes, but most of it I recognized as unchanged. As I made my way out, all the stores were just opening, and people were busy cleaning windows and putting things in their displays and sweeping off the board walkways in front. Most of the men nodded or tipped their hats at me. I didn't recognize anybody as I made my way along the main row of storefronts.

Suddenly I stopped. I couldn't believe my eyes. Right in front of me was a big red-painted sign hanging across the sidewalk with the words "Belle Hardware."

I'd completely forgotten! Grandpa Belle's cousin's store! But I remembered it as a tiny little place without much of anything in it, and I thought it had died out years ago.

I walked inside and up to the man who was sweeping the floor in front of the counter.

"Morning, miss," he said.

"Good morning," I replied. "Are you . . . are you Mr. Belle?" I asked timidly.

"No," he laughed. "There's no Mr. Belle here."

"But what about the name?"

"Just the name of the store, miss. Nothing more."

"How did it get the name?"

"Beats me. That was the name on the front when I bought the store five years back."

"Did you buy it from Mr. Belle?"

"No, from a fellow named Smothers. He'd had it for five years, and he didn't know of no Belles associated with it either. But it's been the name of the place all this time, so both he and I figured there was no reason to change it. Why you asking, miss?"

"Oh, nothing much," I said. "Belle's my middle name, that's all. I thought maybe there was some relation."

"Not likely, miss."

Slowly I walked back outside, disappointed. I suppose something inside me had hoped to find some link to the past. Being totally isolated, cut off from your childhood is an empty feeling. To be completely whole you need to feel the connections to your roots, places and people and events from out of your past. And as I walked through the town, a part of me so desperately wanted to *touch* my own past, to get back to it somehow, to get "inside" those former times again, to relive what I felt then, but through the perspective and spiritual awareness of an adult. Somehow, to complete the wholeness of adulthood, I needed God to reopen my childhood to me in a way that joined the two into one.

Part of this was seeing and touching all these familiar places, remembering what I had felt so many years ago. I walked out of the hardware store, stopped, and leaned up against a pole standing at the outer edge of the walk holding up part of the store's sign. Unconsciously I stood there a moment, my arm draped around the rough piece of wood, my fingers rubbing at its cracks and the roughness of its grain. Suddenly my fingers remembered something! But it wasn't here, not on *this* pole!

The next instant I was running along the boards, my shoes making a loud *clomp, clomp, clomp*! To the end of the row of buildings I ran, then across the dirt street, right on the sidewalk on the other side, and to the end of the street . . . to the livery stable.

There it was! I ran straight to it, nearly out of breath. Out in front sat an old wood watering trough, still full of dirty water, with a long rail for tying up horses behind it. I ran to the end of the rail.

The day was so clear in my memory it could have been yesterday! Pa had come into town with Zack and me. I was seven or eight. Zack must have been only five or six. I can't imagine that Pa would have given him a knife when he was that young, but wherever he got it, he had it that day. Pa went into the livery. I remembered his voice as clear as day now, saying to me, "You stay here, little girl, an' watch yer brother."

The minute he was gone, Zack pulled out his knife and started to scratch and carve away on the rail. I was afraid he'd cut his finger off and then it'd be my fault. But he handled that knife better than I'd figured he could and had his job done in less than five minutes.

"Let me try, Zack," I'd said

"You can't do it. You're a girl."

"I can too. Give me the knife," I replied, then grabbed it from him. But before I could get much done I heard Pa's voice saying he'd see the man inside next week, and then his steps coming back toward us. I quickly folded up the knife and handed it back to Zack, who stuffed it into his pocket.

Now, more than twenty years later, my fingers ran through the grooves Zack had made, as weathered with time as the wood itself, and the awkwardly shaped letters that spelled out the words: Z - A - C - K.

I smiled at the spelling. And yet before my finger had completed the C - O - R - R, which was all there was of my own name, a great lump filled my breast and tears flooded my eyes.

I don't know why. The memory was a happy one. But something about reliving it so vividly brought such a stab of nostalgic melancholy that I could hardly stand it. So many feelings came pouring into me as my fingers caressed the ancient letters whittled out of that tie pole—arguments I'd had with Zack through the years, and happy times too, but you usually remember more of the hurtful things you did to other people, and tend to forget what they did to you. I remembered Zack's and Pa's differences and Zack's leaving home, and then that day he came back. Even as I was hearing Zack's five-year-old little voice talking to me and Pa from that day outside the livery in New York, I was at the same time seeing Pa and Zack in each other's arms the day Zack returned from Nevada, saying words to each other that no one else ever heard.

The memory was too full. I could hardly take another moment of it! Blinking back the tears, I turned and walked back toward the town and away from the livery, struggling to draw in deep breaths to steady my emotions. I hadn't counted on God's answering my prayers in such a personal and emotional way!

I walked slowly down the main street, grinning inside as if I had a secret, almost expecting everyone to know me, memory after memory now coming to me. In spite of the changes, everything was so familiar. I felt as if I were walking in two worlds at once, fully conscious and awake and being both a twenty-eight-year-old and a seven-year-old at the same time. I even *felt* things in both a seven-year-old and a twenty-eight-year-old way, which made my tears and the lumps in my stomach and throat and chest all the more keen and vivid.

I walked along, hardly noticing the shop windows I passed. Off in the distance I saw the white spire of the church rising above the other buildings. I wanted to see the church. There were memories there too, good ones. I hoped it would be open. I began making my way toward it.

As I passed the General Store, I glanced inside. A balding man was arranging some cans in the window. I continued on, then stopped. I turned for a closer look. I recognized him! His head was bald now, and his cheeks were more plump, but there could be no mistake.

I hurried inside. "Mr. Alexander?" I said.

"Yes, ma'am?" he replied, glancing up from where he stood bending toward his window display case.

"Do you remember Agatha Hollister?" I said.

He straightened himself up, screwing his face up into a thoughtful expression. "No, young lady," he said slowly, "can't say as I do."

"How about Nick Belle?"

Immediately his face lit up in recognition. "Not likely I'd forget him!" he said. "Oh, you must mean Aggie *Belle*," he added quickly. "Nick and Aggie—sure, I remember them. Went to school together, sat in Sunday school together. Why? They some relation of yours?"

"Agatha was my mother," I said.

He turned and walked toward me, busily looking me over from head to toe. "You don't mean to tell me," he said slowly, "that you're . . . you're—"

"Corrie," I finished for him.

"Corrie! That's it. Aggie's little girl!"

"That's me," I said, smiling.

"No fooling! I haven't heard a thing about you all since you packed up for California. How is your ma?"

I told him she'd died on the way across the desert.

"I'm sorry to hear that, Corrie. How about your uncle . . . you ever get onto his trail?"

"We found him, and our pa. We're living with them."

"All you kids . . . living with those two wild men," he said, half in question, half in disbelief.

I laughed. "They're not wild, and we're not kids anymore, Mr. Alexander. Uncle Nick's married, Pa's remarried, and even little Tad's twenty years old."

A cloud passed over his face. "Well, they were wild enough years ago," he said. "Nick gave my father such a bad time in Sunday school, and then the older he got, the wilder he got."

"He's as nice a man as you'd ever want to meet now," I said.

"Well, you tell him hello from Jeb Alexander next time you see him, Corrie," he said. "Not that he'd be likely to remember a little kid he thrashed a time or two. But it was a long time ago, like you said, so you give him my best."

"I will. Did you know my father too?" I asked.

"No, can't say I did, not well at least. Saw him around town of course, after he and Aggie were married. But then Nick got himself in that trouble, then your pa was gone too . . . you know how it was. So I reckon I never had the chance to know your pa real well."

We talked for several more minutes. I told him what I'd been doing and why I was there. He was real friendly and invited me to have dinner with him and his wife before I left town.

"Is the minister still here?" I asked. "Rev. . . . hmm, I guess I've forgotten his name."

"Rev. Gilman?"

"That's him," I answered.

"No, he passed on, oh, I'd say five or six years back. He'd retired from the pulpit four years before that. He was an old man."

I nodded. "I suppose so. He seemed pretty old as I remember him, but I thought he'd still be alive."

"We got a young preacher now. He's all right, I reckon. Little too much fire and brimstone for me, though."

We chatted a little more, I said I'd come back and talk to him about dinner, and then I left, thinking I'd walk to the other end of town and visit the church.

About halfway there, along a street that ran perpendicular to the main street, I saw the sheriff's office. Without even thinking about why, I found myself crossing the street and heading toward it. By now there were people and horses and wagons about, and I had to cross with care. The town was busier than I'd remembered it. A few people nodded or smiled or greeted me, but most folks seemed to be about their business and didn't seem too concerned about a stranger in town.

I shuddered momentarily as I walked through the door, taking in the wanted posters on the wall opposite, and the iron bars of the jail cell down a corridor to the right. A young man about my own age sat at a desk in the middle of the room. He glanced up as I entered.

"Howdy, ma'am," he said. "Something I can do for you?"

"I'm just visiting in town," I answered, not even knowing quite why I'd come here, maybe just to satisfy any lingering anxieties about the past. "Have you heard of a Drummond Hollister?"

The man shook his head slowly and thoughtfully. "No," he said, still mulling the name over. "No . . . don't believe I have."

"Or a Nick Belle?"

"Nope. Never heard of neither of them. Why? They causing you some kind of trouble, young lady?"

I smiled. "No, no trouble. I just wondered if you'd heard of them, that's all."

"Should I have?"

"No . . . probably not," suddenly thinking about how I could get this young sheriff or deputy from thinking any more about Pa and Uncle Nick. "What about the Catskill Gulch gang?" I asked.

Now his face showed an instant recognition, and he let out a long whistle. "You bet I heard of them! Who around here hasn't, though none of them have been seen for twenty years. What's your interest in varmints like that?"

"Just curiosity. What did they do?"

"What *didn't* they do's more like it. Mostly they was robbers, though there was killing that went along with it."

"Are . . . are all of them still wanted?"

"Nah, most of the warrants got canceled when old Judd's son went into Catskill and turned in all the loot."

"I didn't hear about that," I said.

"Judd, he was the ringleader. Well, I guess when he was on his deathbed he told his son everything that had happened on one of their big bank jobs, including where they'd stashed the money. When he died, his son didn't want no part of it. He found the loot, turned it in, and told the sheriff there everything Judd had said. Cleared up most of the warrants, all except for two fellers they never found . . . let's see what were their names—the two

258

the sheriff figured had done most all the killing."

"Do you remember the names?" I asked, hardly able to keep from showing the nervousness I felt inside.

"I forgot—let's see, I think I got it here someplace." He opened a drawer and sifted through a bunch of papers, then pulled one out and held it up.

"Yep, here it is," he said. "Only two Catskill boys still wanted—Jesse Harris and Big Hank McFee . . . a couple of nasty coots, those two are."

I breathed a hugh sigh of relief. I couldn't wait to tell Pa and Uncle Nick!

"Those are the only ones?"

"Yep, though neither of those boys, or none of the old gang, for that matter, have been around here in a coon's age that I know of. You sure you're just curious?"

"Yes, that's all," I said, then thanked him and left.

I didn't know why I'd asked about Pa and Uncle Nick. I suppose I'd been thinking about Pa ever since the livery stable. I was glad I did, though. This news would bring him such a sense of relief.

Now that I was thinking about Pa again, I realized that day Zack and I'd come into town with him was the last day I remember doing that. Maybe that's why it had come to me, because by the next month he was gone, and Zack and I didn't see him again until that day outside the Gold Nugget in Miracle Springs.

People talk about things going around in circles. Here I was in the very town Pa had left twenty years earlier, standing right in the very sheriff's office where wanted posters about Pa and Uncle Nick had once hung up on the wall. Now I had come back, Pa's own daughter, just like a great big circle that stretched all the way out to California and back.

Pa and I'd talked plenty that first couple years we were together about the pain his leaving had caused me. Zack hadn't faced what it had done to him inside until that year after he'd joined the Pony Express. Both of us had said some pretty strong things to Pa about the hurt it had caused us.

But it's funny, the older you get the less hurtful become the things that other people have done *to* you, and the more you regret the words you've said to others that caused *them* pain. And now as I walked along through the town, snatches of conversations, words, images, and faces began to come back to me, all related to Pa's leaving us as he did. But there wasn't any pain I felt for what Pa'd done to me or to Ma or to our family. That had all been taken care of long ago for me. I could no more hold anything against Pa than I could hold it against Ma for dying. I loved them both too much for that! The pain I felt was for Pa himself, knowing how bad he felt for what he'd done.

Now began to echo through my ears things I had said to Pa that day not long after we'd gotten to California when Pa had flown off the handle to Uncle Nick for talking to us kids about Ma. It felt like a knife going straight into my heart to hear my own words.

You're a mean man . . . maybe we all oughta just leave just like you left Ma. If it weren't for you, Ma'd still be alive. You ran out on her. You deserted us. . . . I hate you for what you did to Ma!

"Oh, God, forgive me for those awful things I said!" I whispered, not even trying to keep back the tears.

All I could think was how sorry I was for Pa. *He* was the one who faced the worst pain of all from what had happened—the pain of guilt. And I had only made it all the more agonizing for him by the things I'd said!

Somehow being right here, coming out of the sheriff's office, brought it all so close to my heart. I wanted so badly to be able to put my arms around Pa right then and tell him how much I loved him!

I wondered how old Ma and Pa were when they were married and lived here together. Probably about my age now. I think Ma was twenty-four or twenty-five when I was born. Now I was twenty-eight. When you realize you're as old as your parents were when you first have memories of them, it opens your eyes to lots of things. All of a sudden you find yourself inside your parents' skin looking at things from *their* point of view. All your life growing up they are separate from you and you see things only through your childish eyes. But then that day comes when suddenly you realize what it all felt like—for *them*.

There's a lot of growing up that happens in that moment.

Maybe more than at any other time in life, you suddenly realize what your ma or pa felt, especially what they might have felt about you. That's a pretty grown-up adult thing to be able to feel.

As I walked through the streets, thinking about all this, I realized that Ma and Pa were near my *own* age when they lived here right after I was born. Somehow that made them so real and close to me—for the first time in my life in just this way. I felt so close to Ma, even though she'd been dead for thirteen years. And I felt so close to Pa after leaving that jail, even though he was three thousand miles away, and suddenly I could hardly stand to be away from him for another second!

I breathed in deeply and brushed away a few remaining tears. I'd nearly reached the church.

I walked the remaining fifty yards or so, climbed up the four steps, and tried the door. It wasn't locked. Slowly I opened it and went inside.

The church was empty and still and dark. I glanced around. It was all so familiar, especially the smell. A thousand things came flooding back the instant my nostrils took in that first breath. If anybody had asked me a month before to describe the church we'd gone to when I was a child, I wouldn't have been able to so much as tell one thing about what the inside even looked like. Now *everything* came rushing back. The windows . . . the carpet, still threadbare in the same spot . . . the third pew on the right that was rickety from not sitting flat on the floor . . . the room where we kids had had Sunday school.

I sat down on the left side, where all the pews and benches were firmly on the floor. I just sat there in the solemn quiet, not thinking so much of God but just letting the flow of sights and sounds and memories wash past me, looking and listening and watching as they went, but not reaching out to grab at any of them for a closer look.

Gradually all the images faded and the quiet silence of the church came in and filled up all the places of my mind with the sense of God's presence.

I sat a long time. At last I began to pray.

"God," I said quietly, "whatever else you've got to show me while I'm here, whether it's about Pa or about Ma or Uncle Nick . . . and especially about *me*, open the eyes of my heart to see what you want me to. Lord, I do pray for Pa and for all he's gone through. Help him to know how much we all love and care for him."

I stopped. As much as I did love Pa, the thought struck me even as I was praying for him that my visit here wasn't mostly about him. Things had been settled between him and me a long time ago.

Mostly, I realized, it had to do with *me*. "Lord," I prayed again, "I know you're speaking to me, maturing me, showing me things, and preparing me for my life ahead. I know you're putting the past of my childhood behind me and that's why you wanted me to come here. I know there's probably lots of reasons you wanted me to come here, but help me to see the main thing about myself that you want me to see. I want to look forward from now on, and not have to look back anymore. Show me what you want to show me, and help me be who you want me to be."

It was enough to pray. I had to let God do the rest.

I got up. It was time to go visit the farm.

CHAPTER 47

THE OLD BROKEN WINDOW

It was two hours later when I slowly approached the house that had been my home for fifteen years of my life.

I'd gone back to the boardinghouse for a while, then rented a horse from the livery stable and ridden the two miles out into the country farmland.

I was surprised at how familiar everything was. I thought I had forgotten what the area looked like. But being here again, just as had happened everywhere I'd gone in town, suddenly the sights were as recent as yesterday.

Once out on the road out of town, all looked just as it had been. I felt as if I could have been walking along at fifteen with one of my younger brothers or sisters. I passed the farmhouses and barns of many neighbors whose names now began to come back to me.

I passed the lane off toward the house of our nearest neighbors, what we used to just call the Lucas place. Alma Lucas was Ma's best friend, especially after Pa left, though about all I could remember of her was trying to talk Ma out of going to California. "A fool's errand," was what she called it. "I don't know what you're thinking, Agatha Hollister, to head off west with five young'uns!"

Just thinking of her and her friendship with Ma brought Mrs. Lucas back more closely to my mind and I began to remember her more vividly. I turned the horse and guided him down the lane to their place.

When I reached the farmhouse, I dismounted and tied the

horse to a rail in front of the house, then walked up onto the porch. I knocked.

A minute or two later a man appeared. I didn't recognize him, and he didn't seem to know me.

"Is Mrs. Lucas at home?" I asked.

"Alma?"

I nodded.

"No, she ain't. She's upstate t' her brother's. His wife fell sick an' she's tendin' her."

"Thank you," I said, and turned to go. I paused on the first step and glanced back. He was still standing there watching me.

"Who's living in the place next up the road?" I asked.

"Nobody."

"How long's it been empty?"

" 'Bout a year. It's fer sale, miss. You need a run-down ol' farm?"

"No," I smiled, then turned and walked back to the horse.

A minute or two later I was back on the road, and I soon reached the lane leading to our old place. A "For Sale" sign was stuck in the middle of the pasture in front of the house. It looked as if it had been there a long time.

I approached the house. Grass and shrubs were grown up all around it, and the house looked lifeless and vacant and cold. And silent. Even as I rode up, I could remember the sound of voices and running and laughter and cows and pigs, and Ma's voice calling out now after one of us, now after another, all filled the air in the ear of my memory. I heard all the sounds of life with part of my senses, even as the steady clomping of the horse's feet beat out an empty cadence in the silent air surrounding the desolation that our old home had become.

I stopped and just sat there in the saddle. The sounds in my mind faded. Only the silence remained. What a contrast to the place at Miracle Springs! Except for Ma's dying, the life that used to be here wasn't really *gone*—it had just moved . . . all the way across the continent!

Life still existed there . . . but not here. It had left. The spirit of the place had departed, and only the shell remained. Was this what happened when someone died—the body staying but the soul going to heaven? I felt so strongly as I sat there that the *life* that had once been here was now elsewhere.

I dismounted and tied the reins to a shrub next to the porch. I walked up the steps. My boots sounded so loud. I tried the door. It was locked. I stuck my face up to the window and shielded the sun's reflection with my hands, but there wasn't much I could see inside.

I wished I could get in. I stepped down off the porch again and slowly walked around to the side.

Suddenly I remembered. The storm window that wouldn't latch all the way! It couldn't be, I thought, not after all this time!

I was running now, toward the back. Even as I ran I could almost feel the years falling off, and by the time I was by the back door, I was seven again, imagining little Zack running along behind me.

"The window, Corrie . . . we can get in the window. Boost me up, Corrie, I can get in!"

We'd used our "secret entrance" hundreds of times, Zack climbing up first onto my bent knee, then me stooping and getting my shoulder under his rump and hoisting him high enough that he could fiddle with the broken latch and shove the window up and open wide enough for him to scamper through. I was alone now, and though feeling inside like a seven-year-old, I still had the grown-up body of a twenty-eight-year-old. As I slowed from my run and found myself standing in front of the memorable window, I was surprised to see that it wasn't so high anymore. I could reach it easily all by myself.

Everything in the back of the house was run-down and over-grown, weeds and shrubs climbing up against the cracked boards and peeling paint of the house. Several boards of the back porch were loose, a couple were missing altogether, and some of the windows had cracks in them.

I reached up and tried the shutter. The same broken latch was still there! I jiggled it. The latch was so rusted through that a piece of it broke off and fell in the dirt at my feet. I swung back the shutter, then squeezed all the fingers of both hands under the sill of the window.

It gave! With a scraping sound, I shoved the window upward

as high as my arms could reach. Then almost in the same movement I jumped up, stuck my head and shoulders through the
opening, scraping with my feet against the side of the house to
find a crack or ledge to hook the toe of my boot into. Struggling
with my arms inside and my boots against the boards, I inched
my torso through the open window, hardly conscious of scraping
my knees almost raw in the process.

Then all at once I tumbled through, landing in a lump on the
floor. I sat up and looked around. I was sitting inside my old
bedroom!

CHAPTER 48

MEMORIES FROM LONG AGO

I sat there in the silence for what seemed like ten or fifteen minutes. Everything was so quiet and still. The feeling that descended upon me was not a sadness but an overpowering sense of nostalgia. It was almost a warm feeling, and I just drank it in, letting it fill me with an old and pleasant enjoying of the past.

There was a smell I recognized, and the memories and words and images that came with it were so rapid in their passing through my brain that I scarcely had time to concentrate on any single one.

Slowly I rose, then walked from room to room throughout the house, almost on tiptoe, as if to make any sound would be to disturb the peacefulness, the holiness of the memory. There was even a sense of being in a graveyard, of not wanting to disturb the dead. Here in this place, Ma was as alive as I'd felt her in years. The memory of her filled every room, and therefore she *was* alive within me, within my mind, and that memory was sacred to me.

"Oh, Lord," I silently breathed, "thank you for making this possible. It is so good to be here again, to see the house, to remember Ma, to remember Zack and Becky and Emily when they were so young. Take care of them all, Lord. I love them so much! Show me what you have for me, God. Open my eyes here, to my own past, to myself. Whatever you have for me . . . speak to me, Lord. I desire to hear your voice, to grow, to have your finger probe into the deep parts of my heart so that none of my being is hidden from your gaze."

I continued to walk around, breathing deeply and slowly, thinking, reflecting. There was no furniture, nothing but bare

267

walls and floors to hang the memories upon. I heard the voice of a baby crying. Tad? No, he wouldn't have been born yet . . . Becky—that's it. Becky was a baby.

Where was Pa? I searched my mind to see if I could hear Pa's voice anywhere in the house. But it wasn't there. All I could hear were feminine voices. Where was Pa? Had he already left?

When did Pa leave? And why now, with Ma the way she was?

I could see Ma now . . . she was plump . . . of course, she was carrying Tad. . . . Pa must have just left.

Now there was another voice . . . someone else . . . was it Pa? Maybe he hadn't left, after all!

No, it wasn't Pa. It was a stranger's voice. No . . . not a stranger . . . a woman . . . a friend . . . I could hear someone talking to Ma . . . I was listening . . . but . . . now I remembered! I wasn't supposed to be listening. They didn't know I heard! And . . . the voices were talking about me!

As all these fragmentary thoughts tumbled through my brain, I continued to make my way back and forth through the old silent farmhouse. I passed the closet a few feet inside the back door. It's where Ma'd kept brooms and boots and some of our coats. The closet door was ajar. My eyes fell on it, stared for just a second or two, and then a huge stab of pain slammed icily into my heart and I suddenly remembered the conversation that had been gathering itself in the back of my mind.

I slumped to the floor, leaning against the jamb of the half-open closet door, my eyes filling with tears as the words came back to me now as clear as the first time I'd heard them.

" . . . but Corrie wasn't even what you'd call a pretty baby. Why, her brother Zack was prettier'n she was."

"Now, Aggie, you mustn't fret over her."

"But you know, Alma, I just gotta figure how to lead her a different way than I've gone. Her expectin' she'll be gettin' married and everything that goes with it someday, it's gonna cause her too much heartache."

"Corrie'd be as apt as us, or any other young woman, to marry and settle down."

"She ain't the kind men take a shine to, Alma."

" 'Sides, her bein' pretty or not has nothin' to do with what you're *thinkin' right now, and you know it."*

"I reckon you're probably right, Alma, but I'm anxious for her just the same."

"I think I know exactly what's bothering you, Aggie. It's Drummond, isn't it?"

It got so quiet before Ma answered, I remember nearly going faint from holding my breath so long. My legs were nearly numb from standing so still behind the closet door the whole time they were talking. When Ma finally did answer Mrs. Lucas, all the words from before and the ones I now heard all combined to pierce my heart quicker than any needle into the skin, and left me bleeding inside from the ache I heard come with her words.

" . . . I suppose you see right into my mind, Alma," Ma replied slowly. *"I'm just plain scared for my little girl. I don't want her puttin' no high expectations on marriage, with it bein' such an unpredictable thing as it's been for me."*

"Corrie's special, Aggie. She's not like you and me. The Lord put somethin' different inside that girl of yours, that's plain to see."

"I know you're right. Maybe it's on account of seeing that and loving her so much that I don't want no man ruinin' her life before she finds out what that special thing is."

"If the good Lord above put it there, then he ain't gonna let no man ruin it."

"Just the same, I'd rather she didn't take no chances, and the sooner I can convince her that marriage ain't for her, the sooner I'll rest easy."

"Aggie, you're too deep in your own feelin's right now. Look at you—you're nearly ready to have that baby any day, you're tired, you're afraid, you don't know where your man is. You can't be thinkin' clearly at a time like this. Ain't no one who'd expect you to. This ain't no time to be tellin' Corrie things that'll make her feel hard toward her pa. She's too young right now to understand any of this."

I had come home from school earlier than expected that day. I'd gone into the house looking for Ma to tell her I wasn't feeling well, but couldn't find her anywhere. Heading back outside, I heard voices, and then was startled by the sound of my own name!

Seized with fear and uncertainty, I had jumped into the closet, which was right beside me, and closed the door as best I could just as Ma and Mrs. Lucas walked in from the backyard, still talking about me. I stood there, frozen as their voices fell upon my ears, and continued to listen to every word.

My naive broken little heart did not understand what they were saying. Some of the words went only into my ears, others penetrated right down into deep places. . . . *Not pretty . . . gonna cause her heartache . . . ain't the kind men take a shine to.*

I felt an agonizing ache in my heart. I wasn't even sure why. Did it have to do with what Ma had said about me, things she'd said about Pa, things I'd heard her say at other times about our life?

I did not know that Pa would not be returning. That realization would not come till later. I thought he was away for only a short spell. He'd gone away several times in the past.

But Ma's words and the whole tone of her voice made me realize that something had come up all of a sudden to seriously change our whole life. Though I didn't understand, I knew it would never be the same again.

When I began to feel the impact of Ma's words, my eyes swelled with tears, and an uncontrollable urge swept through me to burst out in sobs. I could not keep it back. Suddenly the hurt I was feeling inside became greater than the fear of discovery.

I lunged from behind the door to make my escape out the back door—where, I didn't care. I just had to get outside, into the fresh air, to run and cry and then run farther and never come back.

But I'd stood cramped in the closet too long, and as I ran out into the hallway, my legs crumpled underneath me. I tried to jump up again and scramble to the back door. But the next instant Ma and Alma were at my side, as surprised to see me as I was horrified to have been found out. When I realized I had no place to go, I turned my face to the floor and wept.

The memory of that moment twenty years before became so vivid as I sat on the closet floor again, I found myself filled with all the same emotions again, reliving every second as though it had been yesterday. I was no longer conscious of the separation of past and present. . . . In the huge, silent, stillness of *now* I was in that closet once more, consumed with every fear and doubt a little girl could feel when the whole world around her seems as if it is collapsing.

I hardly know how she did it in her condition. But Ma somehow managed to sit herself down on the floor beside me, right between the closet and the back door, then draw me into her arms and begin to weep with me. Tight in the embrace of each other's insecurities and confusion, we held on to each other for what seemed an eternity.

I'd never felt so close to Ma. Held tight to her bosom, it seemed the safest, most secure place I'd ever known, in spite of all the words I'd just heard. Each of us carried into that precious exchange the deepest despairs of our hearts. Though Ma was a full-grown woman, it was as if we became one, as little girls, as women. Age suddenly didn't matter—each of our uncertainties pouring out in tears, staining the moment with an indelible mark of bonding that would remain in the treasured places of my own being forever.

Tears seem to give the soul that peculiar strength to endure. Emptied and spent, we made no attempt to leave this special moment that had been given us at this lonely time. When or how Alma Lucas left the house, I do not remember. Everything faded into the feeling of Ma's arms tightly clinging to me.

CHAPTER 49

AGATHA BELLE HOLLISTER

Like waking from an endless dream, my thoughts were blurred and timeless. Slowly I became aware of being wrapped in my own embrace on the closet floor, feeling weak and vulnerable, yet strangely at peace within myself.

As my eyes cleared, I recognized once again the wooden-planked floor beneath me. I was sitting just where Ma and I had sat twenty years earlier.

Regaining my senses, I stood, reminded once more of the stiffness in my legs that had caused me to fall on that earlier day. I began walking again through the house, to the now dilapidated kitchen this time. One would never know that a large family had ever lived here. But I could recall everything vividly, now with such detail. Our days here *were* happy . . . and it had been a good home.

That day we wept together, and in the simplicity of Ma's sharing her hurt and compassion with me, she gave me one of the greatest gifts a mother could ever pass on to her child—especially a daughter. I didn't see it then as clearly as it began to come to me now. She had planted a seed in my heart that no deprivation or circumstance could destroy. As a seed lying deep within the soil, waiting for the spring rains and warm sunshine to germinate it into life, so lay buried in my heart the love given to me that day by the one who had passed on her life to me—one who would come to see her own dream die, even as the life ebbed out of her on the hot Nevada desert.

Yet, true to her character, Ma knew the only thing to do was to stand up, shake herself off, and move ahead. She did not know that her day in the desert was coming. Pa may have left, but she would look ahead with a hopeful optimism. There was no time to be lost on what could have been. She knew you had to forge ahead if you were going to succeed at anything.

Ma had never been a complicated woman, yet she was a thoughtful and sensitive one. She didn't go deep into explaining things, and was pretty matter-of-fact about how to get on in life. She said what she had to say, and did what she had to do. I reckon some might even have said she was stubborn because she struck out on her own the way she did.

But Ma wasn't one for wasting time, or for lamenting things lost and broken. She was like the people who laid the foundation stones of this country we had just finished fighting to preserve, and I was right proud of her determination and courage. Ma fought for this great land, too, just by trying to get across it and get free from her past. She was a brave woman.

I suppose in her own way Ma was the one most responsible for me becoming the writer I was, even though her means of encouraging me toward keeping a diary in the beginning had a hurtful side to it. How often had I recalled her words to me two or three years after the incident with her and Mrs. Lucas and the closet: "When a young woman's not of the marryin' sort, she needs to think of somethin' besides a man to get her through life." That was right around the time she started telling me I ought to keep a diary.

I didn't think a whole lot about what she'd said until I was fifteen and we were on our way west. And then after Ma died, the words continued to come back to me more and more often. And that's when my journals began.

But now, in the very home where I'd first overheard her talking to Alma Lucas about my looks and my not marrying and all the rest of it, somehow it all began to widen and grow in new directions in my brain.

We never talked again about that day. I think Ma was so torn up about Pa leaving that she just didn't know what more to say to me. Now that I was up there close to the same age as she had been, I knew how awful it must have been for her. She had no idea how she was going to take care of all us kids, but she was powerfully determined to keep us together. How providential it all seemed now, though I still can't understand why God let Ma die.

Well, maybe I don't really feel that he *let* her die. As a child, I suppose that's how I saw things—God letting, or allowing, bad things to happen to people who seemed to deserve more. I had even thought such things, and even been angry with God about Ma's death, after we'd gotten to Miracle Springs. Ma dying the way she did . . . it just didn't seem right. Then to find out that Pa was still alive made me terribly confused about things for a long while.

And now I could see that Ma did exactly what she wanted to do. No one *made* her decide to take us all west. No one took her life from her. She went because it was a choice she wanted to make—not because she was stubborn and independent but because she knew what she was supposed to be doing. She knew that potential peril lay ahead . . . but she was always one to keep moving forward.

By this time I'd walked through every room of the house two or three times. It had been long enough. I was ready to move on.

The key was still inside the back-door lock, but I didn't want to open it and leave the house unlocked. So I went back to my bedroom and climbed back out through the window, jumped down onto the ground, then closed the window and the shutter as best I could.

I walked back around to the front of the house, untied my horse and headed out across the pastureland. I knew I had at least one old friend that would likely still be here—if it was standing.

CHAPTER 50

UNDER THE OAK

Three or four hundred yards from the house, between two huge expanses of pastureland, stood a small wood made up mostly of pine and fir, with a few scrub oak mingled in. In the very middle of this tiny forest was a grassy clearing of roughly forty or fifty yards in diameter. In the very middle of the clearing stood the most majestic oak tree there had ever been in all the world.

As I made my way along the path through the wood and then emerged into the clearing, true to my childhood remembrance, the great contorted mass of trunk and branches and leaves presented the appearance of filling all space. For several moments I sat there, just soaking in the silent presence of the clearing, empty of all life, with the huge giant rising up out of the grass at its center and then towering above it all. Ma had told me of her coming here as a child (for Grandpa Belle's farm stood adjacent to ours) and playing with Uncle Nick, or sometimes just reading here alone.

In this, as I suppose in many ways, I had followed in Ma's footsteps and had spent more hours in this very place than I could count.

I dismounted and made my way out across the grass. Twenty years had only added to the oak's stateliness. Approaching the mighty giant, I was somehow conscious of being in the company of a faithful, though silent, old friend. As it had on many occasions before we had left New York, my aged companion now gave its patient and unspeaking support as I walked in under his protective umbrella of covering. I thought the special presence and comfort I'd felt here as a child had come from the tree itself, but now I realized that all along it was really from the presence of One much greater.

I eased myself onto the ground and leaned back against the rough bark. A whole new flood of memories came over me, mostly times of laughter and fun with my sisters and brothers. At other times, too, I'd come here to think something through that I couldn't quite understand. I suppose Pa's not coming back caused all of us, except Becky and Tad who were too young to remember, to face silent hurts of our own of different kinds. I found myself wondering if Zack had ever come here to think, as I did. It was interesting to find myself here once more for the same reasons— though having more to do with Ma's presence in my mind than Pa's. Yet it could not help but be different this time. I was no longer a mere eight- or ten- or thirteen-year-old girl as I had been back then.

I was still thinking about Ma, I realized, though Ma was never the kind of woman who talked about a lot of these things; just her very life, and how she lived it, spoke to me of her heart and character. The seeds she planted within me had gone deep into the core of my being. The circumstances of her life, the way she handled the adversity that had come her way, acted like a harrow of truth, always keeping the topsoil of my heart broken and fertile.

But sometimes seeds get planted in the hearts and minds of young children that parents don't intend to plant. Weeds get sprinkled in among the good things, and sometimes what grows up in a young life is a mixture of flowers and nice-smelling things along with weeds and thorns and brambles. Sometimes parents don't even know what seeds they are planting—both good seeds and bad ones. Then the child grows and the seeds sprout roots, and whatever grows—flowers *and* thorns—remains there for a long time.

Seeds get planted wrong, too. A seed that a parent plants, thinking it to be a flower and fully intending it to be a flower, might turn out to be a weed or a thorn. And if the parent knew, he would be heartsick. But by then it's too late and the roots are down too deep to get out. Children can be responsible for lots of the things they *think* a parent did, or the seeds a parent planted and let grow in wrong ways. A child's perception can change a flower seed into a thorn seed, and it's the child who's responsible for seeing it wrong rather than the parent for actually doing anything wrong.

All day long, something had been sticking inside me, poking and jabbing at my mind. I didn't know what it was, but now that I was here underneath the big oak tree, thinking of my mind and heart being like a garden where seeds are planted—both good and bad—the things Ma had said to me kept coming to me. I began to realize that a seed had been planted within me long, long ago that maybe had been acting like a thorn all this time, and was now poking at me from inside. Maybe this was God's way of helping me to see it and pull it out, roots and all, so that flowers could grow in my garden instead, just as he intended.

For years I had been hurt by what Ma had said about me not being the marrying kind, thinking that meant there was something incomplete or wrong with me. I know she didn't mean it like that. She'd been trying to plant a good seed of what you'd call realism. And also what she said about me not being too pretty. Now that I'd remembered the words that had passed between her and Mrs. Lucas, she hadn't exactly said that anyway. She'd said I wasn't a pretty baby, but then I don't reckon a baby's too pretty. Ma sure didn't mean to plant a seed that'd get stuck down inside me to keep flowers from growing. But it got planted anyway and then watered and helped to grow by all the talk later about diaries and not marrying and maybe teaching school.

Ma was just trying to help me prepare for life and not depend too heavily upon a man—as she had done with Pa, only to be left alone with five kids to raise. But I often got confused about what she was *really* saying to me. I was afraid to just ask her.

She didn't want me to put so much importance on the things most folks considered important, such as the way you looked on the outside. I think in her own way, Ma wanted a lot more for me than she'd ever wanted, or even thought she had a right to want for herself. I don't know if she ever quite settled it inside about Pa leaving us. I remember her saying she had forgiven him. But as I thought about it, she must've been awfully concerned about me not making the same mistake. I know there must've remained a powerfully deep hurt in her, though she never let on. Love for him . . . and forgiveness . . . but hurt, too—all mixed in together.

I think she may have been trying to protect me from loving a man on account of not wanting me to ever face the hurt she had. Maybe it wasn't so much my not being the marrying kind as her thinking it best for me to keep my distance from marriage altogether. Then I remembered again the words I'd thought of an hour ago: *I just gotta figure how to lead her a different way than . . . expectin' she'll be gettin' married . . . it's gonna cause her too much heartache.*

All her words came back again. *I'm just plain scared for my little girl. I don't want her puttin' no high expectations on marriage. . . . I don't want no man ruinin' her life . . . the sooner I can convince her that marriage ain't for her, the sooner I'll rest easy.*

Suddenly a whole new light began to dawn on Ma's words! She'd planted one seed . . . but I'd grown another! *She'd* planted a seed of love and protection and wanting only the best for me . . . but down inside had grown a weed of thinking I wasn't worthwhile enough to be married because no man would ever look twice at me.

I had completely mistaken her words!

Mrs. Lucas had said it right to Ma: *Her bein' pretty or not has nothin' to do with what you're thinkin' right now, and you know it.*

And Ma had answered, *I reckon you're probably right.*

Ma wasn't saying I was ugly! She was saying she was anxious for me, and figured she had to find some way to turn me in a different direction from marriage so I didn't spend all my growing-up years thinking about it, and wouldn't get my head turned once I got older.

Her bein' pretty or not has nothin' to do with what you're thinking. The words rang back and forth through my brain like a gong. I'd heard them when I was seven, but only the seeds about not being pretty had planted themselves inside me, and I'd carried them with me like weeds ever since!

Other memories were now flooding through me!

Pa used to call me "his prettiest little lady" when I was young, before he left. It felt good when he said it. Somehow along with his smile, it helped me to know he loved me.

But then as soon as he left, and after I heard Ma and Mrs.

Lucas talking, and through the next years hearing Ma make occasional comments about Pa and Uncle Nick and knowing her hurt, I guess I figured Pa had been lying to me about my looks— or at least exaggerating just to make a little girl feel good.

But I couldn't help being confused, wanting to remember what he'd said, yet knowing that Grandpa Belle said Pa was a no-good man, and Ma saying I *wasn't* pretty.

Now I could see that I had it all wrong, and that Ma didn't intend for me to feel either ugly or confused. She just figured she needed to work as hard as she could to focus my mind in other directions than putting a lot of stock in things that she had found caused grief and pain. She was determined that I not know the hard life she had known in marriage.

More words from the overheard conversation came back to me.

"Corrie's special, Aggie. . . . The Lord put somethin' different inside that girl of yours."

"I don't want no man ruinin' her life before she finds out what that special thing is."

It was all coming so clear now!

Ma used the only way she knew to convince me to set my sights on other things in life than just marriage. Not because I wasn't pretty! Ma and Mrs. Lucas had called me *special*! They said that the Lord had put something different inside me . . . something *special*. And Ma wanted me to find it, and right then she herself was so hurting about Pa that she figured any man in my life might *keep* me from finding it! She could have no way of knowing what a fine man Pa turned out to be!

Even if I had been one of the prettiest girls she'd ever seen, Ma might have done the very same thing, just to discourage me from what she thought might bring me pain someday, and to make sure I found whatever it was inside me that God had put there.

Ma had done her best to protect me! And in a roundabout way she helped to build character into me, because for all the years of growing up, I looked to the things *inside* me instead of the *outside*. She helped me learn to concentrate on the heart—my own and other peoples' too—instead of just their faces. I never fussed much with dresses or fixing my hair the way Emily and most girls did.

Somehow, what Ma said to me through the years about not being the marrying kind put something inside me to motivate me to become important in other ways than what most people might settle for. I doubt she even knew what she was doing or what was going on inside of me. But I think I determined from the time I first heard her and Mrs. Lucas talking that I'd have to do something different in life than counting on just being married. I had to be a different kind of person on the *inside* to make up for what I wasn't on the *outside*.

Without knowing it, Ma had planted dozens and dozens of *good* seeds into my character—seeds of deeper qualities than can ever grow when people are fussing about their looks!

I jumped up off the ground and ran across the meadow, crying and laughing all at once.

I felt so light! I ran and ran, throwing my arms in the air, made a circle, and ran back to my tree.

Ma had never meant that I was an ugly baby or little girl or teenager . . . or even woman! She only wanted me to be the kind of woman who didn't depend on a pretty face . . . who never even thought of it! She wanted me to have a deeper character than that, with qualities that were worth more than the shape of my mouth and nose and cheeks!

I had never been aware of any burden to Ma's words about not marrying. I had grown used to them. They had become part of how I saw myself and how I looked at my life. But now, all of a sudden, a weight from them was gone—a weight I hadn't even known was there!

They didn't matter anymore! Pretty . . . not pretty . . . marrying or not marrying . . . what Ma had said and what Pa had called me when I was little . . . none of it made any difference anymore!

I was just . . . *me*! Exactly how God had made me. I could be a writer or a nurse . . . I could get married or not . . . I could be fat or thin . . . I could be pretty or ugly—none of it changed *me*!

I was special! Mrs. Lucas was right. I *was* special . . . because I was me . . . and I was just exactly the woman God had made. *That's* what made me special! Because he had made me to be the perfect Corrie Belle Hollister . . . *me*, and no one else!

I threw myself onto the ground, rolled two somersaults head over heels, laughing, remembering being young again, but so free of the worry of what Ma or anyone thought. Then I let out a huge yell of delight that quickly died away in the surrounding woods.

Laughing, and still crying, I rolled over on the grass onto my back and gazed up into the sky. One big branch of the oak tree extended out across my vision, and a few white clouds gently passed behind the green leaves of the foreground of my sight.

"Oh, God, oh, God . . . thank you!" I sighed, breathing in deeply of the fresh spring air. "And Ma, wherever you are, if God lets you hear me—thank you too for *everything* you did and said, and for the person you helped make me. Maybe now at last I am ready to be a full-grown woman worthy to be called your daughter. At last I think I understand how much you loved me and all you wanted for me. You once told me, with your hand cupped around my chin, 'I reckon you'll do okay, though, Corrie.' I've never forgotten that, Ma. I hope I have done okay . . . and I hope I will. I hope you're proud of me. I love you, Ma . . . now more than ever!"

CHAPTER 51

TO BELONG IS TO
TRUST THE FATHER

How long I lay under the oak tree I have no idea. It could have been ten minutes, it could have been an hour or more. I had the drowsy sensation that I may have even fallen asleep, but can't be sure.

When I did come to myself, however long it was, I felt such an enormous sense of quiet peace. A peace and contentment inside like I'd never known.

I don't quite know how to describe it. Things seemed settled, ordered, straight inside my mind and heart. Confusion about so much had suddenly disappeared—about Ma, about Pa . . . and mostly about me and what they thought of me. And what God thought of me . . . and therefore about the person I *really* was.

I don't exactly know how to say it, but I felt a contented, good feeling just about *me* . . . about the person God had made me.

Slowly I stood up. I stood tall and stretched my hands high up over my head.

I no longer felt like a little girl. From the moment I'd started walking around Bridgeville early this morning, the past of my early childhood had wrapped itself around me like a cloak, until I even began to *feel* just as I had twenty years ago. I was so glad for every second, every memory, every tear, every remembered word. It was as though each moment was part of a great cleansing flood of fresh water that had swept over me to wash away whatever remaining hurts or insecurities from the past might still have been clinging to me, so that I could go forward into the future whole and clean and secure.

Now as I stood and stretched, the memories from the past contained no pain, only smiles, and I realized my past was just that—past. In these last hours, I had lived out the last of my childhood, one final time in the depths of my heart. God had given me eyes to see everything about it as he wanted me to see it. And now, with that new perspective, the time had come to look ahead.

Funny, I thought to myself, some of my most memorable thoughts and prayer times always seemed to take place around oak trees! There must be something about them that made my thoughts open and reach for heights like the branches of an expansive oak. There was the day of the town picnic when I'd first seen General Grant, and then the day at the convent two years earlier when I'd prayed about what it meant to be a woman. *This* day under *this* oak was such a fulfillment of that day and those prayers!

I walked over to the oak again, wrapped my arms around its great trunk one last time, patted its rough, gnarled bark, and said, "Goodbye, Oak . . . thank you for everything."

I turned and strode across the meadow, bidding this place farewell, then mounted the horse and again made my way through the little wood. All these places had done their cleansing work in my spirit—the oak, the meadow, the house, the town. Now I just wanted to take a long, slow ride through the surrounding countryside, asking God to ready me for whatever lay ahead.

As I rode, gradually thoughts began to come back to me from my train ride a few days earlier, thoughts about belonging, about Christopher, about where I belonged and what I was to do.

You see, Corrie, I felt the Lord saying even as the questions and anxieties floated through my consciousness that had been so on my mind then, *I wanted you to come here. This was the place for you to put away your past, your childhood, your youth, and even the years of your young adulthood. This was the place for you to come to me and discover who you truly are, as my daughter . . . and as my grown-up and mature woman. I am sorry I had to bring remembrances of pain to you. But sometimes I must take my children back in order to ready them to go ahead, to show them things they were unable to see long ago. You are as old as your own mother was when she lived here to raise her children, Corrie. You are no longer a child. You are my daughter and my woman. And you DO belong, Corrie. You belong to me . . . in my heart.*

As he spoke these things to me, I saw that my fears, my anxieties, the loneliness of wanting somebody to care, and the deep gnawing pain of thinking that my value as a person was less because of how I might look. . . . I saw that all these feelings really had only one name—*mistrust*.

Did I *really* believe that God was my Father, that he had made me exactly as he planned, my looks and all? Did I *really* believe that I was of value to him? Did I *really* believe that I had nothing to fear, nothing to worry about, and no reason to feel lonely since I was in his care?

I had always *said* such things.

But was I now ready to take these truths all the way down into the core of my being and believe them in a fully mature way? If today was the day and this was the place to begin, was I prepared to base the rest of my life—an adult life, a life of spiritual maturity rather than adolescence—on them?

Did I really *trust* my Father to be all and everything to me!

Joining a convent would not answer that question. Going somewhere, doing something, traveling here, writing there, meeting people, even . . .

No, I couldn't say that. Those last words were special, words I could *only* write in my journal for my *own* eyes!

No matter where I went or what I did or who I met or what situations I encountered, it was clear that nothing could answer that most important of life's questions from the outside. The only place it could be answered was in my own heart: Did I really and completely and in every way *trust* the Father?

That was the question that separated men and women from children, and determined when true adulthood began.

"Father, help me!" I prayed. "I do want with everything in me to trust you more completely with every part of me and deeper than I have before. God, please do put within me the stature of your being. When people look at me, let me not worry about what they are thinking. Let me only walk as to reflect your character and your being to them. Help me not be anxious or afraid, Lord. I want so badly to lay down every part of my self that remains. Let me do that now, Father—here, in this place where you gave me life. As I have many times before, I give you all of me. Oh,

God, take every piece, every scrap! Take them from my hands and let me cling to them no more. Let me partake of your nature, as Christopher said, Father, by willingly choosing to do as Jesus did, to willingly lay down everything that my own *self* may desire, and want from this day forward *nothing* but what you, my Father, will for me. Help me, God, for I do not trust that I can carry out such a resolve alone. But my heart cries out to live in such communion with you. I do trust you, Father, and love you, and know that my belonging from this day forward is in you."

My heart quieted. As emotional as the prayer had been, no tears accompanied it. Even as the words had poured forth from out of the deepest places within me, a calm sense of God's presence had pervaded it all, as if he himself were prompting and initiating the very words coming out of my mouth, in answer to the desires of my heart that I could not express on my own.

When my voice stilled, a peace of completion and wholeness flooded through me. I *knew* all the words had been answered already because they were *God's* prayers flowing from his heart through mine and out of my mouth. I knew that I had stepped up to a higher plateau. He had taken my hand and pulled me into a higher region of walking in trust with him, a region from which I would never return.

CHAPTER 52

EMPTYING MY HANDS

I rode on across pastureland and rolling hills and a few vaguely familiar pathways and roads. It was time at last to look forward and decide what I was to do now.

"Lord," I prayed, "this is what you've been preparing me for, I realize now. You've ploughed up the soil of my heart, you've pulled up some weeds out of my past, you've shown me some of the good seeds Ma planted inside me, you've shown me that I am special and worthwhile in your eyes because I am just exactly the way you made me, and you've shown me that my belonging is in you and that I can trust you. Now, Father . . . show me what you want me to do."

Almost immediately my thoughts returned to that day when I turned twenty-one, the day I'd ridden Raspberry up into the foothills so I could watch the sunrise over the Sierras. In much broader ways—as I did on that day—I found myself contemplating the same things.

Even though from my earliest memories I hadn't expected to be married, still on that day a lot of my thoughts had focused on the kind of man I would want to marry if I ever did. I thought about the qualities of strength and masculine sensitivity, about *inward* strength of character, about a man standing up for what he believed in, even being willing to make personal sacrifices to do so. I remember thinking a lot about the unusual quality of a man who could share thoughts and feelings, and whose gentleness expressed itself in being able to be open and tender and unafraid of showing emotions. Most of all, I had thought about how wonderful it would be to have a deep spiritual friendship with a man that went deeper than merely being husband and wife.

Then flashed into my mind all the thoughts I'd had on the train when reflecting about Cal, and what a different kind of man than he would be like—a man who looked for opportunities to help people and who was always asking what he could do for others, who always thought about truth, who tried to serve and do good and who was growing to become more loving and kind on the inside.

I now knew such men did exist . . . in the real world, not just in daydreaming fairy tales.

At twenty-one I had been mostly just daydreaming, still doubting either that I'd ever know someone like that, or if I did, there'd be any chance of him being the least bit interested in me.

But now I *had* met a man like that! I knew someone who had all those qualities . . . and many more besides!

Perhaps . . . just maybe, I *could* marry someday. There was nothing to prevent it. Ma'd only wanted to keep me from the suffering and pain.

All of a sudden, it seemed as if the future had opened up before me in a way that involved huge new possibilities!

I knew a man who was so thoroughly God's man that he embodied every quality a woman could ever hope for. How was it possible that a church hadn't wanted him for their minister? *Any* church should want a man of his fiber and depth and wisdom! Any church, any person . . . any young woman would be honored just to know him.

I *did* know him, and I felt honored. So why did the tears keep trying to rise up into my eyes all of a sudden?

Because something deep inside was already telling me I had to set aside even the secret dreams I had harbored on my twenty-first birthday without realizing it.

God had shown me true manhood. Yet he did not want me to place my trust or my sense of belonging even in that, but only in him.

He had shown me that maybe I *could* be the marrying kind. Yet he did not want me to place any trust in that, either. He had shown me who I truly was, not so that I could give myself to a man . . . but so that I could first give myself to *him*. Only in him could I find my deepest belonging, my true heart's home.

Oh, it was such an agony to realize that now God had put within my grasp, for the first time in my life, the very things every woman longs for . . . only to now request me to relinquish them back into his hands!

God, why have you given me all this, only to make me give it back to you? I sobbed, crying in earnest now.

The voice I heard deep in my heart was so quiet, so soft, I had to stop the horse a second and just sit still, straining to make sure it was what I thought it was. But there could be no mistake. Though the thought had come from somewhere inside me, I know it was God speaking in answer to my prayer.

Because I want to show you how much you can trust me . . . in everything. There is no area of your life where I will not give you all that is best for you—only first of all you must empty your hands of your OWN desires . . . and do nothing more than trust me.

I thought of all the possibilities that had been going through my mind for some time about my future. Were all of them things I was still holding in my hands? Were they things I was trusting in instead of in the Father?

I also thought of Christopher. With a pang I suddenly realized that all this time I had been silently hoping for some word from him upon which I might have based a hope for the future.

Then a more recent memory came back to me. At the convent the first time, I'd been so deeply touched by the sisters' devotion to Jesus. I wanted that for myself too—I wanted, above all things, *whatever* God had for me, to be *his* handmaiden.

"Oh, God," I breathed quietly, "that is still my heart's desire. I *do* so want to be altogether and entirely *yours*."

A silence came over me.

Gradually I saw that as neither my work in Washington nor even the convent could be a substitute for my true place of belonging, for trusting God with my future as *his* handmaiden . . . neither could Christopher—even though he was entirely God's man. For me to hold on to my own hopes would be to give God something less than full and complete trust, and a lesser degree of devotion than I had prayed to give him under that oak tree at the convent.

My prayers of that day now rushed back into my memory. "Whatever future you have for me," I had told him, "let me just know that I am completely yours. Use me and fill me with yourself. I am devoted to you, Lord Jesus. Let me love you and serve you."

Even as mature as Christopher was as God's man, and as wonderful a place as the convent was, they could not become a substitute in my heart for what only the Father could provide. Now that I had faced the anxieties and remaining areas of mistrust of my deepest being, and laid them, in willing and choosing relinquishment, into the Father's hands, there need be no fears, doubts, or uncertainties about what the future held. With a foundation of trust in the Father solidly established, whatever was built upon it was sure to stand.

I had to empty my hands before the Father—completely.

"Father . . . Father," I prayed, "I give it all to you—my future, my life, my decisions . . . Christopher, my desires and hopes . . . my writing . . . where I should go, what I should do . . . everything. Oh, God—"

I could pray no more. I leaned over against the neck of the horse and sobbed.

CHAPTER 53

TOWARD THE SETTING SUN

Never, in all my life, had I felt so utterly empty . . . so alone.

For just those few minutes, even God himself seemed to have left me. I had emptied my hands, and my whole being felt as though it had been emptied along with them.

In the few hours of this day, God had given me everything . . . and then he had asked me to give it all back to him.

I felt as if all the *past* was new. Everything had been remade. Memories were new. Words I had heard from Ma now meant more than before. I saw her love more clearly. I saw myself more clearly.

The *future*, too, was new. Possibilities had dawned. God had removed all the limitations I had once placed upon myself.

And yet in the *present* . . . all was gone.

I had emptied my hands of every possibility, entrusting all to the Father . . . and there truly was nothing left for me to hold on to. I *belonged*, in empty abandonment, *only to him*.

I sat there quietly weeping for a while. The tears I shed were not tears of sadness, but the pure, cold tears of empty trust. To make the sacrifice of giving *all* to the Father was my choice, and yet to do so cannot be said to be a *happy* thing. But it was the right thing, the true thing.

As I wept tears of fulfilled abandonment, a quiet sense of God's presence gradually began to steal over me. I felt him wrapping me up as in a giant quilt, with his hands folding the corners of the blanket of his tender love about my raw heart and emotions.

He had stripped me bare of all hopes and earthly desires and ambitions and dreams other than to be completely his. Even in

293

the emptiness there was a certain stark purity and singleness of motive, no longer mingled with the slightest anxiety about all the earthly questions—where, what, who, why, when. None of it mattered anymore—only to be his . . . to trust him . . . to belong to him.

I knew everything had been stripped away. And in that, I *knew* God was with me.

Almost immediately came the clear awareness of what I was to do next. It was time to turn my steps in the direction of the setting sun . . . westward. That was my earthly place. There I would return. It was time to go home.

I turned the horse's head around and immediately started back toward town.

As I rode, the wrapped-around-me presence of God worked its way in tighter and tighter, getting inside me, filling up all the places I had emptied of myself. Before long, it was not just a blanket of God's love *around* me, but a sense of being filled up with him from the inside. Such a new feeling of fullness came over me. But not a fullness with all the thoughts and feelings and dreams and ambitions and possibilities of my *own* that I'd been wrestling with. Rather, a fullness of God's being filling me up and replacing all those *Corrie* things.

It felt so wonderful! The Father's love and Spirit filling me was so much better than *myself* filling me!

As I rode, I remembered my twenty-first birthday, the very words I had prayed on that day. *Lord*, I had said, *help me to cultivate what you've given me. Don't let me waste anything*.

He had done that in so many ways over the years since. He had given me so much, and allowed me so many opportunities to use and cultivate and expand it.

But the most important part of that prayer had come last of all. Back then I'd also prayed, *Help me to grow to the fullest so I can be the person you want me to be!*

I had just turned twenty-one. I *thought* I was becoming a grown-up woman. And in many ways I suppose I was. But twenty-one is still young when later you find yourself looking back from an older vantage point. And the prayer was only the beginning. The fullness of God's answering it would take years. And now today, more than seven years later, I could see that God had been working all this time to answer that cry of my spirit.

How could I have known when I prayed that prayer that to grow to the *fullest* would mean having to empty myself to the *emptiest?* Even today, conscious of abandoning myself more completely to him than ever before, I realized that I would probably, years from now, look back on *this* day and see how much further I had come than what I could envision now. "Growing to the fullest" was an ongoing and never-ending process.

That day at the convent I had had similar thoughts, and I had given myself to Jesus in a fuller way than any time before. Yet now I could see that, even though I'd felt *married* to him in a way, there were still places within myself that I'd held back, not even knowing it. Today's abandonment to him went deeper yet, into corners and recesses of my heart I hadn't even known existed. I wondered if times like this would come again, when he would probe still further.

I smiled to myself. No doubt they would! But today was today . . . and for *today* I was thankful, even if there would come further days of having to empty my hands all over again in the future. He had fulfilled and completed the prayers of devotion I had prayed at twenty-one and at twenty-six, and for right now that was enough.

Today I found myself filled with the wonderful knowledge that God *had* and *would continue* to answer every prayer I had ever offered him. And with that knowledge, such a quiet joy began to escape from my soul—a joy of peace and contentment, and such a freedom from anxiety.

I *belonged*! And I knew where!

Was I to be a writer for the rest of my life? Was I to become a nun, to marry, to travel, to minister to the sick and suffering, to have a family, or to live alone, to work in California, or someday return again to the East? I didn't need to know! I could totally trust that the Father would go before me and direct me in whatever way he intended.

I didn't need to graduate from a university to be a good writer, he had already shown me that. Neither did I need to return to the Convent of John Seventeen to be entirely God's woman. I could live the life of dedication and separation and commitment to Jesus *anywhere*. Neither did I have to marry to be a worthwhile woman. Being "the marrying kind," as I'd thought about for all these years, was no longer of any meaning. I was *God's* woman, and that was the only *kind* of woman I ever wanted to be!

All the rest would fit together perfectly as he ordered my steps! All I needed to do was submit my heart, and my *next* steps, to him, surrendering empty hands—over and over, every day, every week, every year—so that he could fill them with *his* purposes.

I could hardly contain the magnitude of the revelation! And yet, how could I find words to put it on paper? How could I bring into focus the order, the direction, the quiet peace, and the sense of utter contentment it gave me?

I didn't know what was out there for me now—in the *next* three or seven . . . even the next twenty years. But I sensed that today was the beginning of something wonderful—something my eyes couldn't see, though my spirit was already catching a glimpse of it. The emptiness and aloneness I'd felt earlier was slowly replaced by a growing anticipation—that good things were ahead now, even better than I could have planned myself! Service to others, sacrifice, perhaps even pain, but also a deepening trust in the Father, and thus growth and joy as well—all these and much more I knew God had in store for me.

I was nearly back to Bridgeville now. Such a multitude of thoughts and feelings filled my heart. But mostly it was a feeling of being complete and whole and full.

CHAPTER 54

DEAR CHRISTOPHER

DEAR CHRISTOPHER,

As you will see, I am writing this from New York. I am in a boardinghouse in the town near our old home. I have been here two days. Now at last I see the Lord's purpose in leading me back to this place. I feel more prepared than ever to move forward into whatever he has for me, now that I have been here again. I feel more whole than three days ago, and perhaps more at peace with myself, my life, my family . . . and my future.

While here, I believe that God has shown me what I am to do. At least what I am to do now—the next page of the book, even if not the whole next chapter. You have to write one page at a time, you know, whether it is words in a journal or days of a life.

It is not to become a nun, or to remain with the sisters at the convent, as much as I love and admire them.

Neither is it to return to Washington. I feel strongly that my time in the East is at an end. What I am writing to tell you, therefore, is that as soon as I return to the convent, I will immediately begin making preparations to gather what belongings I have and then make arrangements to return, by train and stagecoach, to California. The Lord has shown me, I believe, that for now my future is there.

I remember saying to you once that I didn't belong down there, that I was no Southerner. Well, though I was born here in New York, in this very town where I am now sitting, in fact, I do not belong here either. I do not belong in Pennsylvania or Washington.

297

No, I *belong* in California. I've been gone just over two years. I left Miracle Springs in May of 1863. It is now time I made the return journey.

I wanted you to be the first to know.

I would so much like the chance to talk to you. I am so full of our Father's goodness to me right at this moment that it needs somebody to share it with. Sometimes when you're alone, the Lord is able to show you things and speak to you in a way he maybe can't at other times. Coming here has been like that for me.

I cried a few tears and walked along some old familiar paths. In the end God showed me that he was the only foundation I could build my life on. Maybe someday I'll be able to tell you all of what that realization means and why it was so hard to come to. But now is not the time for that.

Now I know . . . at last—I am such a slow learner, it seems—that I *belong* (no, not really even in California) to him, to our Father! That's what he had been trying to show me all along. *He* is the next chapter of my life, and the light at the tunnel's end . . . the place where my life is full and whole and complete. It's exactly what you said in your letter to me at the convent about tunnels. Now the truth of it is lodged deep in my being where I do not think I shall lose sight of it again.

I am so thankful to God for you, my friend, Christopher Braxton. You showed me what a true *man* could really be made of. I used to dream of meeting a man someday whose life and character reflected the selfless, giving, sacrificial qualities of God's nature. Now I am happy and blessed to say I *have* met such a man, and I will forever be grateful for that. God made use of you in more ways than you can presently know to plant a new level of trust within me for him. I will never forget you, and will always pray for you and give God thanks for you.

I reckon you can read the other letter I sent now if you still have it, and want to read it. It won't matter much now. What I was so worried about is, I pray, gone from me. God took a lot of things out of my hands while I was here. I should say I *gave* him the things I realized my hands were clinging to. But as he always does, he gave me back a hundred times more than what I gave him!

I hope you might think about me sometime, and maybe

want to write again. I enjoy your letters and hope we might correspond. It would be good to have someone to share my thoughts with by mail. A journal is good, but not always enough. Anything that you send to Miracle Springs, California, will get to me. Everybody knows me there.

Remember me as a sister who cared deeply for you, and who will always be grateful to you—for saving my life, for nurturing me back to health, and for showing me many attributes of our Father. And thank you again for the journal! I treasure it, and will fill it only with the choicest gems of truth I can find—some of them things *you* said to me.

God bless you always, Christopher!

Cordially,
CORRIE BELLE HOLLISTER

CHAPTER 55

TRYING TO PUT THE WAR IN PERSPECTIVE

During the train ride back from New York, my mind was strangely clear of distractions and any anxieties about Christopher. I had not allowed myself to build too many castles in the sky anyway, but now that I had settled things within myself about the past, so much about the future was clear, too. I knew at last where my home was—both inside me, and where I physically belonged too—and I was content not to look elsewhere for either.

So my mind was thinking more clearly than it had for a long time, and I found myself reflecting once more on the war and on the articles I had been trying to start that had twice bogged down before. A further perspective began slowly to dawn on me, and suddenly I saw a parallel between the war in the development of our country and what I had just experienced while at Bridgeville.

As difficult as it was, I had written on a moving train before, so I got out my papers and pen and ink and tried to put some of these new thoughts down in writing.

How does a person, or a family, or even a nation grow out of its childhood and adolescence, to come at last into its adulthood?

It must, one would think, reach a certain age in its growth and history where it can begin to look upon itself with a rationality not given to many children. At that point in the development of its personality, it must look upon itself with self-analysis and introspection, and ask, "Who am I . . . what am I . . . where have I come from . . . where am I bound

. . . of what stuff am I made?"

Not only do people ask themselves such questions as they mature, they also find themselves facing such inner issues at moments of crisis, conflict, and crossroads in their lives, when new levels of personhood and character must be sought. Men and women face such times. Husbands and wives, brothers and sisters, families and friends must all learn to weather times of adversity and conflict for their relationships to come out stronger in the end.

Those moments serve to illuminate and define personality and character. Out of such travail, boys become men of valor, girls become women of courage, and brothers learn to put behind them the differences of adolescence, to clasp hands as men and become one.

In every aspect of life, defining moments ultimately come.

This had certainly happened to me! If the last several days had indeed been a "crossroads" in my life, I hoped it had helped me define who I was as a person too.

This truth is seen in the physical world, in relationships, in individual men and women as they grow and progress and live out their days.

What are we made of? Are our muscles of iron, or straw? Who are we . . . really? Down at the core of our beings, what beats in our hearts? The red blood of courage and dignity, or cowardice, selfishness, and greed?

This is also the story of the history of nations. And ours has just emerged from such a time.

Perhaps for the first time since 1776, we can truthfully call ourselves the *United* States of America, and can for the first time summon the maturity to look within ourselves, inside some collective place in our national heart, and ask, "Who are we . . . we who call ourselves Americans? What does it mean to *be* an American? And what kind stuff are we made of?"

Everything I was writing went down so deep into my own heart. For some reason my thoughts again turned to the mirror that I had mentioned before about the war, and realized that the old farmhouse at Bridgeville had been a gigantic mirror for me too—a mirror into myself and into the past. Sometimes those kinds of mirrors didn't reflect comfortable things. There had been pain with some of the memories I'd just lived through, yet I knew the realizations that resulted from it all would make me stronger in the end. I hoped the same would be true for our country. Thinking about the pain and killing brought my thoughts back again to the war.

> We have spent the last four years looking into a red-stained national mirror—looking at the enemy, all the while looking at ourselves.
>
> The images from the mirror are far from pleasant. We learned that Americans are a people capable of killing, killing cruelly, and killing in huge numbers . . . and killing our own brothers.
>
> We have learned, however, that though capable of great evil, there is yet a strength of fiber in the word *American*. This was no war fought by cowards—on either side. As the mirror revealed great flaws in the national character, perhaps it equally revealed a valor that will grow out of the blood spilled on the battlefields into a greater strength than the nation knew prior to 1860.
>
> The war was fought to make this the land of *free* men and women, no matter what the color of their skin. Perhaps one of the greatest lessons of all is that it took *brave* Americans to achieve that freedom. This is indeed now, at long last, a land of the brave *and* free.

I put down my pen. I could write no more. I had begun crying softly even as I wrote, without even realizing it.

I suppose I was crying for the country, for the bloodshed, for Mr. Lincoln. No matter how I tried with my words to find a meaning to it all, a perspective that would see good in all that had happened, I could not forget Gettysburg and the hospital camps and everything else I'd seen. And somehow none of it seemed worth the horror and tragedy and enormous human suffering. Maybe the war had to be fought for freedom's sake. I don't know if I would ever know the answer to that. But it was too high a price to discover that Americans were a brave people. Bravery did not seem worth the death it had caused.

I put the papers away and stared out the window awhile, letting my tears come quietly and softly, dabbing my eyes every now and then with a handkerchief. I had been trying to find some positive lesson to be learned from the war, but it was still so fresh, I didn't know if I believed the thoughts my pen had explored or not. It would probably take a long time to discover, as I had asked myself when I began trying to write my thoughts, what the war *meant*.

I still didn't know.

Before long, however, Christopher began to intrude into my thoughts, mingling with all the images of the last two years. Not in a longing way, but just with a sadness that I would probably never see him again, and that he was just about the finest Christian man anyone could ever meet.

That sadness, along with the completely different sadness over the war, occupied my thoughts all the way to Pennsylvania, and I spent the rest of the day just looking out the windows.

It was definitely time for me to go home. Suddenly I was very, very homesick and anxious to see everyone again!

CHAPTER 56

FINAL GOODBYES

Back at the convent I immediately began gathering my things and making the preparations necessary for my return to California.

Now that the decision had been made I was anxious to be on my way. I checked the train schedule in Lancaster and determined, if I was able, to be back in six days to board the westbound train to Pittsburgh.

I told Sister Janette and Sister Mary and the others that while I was in New York I'd realized it was time for me to go back home to California, and what my plans were. They all expressed regret at my words, yet none of them were surprised by the decision. I could tell that Sister Janette had expected it, and even knew within herself that it was the right thing for me to do.

The next five days were ones of unexpected delight.

Knowing that these were my final days with the sisters I'd grown to love so deeply, I made every effort to make the days as full and rich as possible. We worked and prayed and laughed and sang together, and I accompanied whoever had any errand out in the community, no matter how small. I didn't want to lose a single opportunity to fill my last week here with every possible memory and growing experience I could.

I wrote notes to myself about everything that had happened in New York to insure that I wouldn't forget a single detail. But I didn't want to take the time to write everything out in my journal just then. There would be plenty of hours on the train for that. It wasn't likely I'd forget any of it anyway.

I got out the things I'd written on the war and General Grant

305

and General Lee and read them over a few times, wondering if I could make an article or two out of them. Yet somehow my mind was already looking beyond the war, and it was hard to focus my attention on what I had written. Maybe when I got back home I'd show them to Mr. Kemble, and if he wanted to use them he could.

The day finally came. All the sisters wanted to go along to take me to the train. So two full wagons—with sixteen Catholic nuns and one young lady on her way back to California—jostled off northeastward toward Lancaster, singing and talking and laughing together. I don't think there has ever been a time in my life I remember such pure, happy fun as that day's ride.

We all spent the night at a church there. I was to catch the train eastbound out of Philadelphia the next morning at 9:37.

I didn't feel as sad as I had expected to. I already missed the sisters terribly, even though I hadn't left yet. But at the same time a great thrill of excitement was coming over me, too, just at the thought of being home. Now that I had turned my steps westward again, I couldn't imagine how I could have remained away from Miracle Springs so long without positively dying of homesickness. Suddenly I was so homesick I didn't think I could stand it another second!

So the sadness of leaving was only in a small part of me, while the rest of me was eager and ready.

The next morning two wagonloads of nuns pulled up to the station at 8:30 with their passenger, and we all piled out, causing quite a scene in the small train station. I bought my ticket, while the station manager kept glancing around at all the sisters with an inquisitive look on his face.

We walked to the platform with my two bags, then stood talking and hugging and crying for the next forty minutes.

The train came.

I'd already said goodbye to Sister Janette, but again I found myself embracing her. "Sister Janette," I said, "I'm so glad we met on the train two years ago!"

"So am I, dear Corrie!" There were tears in her eyes.

"The trip won't be the same without you to share it with."

"You will manage, I'm sure," she said, trying to laugh but not succeeding very well. "You'll be too busy thinking of home to be lonely for us. But *we* will be lonely for *you,* Corrie. Our wagon ride home, I'm afraid, will be very somber and quiet."

"Oh, Sister Janette, don't make me cry again," I said, trying to laugh, but succeeding no better.

"The conductor seems to be about ready to make his announcement."

"I suppose I can't delay my going forever. I'll miss you."

"And we you, Corrie!"

"*All aboard!*" came the call behind us.

I turned to go.

"Corrie," Sister Janette's voice said behind me, "I have one last thing for you."

CHAPTER 57

GOING HOME!

My hand trembled as I took the letter from Sister Janette's hand.

I didn't even need to look at it. I could almost *feel* the presence of its sender from the very paper itself, though the briefest glance downward at the handwriting told me everything I needed to know.

All the rest of my goodbyes—stepping aboard the train, waving to all the smiling faces of the nuns out the window . . . everything is only a blur in my memory. All I was conscious of was a tremendous burning sensation in my hand! I couldn't tell if it was the burning from a white hot flame, or the burning of freezing white ice. But once I felt the bouncing of the track beneath me and knew we were underway, I looked at my hand again, almost surprised to see the envelope still intact and not smoking and burning right in my fingers.

I could hardly think what to do!

After all that had happened in New York—at the house, under the oak, and then while riding throughout the countryside—a wave of fear and confusion came over me briefly. I thought everything was done . . . over . . . settled. What was . . . what could this be about?

Almost the next instant, however, a slow sense of expectation began to replace the confusion. It sent me back to the anticipation I had felt that day as I rode back to Bridgeville when I realized that God had already ordered my steps according to *his* purposes.

"Lord. . . ?" I prayed, but I could say no more. Some feeling

I had never known began rising within my breast.

Frantically my fingers tore into the envelope and yanked out the five thin sheets of paper inside!

DEAR CORRIE,

By now you are seated on the train, presumably heading west the way you came two years ago. I imagine you are clattering through the green Pennsylvania countryside, looking out the windows, probably thinking about hundreds of things. I can almost picture you, though I try to keep myself from dwelling on your face, for it causes an uncomfortable tightening somewhere in my throat. How I wish I could be with you right now, and look into your eyes, and say what I have to say. But as you will see, there are reasons why I cannot, why it must be said by letter, and why I asked Sister Janette not to give you this until you were well on your way.

What I have to tell you would probably sound utterly ridiculous to those accustomed to the ways and methods of the world. I hope and pray that it will not seem ridiculous to you. You are the one person in all the world I want to understand! It has been my goal for some time now not to weigh my actions by what the world thinks, but in fact to judge the rightness and wrongness of a thing by the inverse of its worldly acceptability. In any case, what I have done in these matters about which I will speak, I have done by attempting to follow what I perceived God instructing me to do.

My breath was coming in short gasps as I read. In vain I struggled to fill my lungs, but it was no use.

When men and women meet, especially when they find the bond deepening, the normal and accepted mode of their discourse and interaction often becomes such that gratification of each individual self is the sole ambition and motive. I have seen many marriages founded on such flimsy footings, and the edifices constructed thereon always end in misery.

My heart was pounding as I read. The mere words *men and women* on the page in Christopher's flowing hand was enough to send chills and tingles all at once up my spine and into my neck!

I'm certain you recall the day, for you made mention of it

in your letter from New York, when you said you didn't belong here. You meant, of course, in Richmond . . . in the South. But even as you said it, your words smote my heart and I know I was unduly quiet for a few minutes. Forgive me. But I had already begun to cherish a quiet and prayerful hope that perhaps you had been sent to me, and I to you, for reasons beyond our sight at that moment. The bonds of sharing that had already sprung to life between us went far deeper of root than any plant that had till then grown in the garden of my heart. And I must confess that I did not want to see it end.

Your words about returning to Washington fell icily upon my ears, like a quick frost on a tender green sprig. And a further chill swept over me to hear you say, "I don't belong here."

I wanted to cry out, "Oh, but Corrie, you *do* belong here! You belong with me!"

But I could not. For to do so may have been to inhibit the way of God's appointed destiny that he had marked out for you to follow.

I could hardly keep reading! If I didn't force them to stay inside, tears would well up and flood my eyes. I couldn't let that happen, otherwise I would not be able to see the words on the paper.

I already sensed, Corrie, that there were several things which it was the Lord's purpose to resolve in your life with him, and that for me to intrude could have been to prevent or delay that process. You can have no idea how many hours I spent at your bedside before you came to yourself, praying for this unknown life whom God had suddenly deposited into my care. Even then, in the tiniest flutter of your sleeping eyelids, sensations and thoughts and feelings unknown to me before began to come awake. I pondered your face, your every feature, knowing you after the manner of the Spirit of your Maker, even though I knew nothing about you. I knew that you were a daughter of the Most High God. I had a vague foreshadowing that your life would be intertwined somehow with my own, and yet I felt a sense of revelation as well that paths lay ahead for you that must be walked alone, and that

312

for me to intrude prematurely would only be to inhibit the Lord's greatest work which he desired to accomplish in you.

Before many weeks of your waking, I knew I cared far too much for you to lift so much as a finger or utter so much as a word that might sway your affections toward me before the Lord had carried out whatever that work was. I knew, therefore, that my duty before you was clear: it was simply to wait.

Oh, how many times during those final two days of yours at the farm—during those dreadful hours after learning of Mr. Lincoln's death—did I long to shout out to you, "Corrie, Corrie, don't go! Stay here with me! You belong here . . . with me!"

But I dared not. And thus in my silence I fear I offended you or caused you to think me annoyed with you. I wrote to apologize, but even that seemed pale and insufficient.

I was constrained to silence. I felt the hand of God upon my tongue, and upon my pen. *Something* required resolution before you would be ready to think and pray clearly about the things that were already filling my heart. I did not know what it was, but I knew that our mutual Father knew, and that he must speak to you before I would be at liberty to. His was the voice your deepest being needed to hear at this particular hour, not mine. How long I must endure the waiting, I did not know. By then I had prayed in the midnight hours of my lonely silence, and had given you, as well as my full heart toward you, into the hands of our Father. But that did not stop the agony from pressing so hard against me that Monday when you boarded the train as to make me sure I was about to be crushed under the weight of it. How I ached to see you go!

The worldly-wise of our society would hear my words and consider them the rantings of a lunatic. "Take what you want," they would say. "Don't be a fool. Get what you can. Coerce people and events to suit your own designs."

Therein lay the greatest trial of all. For I was aware that you cared for me as well. When eyes meet as ours have, many secrets are revealed. I was aware that one word from me might have turned you in a direction it would not have been right for you at that moment to go.

I was also aware that things are not always as they appear, and that the world's perceptions are not to be counted on any more than ice an eighth of an inch thick is to be trusted to cross a winter's lake. In the kingdom of which we are citizens, Corrie, only those things that we let go and give up to the Father do we truly possess after the manner in which the Father would have us possess. Therefore, I knew that to truly have you I must give you to him, and to truly care for you, I must care more that you belonged to the Father than to me.

He had given you to me for a season. Then I had to give you to him for a season. For everything there *is* a season, and this was his time to carry out his purpose. I could not, I *would* not stand in his way. I have, in truth, been miserable since the day you left. Mrs. Timms, I fear, is about to fire me and cast me adrift among the carpetbaggers who are roaming the South to pluck it clean of every tangible scrap that yet has worth. But even in my misery, I rejoiced because I had known you, and in my heart of hearts I knew it was not the end.

The Lord revealed to me, I feel, that—whatever I may have wanted to shout to you—your sense of belonging had to come from him first. Beyond that, I knew that this was not your home. It was right that you pray through the things that were weighing on you about your family and your writing and how the Lord desired to integrate them in your life. I could not be in the way of his voice speaking to those concerns. For me to have spoken prematurely could have kept you from hearing him clearly in these other areas.

Oh, how I wanted to be part of your future, Corrie, and for you to be part of mine—but as our Father directs, not as our human emotions and even loneliness might. All we could do to keep from intruding with our own ambitions, while leaving matters to the care of the Father, would only insure that in the end we find ourselves in his house with *all* that belongs to him likewise ours to enjoy.

Your letter from New York came with such a sense of anticipation. Does it display weakness for a man to admit that he read a letter from one he cares for with trembling fingers and pounding chest? If so, then I fear I must admit to that weakness! A joyous trembling!

I could tell immediately as I read that a change had come, that you had crossed a threshold of decision and had entered into a new depth of trust in your Father. The very tone of your expression revealed a calmness that told me quickly the work which God had to do had been done. He had purified his scalpel in the fire, and had sent it in search of that hidden place in your heart where the final surgery was required.

Line by line as I read from your hand, I felt the huge weight of waiting slowly lifting from my own shoulders. He had secured the roots of your being in him. No longer could there be any danger in my inhibiting that work by whatever declaration I might make. By the time the pages of your letter dropped from my hand, I was weeping in abandoned happiness, for your final words were accompanied by a silent thundering sensation, as if the heavens were shouting, "Now, my son. You have waited patiently for me to make the two paths straight in preparation. At last you may speak. As your heart told you, I intend now to join the paths and make them one!"

I was sobbing by now. How could I read such words and not weep with a thousand unexpected feelings? *God . . . oh, God, are you truly doing this remarkable thing!*

I grabbed up my pen and a sheet of paper to begin immediately writing my heart to you. But then the next instant I jumped up and ran to my bureau to find the unopened letter. Throw it away? Did you possibly think I would—never! Even unopened, the mere fact that it came from you made it a treasure. I was by now so feverishly hungry for any further word from you, I tore it open and hastily read.

What you wrote that compelled the telegram I have not an idea! I read with renewed tears. Oh, Corrie, Corrie! With all respect to your mother, yours is the face that has filled my entire consciousness now for months. Comely enough to fetch a husband? Someday many years from now I may argue the point with your mother! But for now I will only say that you are so beautiful in my eyes as to reflect the very nature and purity and radiance of the God who made you, and I know of nothing in all the world so beautiful as that! I grew to love every inch of your face as you slept peacefully after your accident—your mouth and eyes, your chin and cheeks, your neck and the dimple and the few freckles, the color and gentle waves of your hair. Do you know that after praying for you, I kissed your forehead every night? Beautiful Corrie . . . you are all the world to me!

I could not keep reading! I was positively bawling like a baby, glad there was nobody right next to me. There were enough people scattered through the coach that some of them were starting to stare, because I'm afraid I was by now crying and sniffling with almost a loud groaning of uncontrolled emotional happiness. But who cared what any of them thought. For the first time in my life I was ready to shout out to the whole world that I was in love with a certain fine man named Christopher Braxton!

Oh, there is so much to say! It may be difficult for you to understand, but in time I'm certain you will, but I read of your decision to return to California with gladness. My heart will be sore for missing you. And I flatter myself that you will feel a certain loneliness as well.

But in matters such as these, haste is almost certain to cause men and women who live in the flesh and the soul to run ahead of the pace by which God establishes his purposes in the Spirit. Speed is often alien to the ways of the Father. The purposes of God take time and cannot be rushed.

Additionally, I feel you need to see your family and home before you see me again. You need to talk with your beloved Almeda and your father, and your dear Rev. Rutledge. I will not tamper with the rightful order by which these things must be done so as to bear the greatest harvest of fruit in the end. Your sensing God's prompting to return confirms to me that he has been speaking to us both, even apart, as with one voice.

It was for all these reasons I wrote, as you of course know well enough by now, to your Sister Janette with instructions to give you this letter as you boarded the train. I feared one of us might grow weak, and the desire to set eyes upon each other grow too strong, that your journey could have been forestalled. I keenly felt that now was the appointed time for your return, and thus I waited as I did to speak to you from my heart.

But you *will* see me again, I promise you that. I know that the appointed path marked out for my steps to follow will lead me also to California. Wherever my own future lies beyond that, let me only say it is my prayer I do not have to make that decision alone.

You will see me one day, not too far off I hope, in the town of Miracle Springs that I have already grown fond of because of someone who lives there. One way or another, I will get there. I have got two very important things I have to do there. I have to see a man by the name of Drummond Hollister to ask if he will consent to give me the hand of his daughter. And I have to see you to ask if you will consent to give me your life, and do me the honor of allowing me to call myself your husband.

Oh, my sister and friend, it seems I always use far, far too many words to say what could be said in only a few. The few I would say now, for all to hear and know, are these: Corrie Hollister, I love you!

How can I end except by saying again, I love you!

Yours forever,
CHRISTOPHER

I broke out in a suppressed sob. I tried to stifle it, but they kept coming in waves. I know every eye on the coach was watching me. I tried to pretend I was looking out the window, but from the sniffling and crying and handkerchief, already wet, going all about my eyes and nose, it was obvious I wasn't much interested in the scenery.

I could hardly remember what state we were in . . . and barely what country.

"Are you all right, miss?" said a voice beside me.

I glanced up. There stood the conductor, with a kind look of concern on his face.

"Oh, yes," I cried, my eyes red and wet and puffy. "I'm just . . . just so . . . so very happy!"

I guess I wasn't controlling my voice too well and must have been talking a little loud, for behind me several people laughed lightly at my words. I took no offense. I think they were relieved, though it must have sounded funny after all the time I'd been carrying on like I had.

"Where you bound, miss?" the man asked.

"I'm going *home*," I answered. I hadn't used the word for a long time. I suppose I'd been confused about just where my *home* was. But not anymore.

"Where's home?"

I finally managed a smile through my tears. "California," I said. "Miracle Springs."

"You got a long ride ahead of you."

Not so long, I thought. I had the memory of a certain man to keep me company. And I intended to read and reread and reread his letter every mile of the way!

ACKNOWLEDGMENTS

Three books stand out above all the rest in their perspective on the Civil War, which I would like to cite for their helpfulness in the research and preparation of this manuscript.

The Civil War, An Illustrated History by Geoffrey Ward, Ric Burns, and Ken Burns (New York: Alfred A. Knopf, 1990).

The Union Sundered and *The Union Restored* by Harry Williams (New York: Time-Life Books, 1963).

Christian History magazine, Vol. XI, No. 1.